THE SILENT QUARRY

A gripping Welsh murder mystery

CHERYL REES-PRICE

THE
BOOK
FOLKS

Published by The Book Folks

London, 2020

© Cheryl Rees-Price

ISBN 978-1-913516-55-0

www.thebookfolks.com

The Silent Quarry is the first title in a series of murder mysteries set in the heart of Wales.

Chapter One

1999

Gwen felt her foot slip and her body tilt backwards as the object she held in her hand fell from her grasp and clattered against the cliff face before falling into the depths below.

I'm going to die, she thought.

She could see the leaden grey clouds drifting across the sky as drops of rain fell on her face. There was no sound other than her heartbeat ringing in her ears. Adrenalin pumped through her body, kicking her brain into survival mode. She flailed her arms, trying to grasp at anything that would stop her falling, but only air swished through her fingers.

Time slowed as gravity pulled her down, the air whistling through her hair. Fear froze her thoughts. She closed her eyes and waited for the impact.

Gwen became aware of her body, weighted down in the darkness, and struggled to grasp thoughts through the dense fog in her mind. Something was trying to pull her up from the darkness but she didn't want to leave, it was safe here.

As she allowed herself to sink into oblivion, a noise filtered through, pulling her back. She concentrated on the faint rhythmic bleeping in the distance. As the bleeping became clearer the darkness changed hue from black to brown, then became lighter – an amber glow. She opened her eyes and a blurred figure appeared muttering soothing sounds. The bleeping sound grew clearer, now matching the strumming of her heart. She blinked until the face of a nurse came into focus.

'Hello, pet,' the nurse said with a smile.

Gwen tried to speak but her tongue lay thick and heavy in her mouth. She inched her head off the pillow and looked around. She was covered in a white sheet. Wires ran from her chest to a monitor. One arm was weighted down with a cast and a drip stood next to the bed emptying fluid into the other arm. Her gaze travelled down to her right leg, which was elevated and surrounded with a metal brace. She could just make out the rods protruding from her skin. She felt bile rise in her throat. She struggled to sit up and pain stabbed at her ribs. Panic constricted her throat. The sound from the monitor increased with her rapid heartbeat.

'Take it easy, honey,' the nurse said. 'Come now, I'll help you sit up.'

Gwen allowed the nurse to help her into a sitting position then watched as she took a glass from the bedside table and filled it with water from a jug.

'Try to sip slowly.' The nurse held the glass to Gwen's lips.

The cool liquid soothed the soreness in her mouth and freed her tongue.

'Why am I here?' The words came out in a croak.

A worried expression flitted across the nurse's face but she quickly forced a smile.

'The doctor will come along and have a chat with you shortly. Try to rest now. Don't look so worried, you're perfectly safe here. Just press the buzzer if you need me.'

2

The nurse walked away, leaving Gwen alone. She let her head fall back against the pillow. She wanted to stay awake and find out what was going on but her eyes stung with fatigue and a heaviness spread through her body. She closed her eyes and sank back into the darkness.

* * *

'Gwenny, Gwenny love, can you hear me?'

Gwen opened her eyes. Her mother was sat next to the bed, tears streaming down her face.

'They called to tell me you'd woken up. I came straight away.'

Gwen stared at her mother. She couldn't believe how thin she looked. Her mother had always kept her hair pristine, now dark roots showed through her blond hair. She felt her lips tremble as confusion and fear constricted her throat.

'Oh, my poor darling.' Her mother stood and leant over the bed, gently cradling Gwen in her arms.

'Hello, Gwen, I'm Dr Powell.'

Gwen peered over her mother's shoulders and saw a portly, bespectacled man in a white coat. A smile crinkled his eyes as he moved closer to the bed. Her mother straightened up and sat back on the chair before taking a tissue from her handbag and wiping her eyes.

'How are you feeling?' Dr Powell asked.

Gwen couldn't find the words to describe how she felt. 'OK, I guess.'

'Good. Now, I just want to check you over and then we'll have a little chat.' Dr Powell checked Gwen's blood pressure and reflexes before shining a torch into her eyes.

'Everything looks fine, I think she'll soon be on her feet and you can take her home, Sue.'

He smiled at her mother before turning his attention back to his patient. 'Now, Gwen, can you tell me what day it is today?'

Gwen chewed her lip in concentration. 'Um, Wednesday, I think.'

'And the date.'

'Twentieth of May, 1999.'

Sue gasped and took her daughter's hand.

'It's July, darling, you've been asleep since' – she looked at the doctor then back to Gwen – 'for a few weeks.'

'But that can't be...' Gwen's mind raced as she tried to pick through memories.

Dr Powell pulled up a chair beside the bed.

'Please don't be alarmed. Temporary amnesia is quite common following a head trauma.'

Gwen touched the side of her head and felt the spiky regrowth of hair. 'My hair!' she shrieked. 'You've cut off my hair.'

'I'm sorry, Gwen, we had no choice. We had to operate to relieve the pressure on your brain. It'll grow back.' He smiled and patted her hand.

'But I don't understand.' Gwen fought to control the rising panic. 'Did I have an accident?'

'What's the last thing you remember before waking up here?'

Gwen turned her head away and stared at the glass on the bedside table as her vision blurred with tears.

'Do you want some water, darling?'

Sue stood, filled the glass from the jug and handed it to Gwen.

Gwen sipped the water slowly as she searched her memory. Everything appeared clouded like she was watching an out-of-focus film. Pain stabbed at her temples.

'The bus. I was on the school bus with Beth. We were sat in the front and were talking about my birthday. Did the bus crash?'

'No–' her mum began.

'It's better that it comes back to you naturally,' Dr Powell cut in. 'Give it a few days.'

'Exactly how long have I been here?' Gwen asked.

Her mum looked at Dr Powell who nodded his head. 'Since the twenty-first of June.'

'But it's only May.' Gwen felt tears sting her eyes.

'It's OK, love,' Sue said. 'I'm sure it'll all come back to you. Try not to think about it now, you have to rest and concentrate on getting well.'

After the doctor and her mum left, Gwen rested her head against the pillow. She strained her mind to remember but nothing surfaced. She was sure she would have remembered if the bus had crashed.

* * *

The days blended into each other as Gwen attended physiotherapy and counselling. Her mother came in every day and some of her school friends and teachers came to visit but there was no sign of her best friend Beth. Gwen went through all scenarios in her mind, but none made any sense. The one thing she was sure of is that Beth was somehow involved. She was her best friend and the only reason she wouldn't visit is if she had been injured herself. Gwen had tried searching the other wards in the hospital for Beth and had given up asking questions. She saw pity in the eyes of her visitors but no one gave a hint of what had happened, they just chatted away with forced cheerfulness.

At the end of the second week, Gwen's uncle David visited along with her mum. Both looked tense as her mum took a seat and fiddled with her handbag. Uncle David hovered at the bottom of the bed.

Gwen felt her body stiffen. 'What's wrong?'

'Nothing, love.' Her mum glanced at David then forced a smile. 'Dr Powell will be along in a moment, he wants to talk about your progress.'

'What's there to talk about? I still can't remember a sodding thing.'

'Gwen! There's no need to use that language,' Sue scolded.

'Well, what do you expect? I've been stuck in here for weeks. No one will tell me what happened and Beth hasn't bothered to come and see me. I'm pissed off!' Gwen folded her arms across her chest and glared at her mother.

Dr Powell entered the room and approached the bed. 'I hear you are making good progress with the physiotherapy on your arm and leg,' he said. 'I also understand that despite the intensive counselling you haven't had any recall of your memory. I understand your frustration but with this type of amnesia it could take months or years before you recover your memory. There's also the possibility that this missing period of time may never be recovered.' He looked at Sue and nodded.

'Gwenny, love, you were attacked.' Sue paused and drew in a steadying breath. 'You were up the quarry with Beth.'

'When? I don't understand. We were on the school bus. That's the last thing I remember.' Gwen heard her voice quiver; she suddenly felt afraid but didn't understand why. 'Are you saying Beth attacked me?'

'No, both you and Beth were attacked,' David said.

'By who?'

'We don't know.' Sue twisted her hands. 'The police want to talk to you, they were hoping that you'd remember.'

'Is Beth OK?' Gwen felt a chill pass over her body and pulled the sheet up to her chin.

Tears filled her mum's eyes. 'I'm so sorry, love. Beth didn't make it. She was already dead when they found her.'

'No!'

Gwen heard a high-pitched shriek and it took her a moment to realise that she was the one making it.

Chapter Two

About twenty years later

Gwen stood in the shower and felt the water pound her sore head like hailstones. Shouldn't have drunk so much last night, she thought as she took the bar of soap and worked up a lather. As she rubbed her hands over her body, she felt the familiar contours of the scars that ran down her right arm and leg, where the surgeons had operated to repair her shattered bones. They were a constant reminder that somewhere in the depths of her mind lay a memory too horrific to surface.

She finished washing, then vigorously dried her body before leaving the bathroom. Blue, her Siberian husky, was waiting outside the door, his tail swishing through the air.

'Morning, boy.' She patted his head. 'Looks like it's just you and me awake.'

In the bedroom she looked at Matt, her husband, lying on his back in bed, his mouth hanging open as snores filled the room. Irritation crawled at her skin as she observed him. His hair had thinned, revealing the pink scalp beneath, and the bulge of his stomach was visible beneath the sheets. He still thought himself a stud even though he could hardly pull his own weight, let alone pull some woman. Gwen thought him pathetic. She scowled at the slumbering form and turned away. Last night's party had been Matt's idea; she never cared much about celebrating her birthday. For Matt it was just another opportunity to flirt. She pulled the curtains roughly and let the sunlight illuminate the room. Matt grunted and turned onto his side.

'I guess it's me who has to deal with the mess downstairs,' she hissed. She pulled on a pair of cropped jeans and a vest before plugging in the dryer and running it over her blond hair.

Matt still hadn't stirred so she slammed the bedroom door as she left the room. Downstairs she made a cup of tea and surveyed the scene. Overflowing ashtrays, empty bottles, and discarded cans stood among half-eaten plates of food. She took a few deep breaths and felt the irritation thaw. Blue danced around her feet so she opened the back door for him, then set about cleaning the kitchen.

* * *

'It was a good night.' Matt ambled into the kitchen two hours later, hair dishevelled and stubble covering his chin.

'It was OK.' Gwen pulled the plates from the dishwasher and stacked them in the cupboard. 'It would've been nice to have some help to clean up.'

'You should've woken the kids.' Matt yawned as he poured boiling water into a mug and added a teabag. 'I think I'll lie on the sofa for a while. My head is killing me. That's what Sundays are for.' He winked and slouched into the living room.

'Yeah, if you're a man. One of us has to cook the Sunday roast.' Gwen popped two painkillers into her mouth before filling a bucket with water and mopping the floor.

Alex, her seventeen-year-old, soon surfaced; he padded across the wet floor and made himself a piece of toast before mumbling something incoherent and joining his father. Gwen had yet to master teenage boys' mumble language and conversations with her son were a rarity. Ariana was last to emerge. Gwen's once pink-loving ballerina daughter had turned fifteen and morphed into the princess of darkness. Long black hair hung over eyes barely visible beneath heavy eyeliner. Black clothes decorated by skulls were topped off with a lip piercing.

Gwen smiled at her daughter. 'Morning, love.'

'Morning.'

Ariana sat at the kitchen table, brooding.

'Got any plans today?'

'No, I have to do homework.'

Gwen was glad all that was behind her. Trying to fit in with the popular girls. Heartache over boys and parents that don't understand you. Life is one big, dark abyss as a teenager, she thought. She smiled to herself as she watched Ariana send a text then glide into the living room to join the others.

The kitchen now restored to order, Gwen put a joint of meat into the oven, set the temperature, and grabbed Blue's lead. The dog whined with excitement as she attached his collar.

'I'm going out for a walk to clear my head,' she called into the living room. No one took any notice so she grabbed her handbag and shut the door.

* * *

The June sun beat down from a cloudless sky, bringing unseasonal warmth as she walked uphill to the park. Ahead the Black Mountains rose sending down a gentle breeze. The aspirin had taken away the worse of the headache and the fresh air cleared away the last of her irritation. Apart from the occasional car passing, all was quiet in the small Welsh village of Bryn Melyn. As she approached the gate to the park her peace was shattered by the shouts and squeals of children playing on the swings. Gwen stopped and Blue sat down, panting.

'Too hot for you today, isn't it, boy?' She ran her hands through his thick white fur. 'What you need is a swim, but I don't think I've got the energy to walk to the river today. Sorry.'

An image of a stream gently tumbling over rocks entered her mind. She felt her body tense. As she took another step towards the park, the image grew stronger. She could almost feel the cool water running over her feet and pictured Blue splashing around.

Oh, why not, what's there to be afraid of? she thought. She turned and walked in the opposite direction, Blue plodding alongside. She entered Quarry Road, walked past the terraced houses and the entrance to the disused quarry, then through the archway of trees that led to the footpath.

At the gate she paused. She hadn't been up the quarry since the attack, not even to see where they found Beth's body. As she stood lingering at the gate, she wondered if the teenagers from the village walked the path. She imagined them daring each other to go through the gate and to the place where they found the dead girl. She even forbid her own children to come here. An image of Beth stepping through the gate flashed across her mind. They used to come to the quarry to hang around in the shack drinking and smoking. A melancholy mood settled over her as the image grew stronger and she pictured Beth in her low-rise jeans, long blond waves bouncing off her shoulders as she walked.

Blue scratching at the gate brought Gwen to the present.

'OK, let's go.'

Gwen pushed open the gate and stepped through. As she took hesitant steps forward, she felt her stomach twist with anxiety. She could hear the stream now, and as her senses heightened she picked up other noises: birds flitting from branch to branch of the sycamore trees, snapping twigs as they went. The smell of a promised summer lingered in the air. She tried to relax as she followed the footpath down until there was a clearing in the trees. There she unclipped Blue's lead and watched him bound towards the water. She followed him down the bank, slipped off her loafers, and dipped her feet in the water, a gasp escaping her as the cold water stung her toes and sent a shiver up her body. She stepped back and found a large rock to sit on as she watched the dog swim. Pure pleasure lit up his eyes and Gwen couldn't help smiling.

When Blue was satisfied with his swim he bounced over to Gwen and shook his coat, spraying her with water. 'Thanks!' She giggled, wiping the water from her arms. 'I suppose we'd better start back.'

She stood and clipped the lead to his collar before leading the way back to the path. At the gate she stopped, she didn't feel like going home.

'We could walk a little bit more.' She patted the dog's head. 'There's no one here, nothing to be afraid of.'

She turned and walked further along the path until she came to a set of steps. A deep foreboding settled over her but she pushed herself on. With each step up, her unease grew; her mouth felt dry and the lead slipped in her hand as perspiration covered her palms. She stopped for a moment unsure if she should go on. She felt pathetic, a grown woman afraid of something she didn't remember happening. She took a deep breath and continued up the steps.

As she walked, she tried to imagine what it would have been like if Beth had survived. Would they still be friends? Spend their days in each other's houses, drinking tea and complaining about their husbands? She stopped when she reached the top of the steps, to catch her breath and scan her surroundings. To her right she could see the disused quarry, and the scars left on the landscape by decades of people hacking away the limestone.

She continued along the path until she came to a second set of steps. Blue happily tugged her upwards, eager to explore new territory. Her legs started to ache as she reached the top step and was grateful when the path levelled off. She stopped for a moment to peer down the ravine. Jagged rocks protruded from the cliff face. The height made her legs weak even though a wooden fence protected walkers from falling.

Gwen knew the path ran alongside farmland and onto the mountain, as she had often walked this route with Beth. Sometimes they would walk the rough grassy hills, pick up the road, and walk back into the village just to fill the time. Mostly they stayed in the shack, hidden from prying eyes where they would discuss boys and sex whilst drinking a flagon of cider. If she went any further she would get to the shack. A cold shiver ran over her body and she rubbed her arms. She looked down again at the stream far below, wending its way towards the village, and tried to steady her breathing.

'Come on.' She tugged on Blue's lead. The old corrugated tin shack came into view set back on the side of the path. A snippet of a memory twisted Gwen's stomach. She could see Beth walking ahead of her, hips swaying, and a silver bracelet dangling on her wrist. She couldn't understand why the shack hadn't been pulled down. Tears gathered in her eyes and she blinked them away as she approached the shack. Two wooden sleepers had been used to make crude steps to the door, the rotten wood crumbled at the edges.

Gwen stepped up and put her hand on the door. Her legs shook, threatening to buckle. You have to look, she thought. She pushed open the door and stepped inside. Blue sniffed around sending dust particles dancing in the air. Her eyes travelled over the dirt floor, then to the walls where the old rusty tools still hung on nails. There was no sign that anything bad had happened in this place. She took a step closer to the wall and noticed the axe was missing. A gap lay between a saw and a rake.

'Oh Beth, who did this to us?' She closed her eyes and tried to conjure Beth's face. When she opened them again she saw Beth lying on the floor, her hair matted with blood, eyes staring glazed and lifeless. A pool of blood seeped into the dirt floor. A strangled cry left Gwen's lips as she backed out of the shack. So much blood, she thought as her foot missed the step and she felt herself falling.

Chapter Three

Detective Inspector Meadows turned off his computer, sat back in his chair, and sighed. His report was now ready to hand over to DCI Lester in the morning. Operation Sweetcorn had been a success. The cannabis-producing operation concealed in a disused factory had been closed down and several arrests made. Now Meadows was bored. He knew it would be quiet working as part of a small team in the Welsh Valleys, but thought he would settle in and enjoy the breathing space after working in a major crimes unit in London. Since relocating back to his home town a year ago, though, he had done nothing but deal with drug operations and the occasional fraud. He wanted something to challenge his intellect and keep him awake at night.

Meadows grabbed his jacket and headed downstairs, where Sergeant Dyfan Folland was manning the reception desk.

Meadows leaned against the desk. 'How's it going, Folland?'

'Pretty quiet, apart from some guy complaining about a missing wife. Apparently she put the roast on, went out for a walk, and hasn't been seen since.'

'So the guy's hungry. Is that what's classed as an emergency in the Valleys now?' Meadows chuckled.

Folland's laughter was cut short by the telephone ringing. He picked it up and addressed the caller in an authoritative voice.

Meadows stood and listened to the exchange. He saw Folland's expression turn from irritation to interest as he scribbled down details before ending the call.

'That was the missing woman's uncle, David Collier.'

The name stirred Meadows' memory.

'Were you still living here when those two girls were attacked in Bryn Melyn?' Folland asked.

'Yes, I was taking my A levels at the time. Gwen Collier and Bethan Hopkins. I used to catch the same bus into school as them.'

'Well, it's Gwen that's gone missing.'

'Perhaps I should call in on the family. It's understandable they're concerned after what they went through.'

'I suppose, but I can't see what this has to do with what happened then. Unless they think the murderer has materialised after' – Folland screwed his face up in concentration – 'must be fifteen years.'

'More like twenty,' Meadows said. 'Still, I think we should check it out. What's the name of her husband?'

'Matthew Thomas.'

Meadows felt his body stiffen. 'So, she stayed with him.'

'Do you know him?'

'Used to be in school with him. He was a right arsehole.'

'Well, if the way he spoke to me on the phone is anything to go by, he hasn't changed much,' Folland said.

'Give me the address and I'll head up there now. I'll call and give you an update.'

'She still lives in Bryn Melyn.' Folland copied down the details.

Meadows took the paper from Folland and looked at the address before leaving the building. Bryn Mawr town centre was almost deserted at this time of night. Only a few people could be seen grouped outside the Crown Inn, cradling glasses while they smoked. Meadows drove out of town and onto a dark stretch of road with empty fields on each side.

Matt Thomas, it will be interesting to see him after all these years.

He let his thoughts drift back to the late nineties. Matt had made his life a misery with his constant bullying. Always surrounded by the same group of boys who would strut around the school looking for their next victim. Gwen and Bethan were two years younger. He could picture them now, sitting on the school bus gossiping and giggling. Gwen always gave him a smile whenever they passed in the school corridors. News of the attack had spread quickly through the school, followed by flowers left at the gates for Bethan, and prayers for Gwen's recovery as girls sobbed and clung to each other. After that came the speculation of who was responsible. Then the worry that there was a killer on the loose. Parents became anxious. Teenagers stayed indoors, afraid to go out after dark. Meadows left the Valleys a year after the attack and when he returned to visit some years later, the murder of Bethan Hopkins had been forgotten and the people of the village had moved on with their lives.

I don't suppose Gwen ever got over what happened, he mused as he drove in and out of the villages until he came to Bryn Melyn. He parked the car and looked at the Thomas' house: a detached, red brick house with a neatly bordered lawn. Two cars sat on the driveway, one with private number plates, the other an old hatchback.

Looks like Matt has done alright for himself.

The daylight had faded and a waning moon struggled to illuminate the sky. The lights had been turned on in the house but the curtains left open, and through the window a figure could be seen pacing back and forth. Meadows took a deep breath and got out of the car. The front door swung open as he approached the house and a wiry, grey-haired man appeared. He wore grey slacks with an open-neck shirt.

'Hello, I'm DI Meadows.' He showed his identification.

'It's about bloody time. Do you know how many calls we've made? You should have come out hours ago.'

Meadows ignored the outburst. 'And you are?'

'David Collier, Gwen's uncle. You better come in.'

Meadows stepped over the threshold, followed David into the sitting room, and took in the scene. A teenage boy and girl were sat on a cream sofa. The boy glared at Meadows while the girl kept her head down as her fingers worked furiously over the screen of her phone. A man in his late thirties with receding blond hair stood in the centre of the room and eyed Meadows suspiciously.

'Police, Matt,' David said.

'DI Meadows.' Meadows watched Matt closely for signs of recognition. It didn't take long.

'Meadows?' His eyes narrowed. 'Winter Meadows?'

'That's right.' Meadows walked further into the room.

'Bloody hell, you're a policeman. Well, there's a turn-up.' Matt's lips curled into a sneer.

'Detective Inspector, actually. It's been a long time, Matt.' He noticed Matt had put on a few pounds over the years, which together with the receding hairline gave Meadows a shot of satisfaction. He knew Matt would be eyeing his lean six-foot-one frame and full head of black hair with envy. He struggled to keep his face neutral.

This isn't the time for one-upmanship.

The kitchen door opened and a lady walked in, short ash-blond hair pushed behind her ears. She wore a pair of capri pants and a short-sleeved pink sweater.

'It's the police, love,' David said.

Meadows saw the colour drain from her face and her hands flew up to her mouth. David moved quickly and put his arm around her shoulder, drawing her in close.

'It's OK, there is no news,' David said. He turned to Meadows. 'This is my sister-in-law, Sue.'

Meadows held out his hand in greeting. 'I'm sorry if I startled you. To be honest, we don't usually get involved in a missing adult at this early stage, but given events of the past I appreciate how concerned you must be. At the moment this is just a courtesy call so I can take some details and establish if the situation warrants further investigation.'

'Well, that's good of you,' Matt said, his voice laced with sarcasm.

'Please, take a seat,' Sue said as she shot Matt a warning look. 'Would you like a cup of tea or coffee?'

'No thanks.' Meadows sat down in an armchair.

Matt grinned. 'Maybe a herbal drink then?'

Meadows ignored the comment and took out his notebook and pen. 'Perhaps you can start by telling me what happened this morning before Gwen left the house?'

'Nothing happened, she took the dog out for a walk and didn't come back. She usually only goes out for about an hour.' Matt slumped down in the chair opposite Meadows.

'And how did she seem when she left?'

'Just her normal self.'

'Had there been an argument?'

'No.' Matt clenched his jaw.

'Has she been worried or depressed recently?'

'What is this?' Matt snapped. He jumped up from the chair and started pacing the room. 'What's the point of all these questions? You should be out looking for her.'

'They're just standard questions. I'm trying to establish Gwen's state of mind when she left the house.'

'He's trying to help, Matt,' Sue said sharply.

Meadows got the impression that Sue Collier didn't have much time for her son-in-law. He rubbed his chin then looked Matt in the eyes.

'What was she wearing when she left?'

Matt shrugged his shoulders.

'Ariana,' Sue said. 'What was your mother wearing this morning?'

The girl looked up from her phone and eyed Meadows as if she had only just realised he was in the room. 'Cropped jeans and a green vest top, probably her loafers, she always has those ugly things on her feet.'

Meadows smiled at the girl.

'How did your mum seem to you this morning?'

'OK, I suppose. I guess she was a bit pissed off.'

'Ariana!' Sue scolded.

'Go on,' Meadows encouraged.

'We had a party last night for Mum's birthday. She didn't really want one and there was a lot of mess for her to clean up. Then Dad got drunk and...' She glanced across at Matt, who shot her a thunderous look. 'Well, nothing, she probably had a hangover.'

'Perhaps she was a little fed up and went to see a friend,' Meadows suggested.

'No, she's not like that. Anyway, she wouldn't deliberately stay away and worry her mother,' David said.

'We've called everyone she knows and no one has seen her today. The kids have been out to all the usual places she walks the dog,' Sue added.

'Have you got a recent photograph of Gwen?'

It was Sue who moved to the mantelpiece and took down a photo frame and handed it to Meadows.

Doesn't look any different.

His eyes roamed over her face. Her hair was a shade lighter and fine lines showed around her eyes and mouth.

'Do you mind if I take this with me? I'll get some copies made and return it to you.' He looked over the notes he had written. 'What type of dog does Gwen have?'

'It's a Siberian husky, white. I bought him for Gwen. I thought she might feel more secure if she had a dog,' David said.

'We'll keep an eye out for the dog and check with the dog warden, see if he has been picked up.'

'Blue would never leave Mum. He follows her everywhere.' Ariana's voice quivered.

Meadows turned to Matt. 'Is Gwen on any medication?'

'She takes a low dose of Citalopram and occasionally tranquilisers to help her sleep. She's suffered with anxiety ever since the attack.' Matt squirmed, obviously uncomfortable talking about the subject.

'You don't think this has anything to do with what happened then, do you?' Sue fingered her necklace with trembling hands.

'I shouldn't think so.' *I hope not.* Meadows gave Sue what he hoped was a reassuring smile. 'Where does Gwen go to when she walks the dog?'

'The park or the rugby field. If it's warm she walks up the mountain to the river. We've checked everywhere. Ariana and Alex have been up the mountain.' Matt started pacing the room again.

'What about the quarry footpath?'

The atmosphere in the room darkened. Sue visibly flinched and Matt stopped pacing and glared at Meadows. The silence hung in the air until Alex spoke up.

'Mum never goes up there. She even forbids me and Ariana to go anywhere near the quarry.' He had the same steely eyes as his father – they challenged Meadows to argue.

'Gwen hasn't been up there since the attack. She would never go up there alone,' Sue said.

Meadows stood. 'I'll log the details at the station, check the hospital, and alert uniform to watch out for Gwen and the dog. Can you give me Gwen's mobile number? I take it she took her phone with her.'

'Is that all?' Matt stepped closer to Meadows. His eyes blazed. 'Shouldn't you be calling in a search team or something?'

'At this point, we don't know exactly where Gwen went. It's a large area to search and it's dark. I can assure you we will do all we can to find Gwen.' Meadows turned his attention to Sue. 'Did Gwen ever recover her memory?'

'No, she went to a psychotherapist for years, but nothing ever came of it. To be honest, I think it's a blessing that she doesn't remember.'

Meadows nodded. 'Please contact the station if you hear anything from Gwen. I will be in touch soon. I understand how difficult this is but I'm sure there is a reasonable explanation for Gwen's disappearance.'

David saw Meadows to the door. 'Thank you for coming out. I'm sorry about Matt, I guess he's just worried about Gwen.'

'That's understandable. How old are the children?'

'Alex is seventeen and Ariana fifteen.'

The daughter is the same age as Gwen was when she was attacked.

'They are both fully aware of what happened to their mother and Bethan Hopkins?' Meadows asked.

'Yes, of course.'

'OK. Good. I will be in touch as soon as I have any news.' Meadows shook David's hand and headed for his car. Once inside he called the station and gave Folland an update.

'So what do you think?' Folland asked.

'Well, it sounds out of character for her to go off and not get in contact with her family. The husband is pretty wound up.'

'Any domestic problems?'

'Not that I've been made aware of. There was a strange atmosphere in the house and I get the impression the daughter would have said more if Matt hadn't been there. Maybe something happened at the party last night.'

'She could have run off. It happens. There isn't much you can do tonight and your shift finished hours ago. Go home and get some rest.'

Meadows ran his hand through his hair. He had a bad feeling about this. 'I think I should check out the quarry. It's the only place the family hasn't looked.'

'Do you want me to send up a couple of boys?' Folland offered.

'Nah, I'm here now. Won't take me long. I have a torch in the car. I'll call in when I've finished the search.' Meadows hung up and drove the short distance to the entry of the quarry then stepped out of the car. From this elevated position he could see most of the village lit with streetlights.

She couldn't have gone far without being seen. He scanned his surroundings. The rugby pitch, now in darkness, was just off the main road leading into the village.

She would have been seen going there and there's no cover. The park was on the mountain road, again, visible to passing traffic and the surrounding houses. The kids had searched the mountain so that only left the quarry footpath. Meadows sighed. He didn't relish the thought of walking the path in the dark. The place used to give him the creeps in the daylight.

The streetlights ended at the entrance to the quarry path; beyond, the pathway disappeared into inky blackness, trees arching over it. Meadows opened the boot of his car and sat on the edge as he changed his shoes for walking boots. There was a chill in the air so he slipped on a windbreaker before grabbing the torch and heading into the archway of trees.

A gentle breeze rustled the branches as he approached the gate and an uneasy feeling prickled at his skin. He shrugged it off, turned up the beam on the torch, and entered the gate. He could hear the stream tumbling over the rocks but could only see the part of the path illuminated in the torchlight. He shone the torch around, picking out trees before walking briskly on. By the time he reached the top of the second set of steps, he was breathless. He stood to catch his breath then called out.

'Gwen! Gwen!' His voice magnified in the silence, disturbing birds. The beating of wings and indignant squawks filled the air, then silence fell. He could feel the darkness pressing against his back and resisted the urge to turn around. He continued to call as he shone the torch from side to side, increasing his pace until he reached the shack.

She wouldn't go in there, not after what happened.

He pushed away thoughts of the murder as he shone the torch on the ground. The beam picked up a discarded canvas handbag.

Meadows crouched on the ground, slipped on a pair of latex gloves, and opened the bag. He rummaged around until he found a mobile phone and purse. His heart quickened as he flipped open the card compartment and pulled out Gwen's driving licence.

'Gwen!' he called out again. He stood, the door to the shack was open, dread coiled around his chest as he entered. The torch swept the ground.

She's not here. He released his breath and stepped outside. As the torch illuminated the ground it picked out a stone jutting from the earth. He knelt to take a closer look. Blood. His stomach clenched. *This can't be happening again.*

He fished his mobile from his pocket and called the station.

Chapter Four

Giles Epworth was walking his dog near the quarry when he saw blue flashing lights enter the village. He stood and watched. From his elevated position he could see the cars turn into Quarry Road. He called the dog and attached the lead before drawing back from sight.

The cars drew up near the entry of the quarry and Giles heard doors opening and voices drifting across the night air. The dog yapped.

'Hush!' Giles commanded as he tugged on the lead. He knew the police had probably heard the dog and worried it would look bad if they came in his direction and caught him skulking around. He pulled on the lead and walked towards the police cars.

What's going on? he thought. He recalled he had seen Ariana and Alex Thomas looking for their mother earlier that evening. Giles stopped. He felt his chest tighten at the thought that it could be happening again and this time he would be seen. He raised his hand instinctively, rubbing at his chest as the muscles contracted.

One of the police officers approached him.

'Are you alright, sir?'

Giles took a steadying breath. 'Yes, thank you. Just old age creeping up on me.' He tried to smile but was afraid it came across as a grimace. He took a step towards the officer whilst trying to decide if he should ask why they were there.

The officer smiled and turned away. Guessing the police didn't want questions, Giles hurried home. Once inside, he took off his coat and poured a large glass of brandy. The amber liquid heated the back of his throat and he felt warmth penetrate his chest.

What if it is Gwen they are looking for? Well, it's too late now, they saw me. What if they come around asking questions? He rubbed his hands over his face and realised he was shaking. There had been no questions last time, after twenty years he should be safe.

He thought of the press coverage and the talk that had filled the staff room after the attack. Sweet, innocent girls. He knew better. Bloody little bitches. Prick teasers, that's what they were. Coming into school with their skirts hiked up and plastered in make-up. Begging for it. He felt the anger tense his body and a sharp pain tore across his chest. He poured another glass of brandy and knocked it back. He'd just have to wait until the morning to find out if something had happened to Gwen. The staff room was always full of gossip.

Giles took his glass into the sitting room and sat in the armchair but couldn't settle. He needed to know what was going on now, so he could be prepared. He called the dog and clipped on the lead.

'Sorry, boy, just a short walk.' He patted the dog's head before leaving the house. He hurried towards Gwen's house. All the lights were on and to his relief there was no police car parked outside. He felt the tension leave his body as he turned and headed back home.

Chapter Five

Meadows watched as the area was cordoned off by tape. The search team and forensic experts were on their way but he still felt he should be doing more to find Gwen. The situation left him feeling inept. He knew he would have to justify the use of precious resources but didn't see what other option he had. He saw DCI Lester approach and braced himself. The boss came to stand next to Meadows and surveyed the scene.

'I didn't expect to see you here, sir.'

'I thought I'd stop by, what have you got?'

'Missing woman, Gwen Thomas, hasn't been seen since noon. No history of depression, although she does take medication for PTSD, mild anxiety from what the family tell me. Domestic life seems stable. I found her handbag containing her mobile phone and purse. There's also blood on a stone.' Meadows indicated the area. 'She could have injured herself and gone for help, but as she had a mobile phone, fully charged with a strong signal, I don't think that's the case.'

Lester turned away from the scene and looked around. 'Where does this path lead?'

'Onto the mountain.'

'That's a pretty large area to search, even in daylight.'

'I'm aware of that. I think we will have to start the search in the immediate area and wait until daylight to search the mountain if nothing turns up.'

Lester rubbed his chin then sighed. 'I only see three options here. One, she's depressed and has taken her own life.' He looked towards the fence. 'Two, she planned to disappear and staged this, or three, she's been taken by force.'

'Well, as I said, there's no history of depression, and if she jumped over the fence, where's the dog?'

'Dog?'

'She had a dog with her, a Siberian husky, large fella by all accounts. I don't think she would have staged a disappearance. Not here. You are aware of the family history, sir?'

'Of course. I remember the case well.'

'Well, she wouldn't choose this spot and put her family through hell deliberately.'

'No, then I think we can assume we are looking at a crime scene. Right, I'll leave you in charge. Keep me updated.' Lester took one last look at the scene and started to walk away. He paused and turned around. 'Have the family been informed of this latest development?'

'Not yet. I would like to do that personally. I've requested a liaison officer to meet me at the house.'

Lester nodded and continued on his way.

One of the uniform officers came up to Meadows. 'He didn't hang about.'

'Probably didn't fancy being up all night,' Meadows said.

He liked Lester and knew him well enough to know that being in charge of several stations across the Valleys kept him busy. He wasn't the type of man to jump in and take over for the glory. He would be happy to let Meadows head up the case. 'I'm going to see the family. Forensics and search and rescue are on their way. I shouldn't be more than an hour.'

Meadows walked down the footpath, changed out of his boots, and drove to the Thomas' house.

* * *

The door opened as soon as he pulled up outside the house. David Collier approached the car. 'Have you found her?'

'Let's go inside,' Meadows said. He followed David into the sitting room where all eyes looked at him expectantly. 'Matt, can we talk somewhere private?' He looked pointedly at the teenagers.

Matt led him into the kitchen, closely followed by Sue and David, who closed the door.

'We found Gwen's handbag on the quarry footpath.' He didn't want to mention the blood yet.

Sue gasped and sank into the nearest chair. David put his hand on her shoulder, his own face ashen.

'I've called in a team to search the surrounding area.'

Matt started for the door. 'I'm going up there.'

Meadows was quick to block his way. 'I don't think that's a good idea. It would be better if you stayed here with your family. I promise, as soon as there is any news we will let you know.'

Matt shoved Meadows in the chest, his face contorted with anger. 'Don't tell me what to do,' he seethed.

'I would advise you to calm down. If you go up there now you could hamper the search. These people are trained professionals. They know their job.'

'Yeah, try and stop me. It's my wife out there. I'll fucking floor you!' Matt grabbed a handful of Meadows' jacket and yanked him forward. His eyes blazed and he clenched his other fist ready to strike.

Meadows took hold of Matt's wrist and yanked his hand away. 'Threaten me again and I'll have you arrested. You're not helping the situation.'

The men stood face to face. Meadows had a height advantage and knew he could easily overpower Matt.

'Matt, please stop,' Sue begged. 'You're acting like a prick.'

Whether it was the shock of his mother-in-law using out of character language or the desperation in her voice, Meadows couldn't tell, but Matt stepped back, his breath coming in short bursts.

'A family liaison officer will be here shortly. She will stay with you and keep you updated. She'll also be able to answer any questions you might have.'

'This is just like last time.' Sue's body shook as she sobbed. 'Why would she go up there?'

Meadows wanted to offer some words of comfort but he knew that platitudes were no good. He was relieved to hear a knock at the door. The family liaison officer was led in and took over.

* * *

Meadows headed back up the quarry. Floodlights had been erected and lit the cordoned off area where a forensic team picked at the ground.

'Have you found anything?'

'No, not yet. There's only one set of footprints, plus those of the dog. It looks like she went into the shack. The steps are unstable and there are some scuff marks and broken-off bits of wood. She could have slipped.'

'Or been pushed.'

The forensic officer shrugged her shoulders and continued the search. Meadows wandered over to the search team, who were rigging ropes off a nearby tree.

Meadows peered over the fence and winced at the drop. 'You think she might have gone over?'

'We can't get a clear view because of the trees. The only way to check is to send one of the men down. I'll send the team up to the mountain when we've finished here. I don't think it will do much good, though. It would be better to wait for first light.'

Meadows watched as one of the team climbed into a harness.

If she is down there, she would have had to go over the fence. There's no sign of a struggle.

'Why don't you go home and get a few hours' sleep? I reckon you'll have a bitch of a day to face in the morning. There isn't anything you can do here.' The team leader patted Meadows on the shoulder.

'Yeah, I might just do that.' Meadows headed back to his car. He had to admit he felt drained but he knew he wouldn't be able to sleep.

* * *

Back in his cottage he changed out of his suit, made a strong mug of coffee, and stood in the kitchen gazing out of the window. It was dark outside and he could see nothing of the farmland that surrounded the cottage. He had bought the place from his mother so that she could move into a ground floor flat, his intention being to renovate and sell the place on. One year on, he still hadn't made a start on the work.

He wandered into the sitting room and turned on the reading lamp which created a soft glow on the orange walls. His mother had decorated the room with bright, cheerful colours but the décor did little to lift his sombre mood. He plucked a book from the shelf and opened it. The inside was hollow and held a small bag of cannabis, a grinder, tobacco, and extra-long rolling papers. He rolled a joint, plonked himself down in the armchair, and lit up.

With each puff he felt his body relax into the chair. The cottage was silent apart from the ticking of the wall clock. He let his thoughts turn to Gwen and what lay ahead at first light if the search team didn't find her. He was sure that Gwen was in danger or already dead. He didn't like to think of that possibility but it could well be the outcome.

Unless she was so unhappy she disappeared of her own accord. No, he couldn't imagine that; the Gwen he knew wouldn't put her mother through all this anguish.

You haven't seen or spoken to her in years. You don't really know her or what she is capable of.

As first light filtered through the window, Meadows drifted into an uneasy sleep. The trilling of his mobile phone startled him awake. With a racing pulse, he snatched it from the table.

'Meadows.'

'We've found her.'

Chapter Six

Gwen could feel something wet against her cheek. Hot breath tickled her face. She opened her eyes and came face to face with a large white dog.

'Whoa, get off.'

The dog sniffed at her head then pawed her chest.

'Hey!' She pushed him away and tried to sit up. Pain shot through her head and the ground seemed to move beneath her body. She put her hand to the ground and waited for the dizziness to subside. She tried moving her head again. More pain. She put her hand to the back of her head and felt a sticky bump. She quickly pulled her hand away and brought it close to her face. Her fingers were covered in blood. Her stomach lurched and another wave of dizziness washed over her.

'What happened?' She slowly raised her body to a sitting position and looked around. The light was fading but she could make out the footpath and trees. A vibrating buzz filled the silence, this was followed by a tune. Gwen looked around searching for the source of the noise. Her eyes fell upon a handbag. She was tempted to look in the bag but it didn't seem right to nose around in someone else's property. Confusion clouded her mind. She didn't remember coming up to the quarry. She tried to concentrate and recall the last thing she remembered. She was on the school bus talking to Beth.

'Beth! Beth!' she shouted. She knew she wouldn't have come up the quarry alone and figured Beth must be around somewhere.

The dog whined and pawed her again.

'I don't know what you want.' It was then that she noticed the lead wrapped around her wrist. Panic gripped her body. Her eyes travelled down her body. They weren't her clothes. What the fuck are those things on my feet? she thought. Tears welled in her eyes and her body trembled violently.

She dared to turn her head and saw the shack with its door hanging open. Fear prickled at her skin. She had a strong feeling that she shouldn't look inside.

She got unsteadily to her feet, putting her hand on the dog's back to steady herself. 'I guess you had better come with me. Though why you're here, I've no idea.'

She staggered towards the path. Her mum was going to be so angry. She was not supposed to be out this late. I better get home, she thought. No, I can't; he'll be there. The thought froze in her mind. She rubbed her hands over her face trying to remember why she didn't want to go home. She pinched at her skin hoping to wake up from some weird dream but nothing happened, she still felt afraid. She wrapped her arms around her body and tried to rub away the chill. Tears leaked from her eyes as she changed direction and walked towards the mountain.

Gwen hurried along the path, the dog keeping step with her. Goosebumps covered her arms and she shivered uncontrollably. When she reached the gate she stepped through onto the mountain. It was dark now and she could only make out the silhouettes of grazing sheep that scattered when they saw the dog.

'Come on.' She tugged at the lead. She was glad now she had the company of the dog, she didn't think she could bear it if she was totally alone. She stumbled a few times across the rough terrain but fear pumped her adrenalin and kept her going. Her mouth was parched and she longed for a drink. Salty tears trickled down her face; she wiped them with the back of her hand and tried to swallow down the panic that lodged in the back of her throat.

Eventually she saw the large black outline of a hay barn. She knew it was too early for the hay to be cut but hoped there would be enough to keep her warm. It was then that she remembered that she'd been on her way to hide in the barn. She tried to hold onto that thought but it dispersed like vapour on the breeze.

Inside she found some bales of hay and loose straw. She dragged them together then lay down. The dog rested his head on her chest and she threaded her fingers through his hair. She suddenly felt weary. As her mind closed down she heard someone call her name.

'Stay quiet,' she mumbled to the dog. 'I don't want him to find me.'

Chapter Seven

Meadows rushed to his car. He felt the tension drain from his muscles. He had little information at this time, only that she had been found in a hay barn and taken to hospital. She was conscious but somewhat confused.

It took nearly an hour to drive to the hospital; the traffic was heavy, with commuters either heading into Swansea or picking up the M4 to drive further afield. Meadows had run through all scenarios in his mind and was eager to find out what had happened to Gwen.

Inside the hospital he took the stairs to the ward and as he approached Gwen's room, he saw a doctor step out.

'Can I have a word?'

The doctor turned and Meadows showed his identification.

'Sure, I'm Dr Rowland.' He held out his hand. 'I expect you want to know about Gwen's injuries.'

'Yes, I hope to have a chat with her in a moment, if you think she is up to answering some questions.'

'I don't see why not. All I can tell you at the moment is that she has taken a nasty bump to the back of the head, she needed stitches. As is usual for head injuries, she lost a lot of blood. What's interesting is that she seems to have had some sort of regression.'

'I don't understand.'

'She was very confused when she came in. From what she tells me she lost consciousness when she hit her head. When she came around she thought she was fifteen years old.'

'And now?'

'Apart from being shaken and tired, she's fine. I don't see any signs of concussion. She's aware of how old she is, the day, and date. Gwen told me that she has retrograde amnesia from a previous head trauma. I would like to take a look at her medical records and run some more tests. It could be that this latest knock to the head has somehow, how I shall put it?' Dr Rowland wrinkled his brow. 'Jolted her memory. Meanwhile, I don't think a few questions will do any harm. Just try to keep it short.'

Meadows quickly absorbed the doctor's words and felt a twinge of excitement at the thought of new information on the attack that took place all those years ago.

'Is it possible that she'll regain all of her previous memories?'

'I can't really comment on that until I assess her further. The chances are that she will begin to experience flashbacks, snippets of information. It won't be instantaneous, I shouldn't think.'

'Well, thank you for your time, Doctor. Perhaps I can talk to you again, when you've completed your tests?'

'Yes, of course. To be honest, I'm a little intrigued myself.' He smiled before turning away.

Meadows entered the room and saw Gwen propped up in bed with her head resting against the pillow. Her skin was pallid and she looked delicate and vulnerable beneath the white sheets. Matt sat on one side of the bed with the children standing next to him. On the opposite side stood Sue, looking as pale as her daughter, a tissue pressed against her eyes. David Collier stood in the corner of the room rubbing his hand over his unshaven face. His eyes were fixed upon Gwen.

Meadows walked further in and approached the bed.

'Hello, Gwen, I'm DI Meadows. Do you mind if I ask you a few questions?'

Gwen stared at Meadows and her face creased in concentration. Cornflower blue eyes searched his face, then she smiled warmly.

'Winter Meadows?'

'Yes, that's right.'

She remembers me. An ember from the past glowed in his stomach. He returned her smile.

'How are you feeling?'

'A little foolish, if I'm honest. I'm sorry to have caused so much trouble.'

'We are just glad that you're safe.' Meadows felt a stir in his emotions.

He became aware of Matt's glare and quickly took out his notebook. He thought the family might give him some space but they appeared reluctant to move and he didn't have the heart to ask them to leave.

'Do you feel up to telling me what happened yesterday?'

'I took Blue, my dog, out for a walk. I thought he could do with a swim and I didn't feel like walking up the mountain. I only intended to stay near the entrance of the quarry and let Blue play in the stream.' Gwen paused and sighed. 'Then I just walked a little further up. I haven't been up the quarry since the attack and I wanted to prove to myself that there was nothing to be afraid of.'

'Oh, Gwenny!' Sue cried. 'Why would you want to go up there, and on your own?'

'I know, it was stupid, but I had Blue with me. When I got to the old shack I guess I was surprised it was still there. I thought it might have been pulled down. I walked inside. It was OK at first, but then I could see Beth's body.

Blood pouring out of her head.' Gwen's voice broke and she pulled the sheet up to her neck with trembling hands.

'I think that's enough.' Matt stood and faced Meadows. 'We're grateful for all your help but I don't see the point in questioning her further.'

'Please, Matt, it's fine.' Gwen looked at Meadows. 'I don't mind.' She took a sip of water and continued. 'I don't know if it was some sort of flashback or my imagination but suddenly I felt afraid. I stepped backwards and I guess I must have slipped and hit my head. When I woke up I thought I was back in the past. I thought I was a fifteen-year-old schoolgirl.' She bit her lip as colour rose in her face.

Meadows again felt a flutter of excitement. 'What were your first thoughts?'

'I was confused, the clothes I was wearing were alien to me and I didn't even recognise Blue. It was getting dark and I was terrified. I thought Mum would be mad because I was out so late.'

'Why did you go up the mountain?'

Gwen looked around at her family then down at her hands. 'I don't know.'

Meadows had the feeling that she knew more than she was telling.

Is she afraid of someone in the room?

'Is there anything else you can tell me?'

'No, I just felt afraid, like someone was after me but I don't know who.' Tears welled in her eyes.

'I really do think that is enough,' Matt said.

Meadows put his notebook back into his pocket. He could see that Gwen was tiring and would much prefer to talk to her alone. 'OK, we'll leave it there for now. Perhaps I could come and see you in a few days, when you've had a chance to rest?'

Gwen nodded and gave him a weak smile.

As Meadows left the hospital, a troubling thought entered his mind.

If Gwen recovers her memory, she could be in danger from a ruthless killer.

He just hoped that it wasn't someone close to her.

Chapter Eight

When Meadows arrived at the police station he felt drained. Now that Gwen had been found the adrenalin had worn off, and after only a few hours' sleep he felt his eyes stinging in protest. Lester approached him as soon as he walked into the office.

I bet he's pissed off with me after all the overtime I used up last night. Then there's the cost of the search team to deduct from the already stretched budget.

Meadows glanced around the office. Word had obviously spread and DS Blackwell smirked from behind Lester's back. Blackwell, built like a bulldog with a triangular body sat on top of thick stubby legs, made no attempt to hide his dislike for Meadows. He made it obvious from the time Meadows took up the position of Detective Inspector that the job should have been his.

'A word in my office,' Lester said then turned and strode towards his office.

Meadows followed, deliberately avoiding Blackwell's gaze. Once inside the office, he closed the door firmly.

Lester took a seat behind the oak desk and waited for Meadows to take a seat. 'I hear that you were at the hospital this morning interviewing Gwen Thomas. I take it you're satisfied that there was no one else involved in the incident. An accident, I hear.'

'Yes. Sir.' Meadows sat forward in his chair. 'She has however recalled some memory of the previous attack.'

That's got his attention.

'Go on.'

'I spoke to her doctor and he thinks it possible that she will fully recover her memory.'

Lester leaned back in his chair, his brows furrowed. 'Well, I can certainly see how that would be a major development in an old case. I assume that once she's had time to recover from this latest injury she will be able to shed some light on what happened back then.'

'I'm afraid it's not as simple as that. Her memory may only come back in flashbacks. Snippets of information. I'm not entirely sure how it works. The doctor wants to do a few more tests. I'll give it a few days and talk to him again. Meanwhile, I would like to re-open the case and look at all the original evidence and statements.'

'I'm not sure that's a good idea at this time. As it stands, we don't have anything new that would justify opening the case. Perhaps we should wait and see what transpires with her memory.'

'I really think we should act now, sir. If it is known that Gwen Thomas has recovered some of her memory, it could force the killer to act, especially if it's someone close to her. Wouldn't it be better to start looking now and be prepared, make it known that the police are taking an interest in Gwen's safety?'

'I don't think we can justify the expense.' Lester folded his hands and placed them on the desk.

'I didn't mean for her to have a police guard. If I could interview her again, maybe use some of the information from the original investigation to jog her memory, it could help things move along.' Meadows let his words hang in the air and watched Lester consider the request.

I bet he's thinking how good it would look on the department to solve a twenty-year-old case. Go on, take the bait.

'I'm not working any cases at the moment. There are a few minor frauds up for grabs but I think Blackwell is more than capable of handling them.'

'OK, but for now I would like you to keep it low key. I can let you have DC Edris to assist.'

'The new trainee?'

'He's been here six months.' Lester leaned back in his chair and surveyed Meadows. 'I know you're used to working in a large team which did give you some anonymity. Granted, we are a small operation here, but it does have its advantages. The team works well together. Yes, they know the ins and outs of each other's personal lives but that means they support one another. I get the feeling that you're not gelling with the group, you don't give much of yourself away.'

Meadows groaned inwardly. 'I guess I'm not much of a team player.'

'No, but give it a chance. They're a good lot, even Blackwell. He's just pissed that he didn't get his promotion. He'll come around. Meanwhile I think it will do you good to take Edris under your wing.'

'I thought he was assigned to Blackwell.'

'He is, but to be honest, from what I hear he isn't very happy. He scored highly on his exams and sailed through training. Blackwell isn't the most patient of men and it would be a shame to lose Edris because of a clash of personalities. I think it will do him good to work with you on this.'

Meadows sighed. He would prefer to work alone but while he had Lester on his side it was best to agree. He mustered a smile. 'Fine by me.'

'Good. Keep me updated, and I think it would be prudent to spend no more than a couple of weeks on the case, unless of course there is a major breakthrough.' Lester stood to indicate the meeting was over.

* * *

Meadows returned to his desk as Lester called in Blackwell and Edris. A few moments later Edris came out smiling, followed by Blackwell who shot Meadows a thunderous look before plonking himself down at his desk, his biceps straining at his shirt.

'So, we're working on a murder case.' Edris smiled at Meadows, his eyes alight with enthusiasm.

Meadows surveyed the young man that stood at his desk. Dark blond hair, worn long, framed an oval face. His eyes were a strange mix of hazel and blue-green. Straight white teeth were revealed in his warm smile.

Nice-looking kid.

Meadows returned the smile. 'Pull up a chair. It's Tristan, isn't it?'

'Yes, sir.' Edris sat down.

'You don't have to call me sir when it's just the two of us.'

'Oh… DS Blackwell insists on it.'

He would.

'Well, you will find my ways a little different. I don't hold much with titles and superiority. Don't get me wrong, I give respect where it's due, but I don't think myself better than anyone else in this office because I outrank them. Nor do I think that anyone has the right to think they are better than me.'

Edris looked confused. 'Um… what shall I call you then?'

'You can call me Meadows, I prefer it to Winter,' Meadows said.

'That's an unusual name.'

'Yes, long story. What would you like me to call you?'

'Edris will do.'

'Good. Well, now that's sorted let's get down to business. We're re-opening a case from 1999.'

'You're kidding! I was born in the nineties,' Edris said, laughing.

Great, so I'm expected to be a babysitter.
'How old are you?'
'Twenty-five.

'I was seventeen then. I can only tell you what I remember from that time and the rumours that followed. Bethan Hopkins and Gwen Collier were friends. They grew up together and attended the same school. By all accounts they were very close. The girls were fifteen years old. In Bryn Melyn, where both girls lived, there is a disused quarry. A public footpath runs past the quarry and upon to the mountain. It's mainly used by hikers and dog walkers. There's an old shack about halfway up, the girls used it as a hang-out. Presumably to drink and smoke or whatever teenage girls got up to in those days. The shack was owned by a farmer, he kept some tools and animal feed up there. He was aware that kids sometimes used it but as they left it intact he turned a blind eye, or was too old to care.' Meadows paused and ran his hand through his hair. He glanced at Edris who was listening intently.

'The girls went missing on Saturday the 20th of June. A search party was set up by the locals. There was no reason to believe the girls had run away. Bethan Hopkins' body was found on Sunday afternoon in the shack. Gwen Collier was found some hours later at the bottom of the ravine, she had sustained horrific injuries and as a result lost her memory.'

'Did you know the girls?'
'Yes, although not very well.'
Except Gwen, but that was after the attack.
Meadows shifted in his chair.
'Were there any suspects at the time?'
'There was talk. Bethan had a boyfriend, Samuel Morris. He was taken in for questioning but was never charged. Gwen Collier had an accident yesterday. She took a fall and hit her head. It seems that this fall has triggered something in her memory. She experienced a flashback and may continue to have more.'

'What do you want me to do?'

'We need to get all the old case files out of storage. Look at the original statements and evidence. I'll give Gwen a few days to recover, then interview her again.'

'I'll get right on to it.' Edris stood up and hurried to his desk.

Maybe it won't be so bad working with him. Meadows watched Edris tap away at his computer. As his eyes moved away he caught a glimpse of Blackwell watching from across the room, a disgruntled look on his face.

I should have known it wouldn't be easy coming back. Once an outsider, always an outsider. People don't like what's different.

Meadows blew out a slow breath and turned his attention to the computer, where he typed up his notes from the previous night and his subsequent visit to the hospital.

Maybe solving this case will make a difference. I owe it to Gwen.

Chapter Nine

June 20th 1999

Gwen stepped out of the front door and into the hazy morning sunshine. A low mist had hung over the village that morning, dispersing to leave humid air in its wake. She slung her bag over her shoulder and called goodbye to her mother before closing the door.

A sheen of perspiration gathered on her brow as she walked briskly up the road. Gwen arrived at Bethan's house and knocked the door. A shuffle of footsteps could be heard then the lock being turned. The door opened and Bethan's mother, Doreen Hopkins, smiled at Gwen.

'Hi, Mrs Hopkins, is Beth ready?'

'I'm sorry, love, Beth isn't feeling well this morning.'

'Oh, we were supposed to go shopping to Bryn Mawr this morning.'

'I'll let her know you called.' Doreen started to close the door.

'Can I see her?' Gwen stepped forward.

'She's asleep, maybe you should come back tomorrow and see if she is feeling better.'

'OK.' Gwen turned away. Bethan had been well enough yesterday and Gwen knew she'd been out with Sam last night. She stepped back and looked up at Beth's bedroom window. A silhouette briefly appeared then moved before Gwen could be sure of what she had seen. Beth was not asleep. If she didn't want to come shopping she should have said. Bitch!

Her body tensed with annoyance as she stomped away.

Gwen decided to call for Catrin to see if she would go shopping with her. She made her way down Turnpike Road just as the bus was passing. Resigned to catching a later bus, she reached Catrin's and knocked the door. She waited a few moments and knocked again. Harder this time. She put her ear against the door, but no sound came from within. She fought the urge to stamp her feet in frustration as she walked back home. She called out as she entered the house but no answer came.

'What is it with everyone today?' She seethed as she stomped upstairs and into her bedroom. Through the window she could see her mother pegging out the washing. She dumped her bag on the floor and plonked down on the bed. The front door opened and someone entered the house...

A sharp rapping on the door bought Gwen back to the present. Startled, she looked down at the iron she held in her hand. It was pressed firmly against one of Matt's shirts, the fabric smouldered from the heat.

'Shit!' Gwen cursed. She pulled the iron up and saw the brown imprint scorched into the white cotton. Another rapping on the door and Blue started to bark.

'I'm coming,' she hollered. Flustered, she switched off the iron and placed it on the cooling rack before rushing to the door, Blue close at her heels. She grabbed hold of Blue's collar and opened the door.

'Hello, Gwen.' Meadows smiled then his eyes fell upon Blue. 'Whoa! He's a big fella.' He took a step back.

'Don't worry, he's a big bear really. All brawn and no brains, come in.' She stepped back, pulling Blue.

Meadows held out his hand to the dog. Blue sniffed, then turned and padded towards the kitchen. Gwen tried to catch her reflection in the hall mirror as she walked past, feeling conscious of how she looked. She led Meadows into the kitchen.

'It's nice to see you again.' She felt a warm glow radiate from her body.

'You look better than when I saw you last. How are you feeling?' He leaned casually against the worktop.

'I'm fine, thanks.' She couldn't stop her eyes travelling over his face. Malachite eyes sparkled beneath thick, dark lashes. She noticed that age had not thinned his unruly hair.

'Would you like a cup of tea?'

'That would be nice, thanks.'

Gwen was glad of the distraction and busied herself filling the kettle and setting out the cups. She was aware of Meadows' eyes following her movement but he remained silent.

She turned to face him. 'So, when did you get back?'

'About a year ago.' He pulled out a chair and sat at the kitchen table. 'Mum's arthritis has got worse and I needed an excuse to get out of London. A post came up in Bryn Mawr station so I put in for a transfer. I bought Mum's old place so she could move into a flat. I had planned to renovate but haven't got round to it yet.'

She turned away and poured the tea. She could still feel his gaze and suddenly felt self-conscious of the thick scar that run from her right shoulder to her elbow. She felt like a teenager again, shy and awkward in his presence. She drew in a deep breath to steady her nerves then turned and set the cups down on the table before taking a seat opposite Meadows.

'You look just the same as when I left,' he said.

'I could say the same about you.' She felt the heat rise in her face and lowered her eyes. 'I didn't get the chance to thank you when you came to the hospital. I feel like an idiot causing all that fuss.'

'Please don't feel bad.' He smiled and his eyes crinkled at the corners. 'I'm glad, well, we were all pleased with the outcome.'

'Please pass on my thanks to everyone that was involved with the search.' She took a sip of tea just to have something to do with her hands. The hot liquid burned her throat, making her eyes water. Blue walked up to the table and planted his face on her lap. She ran her fingers through his hair, willing her heartbeat to return to normal. The air felt charged with tension.

'So, I guess you are here to talk about what happened on Sunday. I don't think I can tell you any more than I did at the hospital.'

'What made you go up to the shack?'

She twisted a lock of hair. She didn't want to tell him that she was fed up with her husband and life in general. 'I don't know, we had a party Saturday night to celebrate my birthday. It was Matt's idea. I don't like celebrating the fact that I get to live another year while Beth, well, she didn't get the chance to grow up, get married, and have children. It doesn't seem fair.'

'No, it isn't fair, but it's not your fault, Gwen, you have no reason to feel guilty. You survived against the odds. There is someone out there that's responsible for what happened to you and Bethan. Were you thinking about Bethan when you went to the quarry on Sunday?'

'Not at first. Blue was hot and bothered and I thought it would be good for him to have a swim and cool off. I didn't feel like walking up the mountain road to the river. Then I remembered the stream by the quarry. Beth and I used to paddle in there sometimes. I was nervous when I went through the gate. Then I just wanted to prove to myself that I could do it, that I didn't have to be afraid. Didn't turn out like I planned.'

Meadows smiled. 'You said that you had a flashback of Bethan in the old shack.'

'Yes.' Gwen felt a sudden chill snake around her body. 'I think that's what made me panic and fall. I saw Beth lying on the floor of the shack. Her denim jacket was dirty and her skirt had ridden up over her thighs.' Gwen twisted her hands as she fought against the image. 'Her eyes were open and staring and her hair was matted with blood.'

'Has anything like that happened before?'

'No, it's the first time I have been up the quarry since it happened. Up until now I've had no recollection of that day or the weeks leading up to it.'

'And now?' He leaned forward, his eyes searching hers.

She felt a warmth spread through her body and squirmed in her seat. 'I keep having odd moments. It's a bit like daydreaming. I'm fifteen again and I suppose reliving bits of that day or at least that period of time that I lost. It happened again just before you arrived. That's how I managed to burn a shirt.' She indicated the spoilt shirt still draped over the ironing board.

Meadows straightened up, curiosity evident in his manner. 'What did you recall?'

'I'm sure it was the morning of the attack. Beth and I usually spent Saturdays together. I can't think of a time when we didn't, other than when one of us was away on holiday. We were supposed to go shopping that morning but Beth was ill, or pretending to be ill. I got the feeling she was trying to avoid me.'

'Do you recall talking to her?'

'No, just her mother.'

Meadows frowned. 'You must have met up with her sometime that day, though.'

'I guess but I don't remember. I went back home and up to my bedroom. I heard someone come into the house.'

'Who?'

'I don't know, that's when you knocked the door,' she said with a laugh.

'Last Sunday when you hit your head, you said you thought you were fifteen.'

'Yes, it was a bit trippy. I couldn't understand why I was dressed in the clothes I was wearing and I didn't even recognise Blue.'

'You must have been frightened.'

'I was.'

'Why didn't you go home, or at least to your mother's house? I take it she still lives at the same address?'

'Yes, she does. I don't know. I was confused and afraid that he would be there.'

'He?'

Gwen suddenly pushed her chair back and stood up. 'I don't know who he is. It was the first thought that came to my head when I thought about going home. This is so frustrating.' She started to pile the ironing into the washing basket.

'It's OK. I spoke to Dr Rowland again. He thinks it's possible that you will fully recover your memory. It may come back a little at a time. He suggests prompts might help. Like listening to music from that era or reading old news articles.'

Gwen rubbed her hands over her face. 'I don't know if I want to go back to that time. Maybe it's better that I don't remember what happened that day.'

Meadows stood and approached her. Blue, who had been lying on the floor, stood and positioned himself between Gwen and the detective.

'He thinks I've upset you,' Meadows said.

'You haven't upset me.' Gwen stroked Blue, who wagged his tail and sat at her feet.

'Look, I understand how difficult this is for you. To be honest I wouldn't like to go back to the nineties myself,' he said with a smile. 'I had a chat with my boss and he agreed that we should re-open the case.'

Gwen felt her body stiffen. 'What if I don't remember what happened?' Then, as an afterthought she said, 'Will you be in charge of the case?'

'Yes, if that's OK with you. Please think about it. Whoever is responsible for Bethan's murder and the attack on you has got away with it for twenty years. I think you and Bethan's family deserve some answers.'

Gwen sank down in the nearest chair. 'What do you want me to do?'

'Just keep doing what you have been doing and try to prompt your memory. Write down everything that you recall no matter how insignificant it seems. I would also suggest that you keep this to yourself.'

'In a place like this? I already had someone from the paper call to ask for an interview.'

Meadows' face became serious. 'I can have a family liaison officer assigned to you.'

'There's no need for that. I'm not worried. I'm rarely on my own outside and I have Blue.'

'I don't think you understand the danger you could be in. If the killer becomes aware of your memory returning then he may be forced to act.'

'Well, maybe that would be a good thing. It would draw out the killer. Then I could finally put the past behind me.'

'I don't know about that. It's very risky. I think you should keep any further memory recall between us. I'm sorry, Gwen, but you have to consider the possibility that it is someone close to you. I have requested all the files from the original investigation. Once I've had a chance to go through the evidence and statements, I will come and see you again. Maybe something will stand out.'

'You do know I was never told anything about what happened? At first it was because the doctors wanted me to have the chance to recover my memory naturally. They thought any outside suggestions or theories would contaminate the truth. After that, my family felt that they had to shield me. I still don't know how Beth was killed or how we were found. I guess up until now it hasn't bothered me. Once you've read the files, would you be able to share the information with me? I think it's time I knew the facts.'

'I'll tell you what I can but some of it will be confidential.'

'I understand. I remember that Sam Morris was a suspect at the time. I never believed he could be responsible.'

Meadows sat back down and took a sip of his tea. 'Sam was Beth's boyfriend?'

'Yes.' A flicker of a memory flashed across Gwen's mind. Sam standing in the rain and handing her his coat. She bit her lip and tried to hold on to the image but it dispersed like smoke and was replaced by the school bus…

She was sitting next to Beth on the top deck of the bus. 'Are you seeing Sam tonight?'

'Yeah, his parents are out for the evening so we'll be all alone,' Beth said, giggling.

'So you are going to do it?' Gwen felt a stab of jealousy.

'Hell yes, he's been begging for ages.'

'Don't you think you should wait?' Gwen picked at the hem on her skirt.

'What for?' Beth took a lip gloss from her school bag and smeared it over her lips.

'For the chosen one.' Gwen looked around to make sure no one was listening in on their conversation. 'It's supposed to be special.'

'Got to get some practice first,' Beth said. 'No boy is going to be interested in a virgin. You have to know what you're doing.' She tossed her long blond hair over her shoulder.

The bus pulled up at the next stop to pick up a batch of schoolchildren. Gwen peered out of the window and saw Winter Meadows walk towards the bus, followed by his little brother. She felt her stomach squirm.

'What're you smiling at?' Beth followed her gaze. 'Please don't tell me you fancy him.'

'Yeah, he is kind of cute.'

'Yuck, that scabby hippy!' Beth's lips curled in disgust.

'Don't be horrible.' She sat back in her chair.

'I thought Matt was supposed to be the chosen one.'

'He is.' Gwen stared out of the window as the bus continued its journey...

'Gwen, are you OK?'

Meadows' voice brought Gwen back to the present. She rubbed her hands over her face and looked into his concerned eyes. 'I'm fine, sorry, this is how it happens. A random memory just enters my head.'

'What did you see this time?'

'Sam, at first. It was raining and he gave me his coat. Then I was on the school bus with Beth.' Gwen felt the heat rise in her face. 'It's all a bit childish.'

'Anything you remember could be useful. Please don't be embarrassed, I do appreciate you were only fifteen at the time. I promise I won't laugh.'

'Beth and I were talking about the chosen one. We would pick a boy that we wanted to marry, then orchestrate meetings. Find out his school timetable, where he hung out after school. That sort of thing.' Gwen saw the smile play on Meadows' lips. 'I guess I would be called a stalker these days.'

'Oh, I don't know. I think I would have been flattered at fifteen to be a chosen one. So I take it Sam was Bethan's chosen one.'

'No, she liked him and they were going out at the time. She was even going to' – Gwen stopped as guilt prickled her skin – 'I don't feel comfortable talking about

Beth like this. It's like reading someone's diary. I'm not sure I should be giving away all her secrets.'

Meadows leaned forward, his hands on the table close to Gwen's. 'I know it may feel disrespectful but you are doing this to help. Unfortunately, a victim has no privacy. We have to go through their personal lives, but trust me, any information will be handled with sensitivity and compassion.'

Gwen pulled her hands from the table and placed them on her lap. The urge to touch him was too strong. 'Beth had planned to sleep with Sam. She said that he had been asking.'

'Asking or demanding? Do you think she could have changed her mind and he tried to force her?'

'I don't know. She seemed really keen on him and I don't think he was the first boy she slept with. I got the impression she knew what she was doing. I think maybe she used to keep secrets from me.'

'OK, thank you for being so honest with me. So, did you have a chosen one?'

Gwen saw the sparkle in his eyes and squirmed in her seat. 'Well, I, erm…'

'It's OK, you don't have to tell me unless you think it's relevant.' Meadows drained his cup and stood up. 'I think I have taken up enough of your time today. I will review the case notes and if it's OK with you I'll call again and tell you what I've learnt.'

Gwen stood up and Blue fussed about her legs. 'OK, we'll go out for a walk in a minute.' She patted the dog's head. 'I'm here most days so you are welcome to come anytime.'

Meadows reached into his jacket pocket and took out a business card. 'This is my mobile number and contact details for the station. If you have any more flashbacks or just need to talk, call me.' He handed the card to Gwen.

As she took the card her fingers brushed against his and her skin tingled. 'I'll see you out.' She was aware that her voice sounded breathless.

Once she closed the door on Meadows she leaned against the wall. She could feel the thrumming of her heart through the cotton of her T-shirt. She glanced in the mirror and saw the scar on her forehead peeking out from under her fringe. There is no harm in enjoying his company, she thought. A smile played on her lips as she turned away from the mirror.

Chapter Ten

Giles Epworth looked out of his office window and watched the children scurry like ants towards the main hall for lunch. He tried to pick out Ariana or Alexander Thomas among the faces but there were so many pupils it was difficult to distinguish one from another.

He had checked the school computer and saw that they had both registered this morning. He knew they were on the grounds somewhere but he wouldn't be able to question them about their mother. He'd need to be subtle when trying to find out information.

He rubbed his hand over his face and noticed the tremor in his fingers. He had barely slept since Sunday night despite hearing through village gossip that Gwen had been found. It was the rumours of her recovered memory that plagued him.

Gwen's children had been absent from school for a couple of days but now that they were back he expected to hear something more about what had happened. He had purposely passed the boy in the school corridor, looking for any indication that Gwen had revealed something to her son. The boy didn't act any differently.

Giles turned away from the window and put on his jacket before heading for the staff room, knowing this would be the best place to pick up gossip. He opened the door to a high volume of chatter and the aroma of coffee. The chatter petered away as he walked across the room and poured a coffee from the pot, before scanning the room for a seat.

'Good afternoon, Headmaster.' Catrin, the school secretary smiled sweetly as she smoothed down her skirt.

Giles nodded and took a seat before stirring the sugar into his coffee. He wondered if they had been gossiping about him before he entered the room.

'Anything happened today that I should be aware of?' He looked at each teacher in turn.

'Actually we were just talking about Gwen Collier, I mean Gwen Thomas, as she is now.'

'Oh, and?' Giles' stomach squirmed.

'Ariana is in Lynne's class,' Catrin continued.

Giles looked at Lynne Davis, who straightened up in her seat.

'She was telling me this morning that the police have been to see her mother again. They're going to re-open the case.'

Giles felt his chest tighten as a coldness spread through his body. 'Really?' He sipped his coffee, trying to hide his distress. 'I'm surprised, I was under the impression that Gwen lost her memory. Why would the police re-open the case now?'

'It seems that she's started to remember things,' Catrin said. She leaned forward, her eyes wide with interest.

'Weren't you in the same class as Gwen in school?' Lynne asked.

'Yes, we were good friends.'

Another wannabe slut, Giles thought. He let his eyes travel from Catrin's wild, red hair down to her short skirt.

'Well I must get on.' He rose from his chair, he could feel the perspiration gathering under his shirt collar.

He walked briskly back to his office and closed the door before rummaging around in his desk drawer for the bottle of whisky he kept for emergencies. He took a swig from the bottle and felt the grip on his chest loosen as the warm liquid spread.

He checked his watch. Another four hours until he could leave. Then he'd go straight home and destroy the pictures. He took another gulp of whisky before stowing it safely back in the drawer.

The afternoon dragged by as Giles struggled against a throbbing headache. Finally the school bell rang, signalling the end of the day. He stood by the window watching the pupils hurry to catch the bus home. His mind wandered back in time to when he taught English. It was easy back then to get a pupil to stay behind on the pretence of detention or discussing grades. A smile played on his lips as he recalled the sweet memories.

A knock at the door brought him back to the present.

Catrin entered carrying a file. 'Some letters for you to sign.'

'Just leave them on the desk.' Giles turned away from the window. 'That will be all for today. You can go early.'

Catrin raised her eyebrows.

'To be honest I'm not feeling too clever.'

'You do look a bit peaky today.' She smiled. 'Well, if you're sure there is nothing else, I'll be on my way.' She left the office, closing the door gently.

Giles scribbled his signature on the letters without bothering to read the contents, then hurried out of the building. The drive home was a blur, his mind in such turmoil that his focus didn't return until he pulled the car into his driveway. The dog barked in greeting when he opened the door. Ignoring the yaps, he locked the door and entered his study. While he waited for the computer to boot up, he took a large envelope from the desk drawer and tipped out the contents. Photographs scattered across the desk. Some Polaroid, others he had developed or printed himself.

'Beautiful,' he whispered as he ran his fingers over the photos. He didn't want to let them go.

Over the next couple of hours he scanned the photos into the computer and saved them onto a memory stick. He made sure he'd deleted the files on the hard drive then shut down the computer. Outside in his garden he made a small bonfire and burned his entire collection. Only the memory stick remained. He took it from inside his jacket pocket and stared at the small device. He needed somewhere safe to keep it where it wouldn't be found. An idea struck him and he smiled to himself as he placed the memory stick in a tin and buried it under a rose bush. Back indoors he sat down heavily in his armchair, a glass of whisky in his hands. There was no evidence now. Just her word against his.

Chapter Eleven

Meadows sprinted up the stairs leading to his office, his legs still smarting from a run that morning. He knew he had pushed his body to the limits over the past two days trying to rid himself of the frustration that tormented him night and day. Thoughts of Gwen kept snaking their way into his mind, stirring up old feelings that he couldn't act upon. Flexing his muscles as he inhaled deeply, he pushed open the door. He had noticed Edris' car in the car park on the way in and hoped the young DC had some news about the case files.

As he walked across the office he saw Edris stacking files on his desk, who turned and beamed at Meadows.

'Just picked these up – case notes and statements. The scene of crime photographs, physical evidence, and post-mortem report should be here later this afternoon.'

'Good work, you must have hounded the storage guys to move it along this quickly.'

'I used my charm.' Edris winked. 'Where would you like me to start?'

'You can start by taking a look through the statements, sort them into order, then you can start entering the details onto the database. It's a long shot but you might get a match on one of the names.'

Edris hovered by the desk. 'Would you like me to fetch you a coffee?'

'That'd be great, then move your stuff over here. We'll share my desk for now, that way we can discuss anything you find of interest as we go along.'

By the time Edris returned with the coffee, Meadows was engrossed in the case notes. His eyes scanned the document picking out the fine details of the case.

Jack Hopkins, Bethan's father, had been the first to alert the police. The call was logged at 11.05 p.m. on Saturday 20th June 1999. At this stage the call wasn't given high priority as it had only been ten hours since Bethan was last seen. Another call from Jack Hopkins was logged at 11.15 p.m. This time he was insistent that his daughter would not deliberately stay out late and that an officer be sent. Jack, a local councillor, was well respected in the community and a known friend of the then Chief Inspector. PC Aneurin Davies was despatched and called in a report to the station at 12.15 a.m., stating that he believed there to be reasonable cause for concern. Bethan had not been seen since 1 p.m. on Saturday afternoon after leaving the house to go for a walk and saying she would be back in a couple of hours. All her friends and relatives had been contacted but no one had seen or spoken to her.

At 12.30 a.m. a call was logged from David Collier stating that his niece Gwen had not returned home since leaving the house that morning. CID were informed of the missing girls and DS Mike Funning took over the enquiry. After both sets of parents had been interviewed it became apparent that the girls were likely to be together. While Jack Hopkins had insisted there were no problems within the family, Gwen's mother, Sue, had stated that there had been an argument between herself and her daughter that morning.

Neither of the girls had mobile phones and they weren't carrying money when they left the house so it was probable that they were still in the area and could be at a friend's house or hiding in one of the neighbouring farms' outbuildings. A decision was made to wait until first light. If the girls had not returned, officers would start house-to-house enquiries and search the area.

Meadows took a sip of his coffee and leaned back in his chair stretching his arms above his head. He noticed Edris was still engrossed in the statements, his eyes darting from side to side as he devoured each page.

The case notes continued, dated Sunday 21st June. Jack Hopkins had become increasingly agitated during the night, insisting that the officers should be out searching. By first light he had organised a search party, this consisted of friends, neighbours, and relatives. Among them was Gwen's uncle, David Collier. It was suggested that Jack stay home with his wife to await news but ignoring this advice he set off with the party to search the mountain and neighbouring farm buildings.

House-to-house enquires began and a friend of the girls, Catrin Evans, informed officers that although she hadn't seen the girls they quite often hung out around the old quarry. A search was made of the quarry and the footpath leading onto the mountain. At 2 p.m. the body of Bethan Hopkins was discovered in a disused tool shack on the quarry footpath.

Scene of crime officers were called in and the area cordoned off. Officers were dispatched to find the search party and head them off before they reached the quarry. Both sets of parents were informed of the developments but not told at this stage which of the girls had been found.

Meadows felt his skin prickle and ran his hand over his face. He imagined the turmoil the parents must have gone through at that time. Knowing a body had been found but not the identity. Caught between a world of despair and hope.

The search continued for Gwen, up the footpath onto the mountain, in barns and outbuildings. At 4.15 p.m. she was spotted lying at the bottom of the ravine half in the water. It looked like she had gone over just opposite the shack but had not been spotted in the initial search. A rescue team rigged equipment to nearby trees. The operation was difficult but when the crew reached Gwen she was still breathing, although suffering from serious injuries and exposure.

Meadows closed the file and handed it to Edris.

'Have a read through this before you finish the statements. I don't think we should read any further than when the girls were found. Let's treat it as if it were a new case and draw our own conclusions.'

While Edris read through the case notes, Meadows leaned back in his chair and closed his eyes.

The quarry path is isolated, unlikely it would be a random attack, so it has to be someone known to the girls, someone they felt comfortable with. Perhaps someone who had been to the shack with them on previous occasions.

'Must be an interesting case.'

Meadows opened his eyes and saw Blackwell standing at the desk, a sour look on his face.

'Did you need to talk to me about something?' Meadows asked.

'No.' Blackwell sauntered back to his desk.

Meadows stood up. 'I think I'll stretch my legs.' Blackwell was starting to irritate him and if he didn't take a walk he would end up having words with him.

He left Edris reading the case notes and walked around the station, stopping to talk to Folland at the front desk. When he got back to his desk he felt calmer, his focus back on the case.

'So what do you think?' Meadows asked as soon as Edris closed the case notes.

A grin spread across Edris' face. Meadows suspected that he wasn't often asked to give his opinion.

'Definitely someone known to the girls judging by the location and there being two of them. It's a big risk though, one of them could have run for help.'

'My thoughts exactly. Maybe one of them did try to escape.'

'You mean Gwen, as she was found down the ravine while Bethan was killed in the shack.' Edris sat back in his chair and swivelled it back and forth.

'It's possible, but why would she run in that direction? Surely she would have run down the path to get help.'

'She could have tried but he caught her and pushed her down the ravine,' Edris said.

'Which means he would have already killed Bethan.' Meadows tried to imagine the scene.

Bethan would have to be already dead or unconscious for Gwen not to have had enough time to run before the killer caught her, otherwise Bethan would have tried to escape. The killer wouldn't have been able to chase both girls. Gwen went over the ravine opposite the shack which means she didn't get very far. Then again, she might have tried to help Beth, maybe fought with the killer. So was Bethan the target? She must have been attacked first.

'I can't see it being someone their own age.' Edris interrupted his thoughts.

'Why not?'

'Well, he would have to be strong to overpower two girls. A fifteen-year-old boy? I can't see it myself.'

'Not impossible though. Both girls were petite and most boys by fifteen have outgrown girls of their own age. Maybe someone a little older. Girls that age tend to be attracted to older boys. Could be a seventeen or eighteen-year-old,' Meadows said.

'Or an adult they trusted. Jack Hopkins seemed certain something had happened to his daughter from the start. He called the station just after 11 p.m., Gwen wasn't reported missing until later.'

'No one likes to think that a father would do that to his own daughter but it has been known to happen. Find out everything you can about Jack Hopkins. I'll take a look at Gwen's uncle. This would have been done at the time but it won't hurt to look again.'

Edris scribbled down some notes, then turned to Meadows. 'I noticed that there was no mention of Gwen's father in the case notes.'

'He died of cancer when Gwen was eleven years old. It was just Gwen and her mother. No siblings. Her father's brother, David, helped out. I'm not sure how Gwen felt about him. Come on, let's finish the statements and break for lunch.' Meadows said as he picked up Doreen Hopkins' statement.

Doreen stated that Bethan left the house at about 1 p.m., saying she was going out for a walk and would be back in a couple of hours. She was wearing a denim jacket and a blue flowered skirt. Meadows noted down the description of the clothes.

That's what Gwen had described Bethan wearing when she had a flashback.

Doreen also stated that Bethan had left the house alone and there had been no recent arguments in the family.

'That's interesting.'

'What's interesting?' Edris looked up from the statement he was reading.

'Doreen Hopkins doesn't mention seeing Gwen that day or that her daughter had been unwell. Gwen remembered calling at the house that morning. The girls were supposed to catch the bus to go shopping.'

'Do you think that Gwen's memory is accurate? It's been a long time.'

'I've no reason to believe otherwise. Everything else adds up. What have you got?'

'Interview with Sam Morris. He states he met up with Gwen about noon and that she appeared to be upset. They spent some time in the park, then went into the trees behind the rugby field and smoked a few cigarettes. He claims Gwen didn't tell him why she was upset but had mentioned that she was supposed to meet Bethan that morning. I suppose that ties up with what Gwen told you.'

'Go on.'

'They talked about Bethan. Sam said she had been acting odd lately and thought she wanted to break up. He said the last time he saw her was Friday at school. They were supposed to meet up that evening but Bethan didn't show. Later he walked with Gwen to the top of Mountain Road, only as far as the cattle grid. He says he couldn't be certain of the time but thinks it was about 4 p.m. It started to rain and he suggested they go home. Gwen was reluctant so he gave her his coat. He claimed that was the last time he saw Gwen and he did not see Bethan at all that day.'

'Interesting. He was the prime suspect at the time. We'll have to wait for the evidence log to see why. Gwen remembers him giving her his coat. I remember him from school. He wasn't a tall boy, skinny as I recall.'

Edris rubbed his hand over his chin, a look of concentration on his face. 'It sounds like he was very friendly with Gwen. Giving her his coat would perhaps suggest stronger feelings. They could have walked to the quarry path from the mountain end. Then he could have tried it on with Gwen and she became upset.'

'What about Bethan?'

'She could have turned up. Maybe she even followed them to see what they were up to.'

'Did you come across any sighting of Bethan from the statement?'

'No, not yet. Plenty of Gwen and Sam.'

'If Bethan left the house at 1 p.m. where did she go? Sam and Gwen were together until 4 p.m. Someone must have seen Bethan and if they did they didn't come forward at the time. Keep looking, see what you can find out and keep those theories coming. I think Sam Morris is definitely worth a visit.' Meadows smiled at Edris and they continued to trawl through the statements but they didn't turn up any sightings of Bethan.

They took a late lunch in the canteen where they sat discussing the case and when they returned to the office they saw a stack of containers.

'Looks like the evidence has arrived,' Edris said. 'This should be interesting, my first murder case and I get a chance to look at all the evidence.'

'Let's see what we've got.' Meadows opened the first container and pulled out a labelled plastic bag containing an item of clothing. 'Gwen's T-shirt.' He wrinkled his nose at the bloodstains.

Edris opened a second box and between them they examined each piece of evidence. Among the items of clothing were an empty bottle of cider, cigarette butts, and an axe. Blackwell sauntered over and peered at the items lined up on the desk.

'Murder weapon?' Edris picked up the axe and examined it through the plastic.

'Nasty,' Blackwell commented.

'OK, check this lot against the log and send it off to the lab. I want it all re-tested.' Meadows picked up the file containing the crime scene photographs and sat at his desk. The first photo showed the shack taken from the outside. The door was open, as it had been when they discovered Bethan's body.

Why leave the door open? Not a calculated act. The killer would want to conceal the body for as long as possible. If Gwen had tried to escape, the killer would have chased her and that would explain the open door. But surely he would check that Bethan was dead and close the door.

He moved on to the next photo. This one showed footprints leading in and out of the shack. It had rained that afternoon so the earth was sodden, leaving clear prints.

The officers' prints would have been eliminated.

Meadows checked the scene of crime report. There was only one set of unidentified prints. A size ten training shoe, with little wear on the tread indicating that they were recently bought. Gwen's prints were identified but no prints matching Bethan's.

She must have entered the shack before it started to rain, or was carried inside.

The office grew quiet as officers left for the weekend. Some would be on call but the majority would be taking advantage of a quiet period in the station. Meadows could hear Edris' rhythmic tapping of the keyboard.

'You can go now, I'll call you if there are any developments.'

Edris looked up from the screen. 'I'll stay a bit longer. I just want to get the rest of the information onto the database.'

Meadows nodded his approval.

He returned his attention to the photographs; the next set showed the inside of the shack. Various rusting tools were hung between nails in the wall. A close-up of an axe wedged between two nails showed congealed blood and hair.

Why would you hang an axe with the blade facing outward? It must have originally been positioned flat against the wall. Unless the killer used the axe then hung it back on the wall.

He looked at the rest of the tools; all of them were hung at awkward and dangerous angles.

Strange, not the sort of place you would expect teenage girls to hang out.

The next photograph made his stomach contract. It wasn't that he was squeamish, and he had enough experience of violent crime. It was because the image showed a girl who went to school with him, full of life and laughter, lying lifeless on a dirt floor. The Bethan he remembered was not this pitiful grotesque image. She lay as Gwen described. Skirt bunched up revealing her thighs. Denim jacket smeared with blood and dirt, a wild tangle of blond hair matted with blood.

There's nothing pretty about death. No sleeping angel, no look of peace.

The next set of photos showed Bethan from different angles. A pool of blood leaked from her head and was partially soaked up by the dirt floor. A close-up showed part of the skull caved in. She had a torn nail on her right hand and a bruise on her cheek.

Looks like she put up a fight. Scrapings would have been taken from under her nails, which would have matched or eliminated Sam Morris' DNA if the technology had been available at the time.

He moved on to the photos of Gwen. He guessed that as SOCO were already at the scene they were at hand to take photographs of Gwen's position and the rescue operation. It was evident that a zoom had been used and the details were not as clear as they were on the photographs of Bethan.

Gwen lay on her right-hand side, her leg twisted outward. Her arm trailed in the stream, with her head dangerously close to the water. She was wearing shorts, her right foot was bare and her legs dirty. Meadows moved on to the hospital report. Gwen had sustained multiple injuries, among them fractures to the femur, tibia, and fibula of her right leg, open fracture to her right arm, and a fractured left wrist. Broken ribs, one of which punctured her lung. The most worrying of the injuries was a depressed fracture of the skull causing haemorrhaging to the brain.

She must have had some strength to pull through those injuries.

Among the listed injuries was a four-inch cut to the back of the head, not consistent with the fall. Meadows took another look at the photo of the shack and studied the bloodstained axe.

Likely she was thrown against the wall with some force, this would have stunned her and could be the reason she didn't immediately run for help. She would have been dizzy and slow to respond. Easy to catch.

He felt anger rise in his chest and bubble beneath his skin.

Who would do this?

He left his desk and walked to the kitchen where he made two mugs of coffee. He took one to Edris then picked up the post-mortem report on Bethan.

Cause of death was listed as a depressed fracture to the skull, resulting in severe haemorrhaging. Bruising was visible around her throat, consistent with manual strangulation, however insufficient pressure had been applied to cause unconsciousness or death. There were signs of recent sexual activity and traces of semen were found.

'Bloody hell!' Meadows cursed as he read the next paragraph.

'What is it?' Edris stopped typing and turned his chair to face Meadows.

The ringing of a phone shattered the silence in the office. It took Meadows a few moments to realise that it was his mobile phone. 'Hold on a sec.' He pulled it from his jacket pocket.

'Meadows,' he announced.

The pleasure of hearing Gwen's voice soon turned to concern when he noted the panic in it. He listened intently then ended the call as he stood.

'Come on, Edris, we have to go.'

Chapter Twelve

Gwen ended the call to Meadows then paced the kitchen. She heard Matt come in, and turned to face him.

'So you called the police,' he said.

She turned to face him. 'Yes, I had to.'

'Why can't you just leave it alone? It's going to get worse. It's not just you now, it's the whole family. Is that what you want? Drag us all into this mess.' He glared at Gwen.

Gwen sighed. 'No, of course not, but what do you expect me to do?'

'I told you, leave the police out of it and just forget the whole thing.'

'I can't. Win... Detective Meadows is on his way now. Let's just see what he has to say.'

Matt clenched his fists.

'Why does it have to be him?'

'Because he's the one dealing with the case.' She turned away and gazed out of the kitchen window.

'What bloody case? This was over years ago!'

'It's never been over for me.' She could feel the tears sting her eyes but was determined not to cry. She took a deep breath and blew it out slowly. She could feel Matt getting closer. He lay his hand on her shoulder and she felt her body stiffen. She turned to face him. 'What have you got against Winter?'

The kitchen door opened and Alex sauntered in. 'What are you two arguing about again?'

'Nothing. Where's your sister?'

'Upstairs in her room. Probably on Facebook giving all her friends updates.'

'I hope not.' Gwen groaned. 'Go and check on her and tell her that this has to be kept in the family.'

'Well, it isn't going to be now, is it?' Matt hissed. 'I'll go and see her.'

Blue was dancing around the kitchen. It was past his evening walk time and Gwen could sense that her unease was making him restless. 'I'm sorry, boy.' She stroked his head. 'We'll go out soon.'

'Do you want me to take him out?' Alex offered.

'No, you'd better stay here until the police come.'

'What for? It's not like I can tell them anything.'

'OK then, just take him around the block. Thanks, love.'

'It's OK. You shouldn't let Dad bully you.' Alex grabbed the lead and hooked it to Blue's collar.

'He doesn't mean to get angry. I guess he just wants what's best for us all,' Gwen said.

'Yeah, well, he's always bloody angry.' Alex turned and left the kitchen.

Gwen fussed around, filling the kettle and putting out cups. Her stomach felt twisted and the adrenalin pumping through her body made it difficult to stay still.

Even though she was expecting the door to knock, it still gave her a start when it happened. She rushed to the door pausing to check her appearance in the mirror. She heard Matt thumping down the stairs as she opened the door.

'Thank you for coming so quickly.' She smiled at Meadows.

'This is DC Edris. He's assisting me with the case.'

Gwen heard Matt huff from behind and ignored him. 'Please come in.' She led them into the kitchen where they all took a seat.

'You said on the phone that you had received a threatening letter,' Meadows said to Gwen.

'Yes, Ariana found it in her bag.'

'May I see it?'

The printed words on the page jumped out at Gwen as she handed Meadows the letter.

> SOME THINGS SHOULD REMAIN FORGOTTEN. YOU DON'T WANT HISTORY TO REPEAT ITSELF.

She felt a coldness creep over her skin and averted her eyes.

Meadows put the letter into a plastic bag. 'How many of you have handled the letter?'

'Just me and Ariana.'

'Good, was it in an envelope?'

'Yes.' Gwen handed it over. 'Her name was typed on the front.'

'And she found this today?'

'Yes, but she's not sure how long it's been in her school bag.'

'Some pervert is obviously after my daughter. What do you intend to do about it?' Matt demanded.

'It doesn't appear to be a direct threat against your daughter–'

'Of course it is, you idiot. Why was it put in her school bag?' Matt said.

'As not to be seen posting it through the door, perhaps. It's meant to frighten your wife,' Edris said.

'Perhaps we can start by looking at who had access to the bag. Maybe it's best that we speak to Ariana,' Meadows suggested.

'I'll give her a call.' Gwen stood up, glad to have a chance to leave the room. The atmosphere was already tense and she had a feeling it would get worse. She called up the stairs to Ariana then returned to the stony silence of the kitchen.

Footsteps thundered down the stairs then Ariana strolled into the kitchen. She looked around the table and her gaze fell on Edris. Her eyes widened and she altered her stance before walking tentatively to the nearest seat.

'Hello, Ariana. I don't know if you remember me from the hospital. I'm DI Meadows and this is DC Edris.'

Ariana acknowledged Edris with a coy smile then lowered her eyes.

'Ariana, would you mind talking us through how you found the letter?' Meadows asked.

'I was emptying my school bag for the weekend and it fell out from between my books.'

'Do you think it was placed there today?'

Ariana shrugged her shoulders. 'I dunno, I suppose it could have been there since Wednesday.'

'Why since Wednesday?'

'I wasn't in school on Monday and Tuesday, I wanted to stay home to make sure Mum was OK.'

'I take it you keep your bag with you at all times.'

'Yeah, unless I have PE, then I leave it in the changing room.' Ariana sneaked a glance at Edris, who was scribbling on a notepad. He looked up and smiled. Two red spots appeared on her cheeks and she squirmed in her seat.

'What about after school? Do you usually come straight home?'

'I stayed behind on Wednesday to practice drama. Yesterday I went to Jess' house.'

'Jess?'

'Jessica Evans.'

'Catrin Evans' daughter, they live on Quarry Road,' Gwen said, trying to swallow the bitterness that rose in her throat every time she heard that name.

'Anywhere else?'

'Only Gran's.'

'Was Uncle David there?' Gwen instantly regretted the question as Meadows turned his attention to her.

'Yeah, he was there.'

'Why do you ask?'

Meadows was still looking at Gwen. 'No reason.' He turned his attention back to Ariana. 'Do you catch the service bus when you stay after school?'

'It depends, there's a late school bus at four-thirty but I don't always make it.'

'What about Wednesday?'

'I caught the service bus, I stayed till five.'

'Were you alone?'

'No, Jess was with me.'

'Anyone else you recognised on the bus?'

'Not really, I wasn't taking much notice.'

The front door opened and Blue bounded into the kitchen. He jumped up on Gwen, his front paws resting on her shoulders. She patted his head and he moved towards Edris.

'Whoa!' Edris moved back in his chair.

'He won't hurt you.' Ariana giggled.

Alex appeared in the doorway. 'Alright?'

'You were quick,' Gwen said.

'Stupid mutt wanted to come home. Ten minutes away from you and he started whining.'

'Well, I think that's all for now. Thank you, Ariana,' Meadows said. Perhaps I can talk to your mum and dad alone.'

'OK.' Ariana appeared reluctant to leave the room and miss the opportunity to sneak glances at Edris.

'Move it!' Matt snapped.

Ariana huffed then left the kitchen, closely followed by Alex.

'Well?' Matt demanded. 'What are you going to do about it?'

Gwen felt her skin prickle with annoyance. 'Do you think that Ariana is in danger?' she asked.

'I think you should take some precautions. Make sure she isn't alone after school. The note could've been placed at any time. Maybe a parent asked their son or daughter to slip the envelope into her bag or it could have happened after school. We'll start by looking at those who were interviewed in the original investigation and see if they have children currently attending the same school as Ariana. We can also talk to the headmaster about security.'

Mr Epworth, Gwen thought. She felt herself drifting back in time. She didn't fight it but let the memories flood her mind. Meadows' voice faded and was replaced by the clattering of cutlery against plates among distorted voices...

She was sat at a table in the school canteen. Winter was sat opposite, a copy of the English GCSE study book open in front.

'Thanks for helping me. I just can't get into this book, nothing's sinking in.' Gwen could feel her whole body tingle as she looked into his eyes.

'It's no problem. Shakespeare isn't the easiest to study, you either love him or hate him.' Winter smiled at her.

'I heard you got straight A's in all your exams. I'll probably end up with U's!'

'Don't be so hard on yourself, it can't be easy with all the work you had to catch up on.'

'No, but it's better than being put back a year. I suppose I can always resit.'

'I don't think you'll have to.' He leaned forward and turned the pages of the book.

Gwen felt her stomach squirm. It had taken her weeks to work up the courage to ask him to help with her studies. He was one of the few who didn't stare and whisper behind her back. Now the more time she spent with him the more she liked him and looked forward to the time they spent together.

'Are you OK?' Winter reached his hand across the table.

A noise erupted in the canteen, Winter withdrew his hand, and Gwen looked up and saw a group of boys dressed in their rugby kit approaching.

'If you want a study partner I can help you there,' Matt, the leader of the group, said and winked at her.

'I'm fine, thank you.' Gwen turned her attention back to Winter.

'Hey, hippy boy, move over.' Matt sat down and the group followed until Gwen was squashed in between them.

'We'll finish this another time.' Winter stood up and grabbed his bag.

'Don't leave on my account,' Matt called as Winter left the canteen.

Gwen scraped back her chair. 'You're such an arsehole sometimes, Matt.'

Outside she scanned the grounds for Winter but there was no sign of him.

'Gwen, wait!'

Gwen turned and saw Matt running towards her.

'What do you want?'

'Don't be like that, I just came to see if you're OK.'

'Well, I'm fine.'

'OK, but I'm here if you need me. I'm watching out for you so there's no need to worry.'

'What's that supposed to mean?' Gwen felt anger bubbling beneath her skin.

Matt looked at the ground and shuffled his feet. 'After what happened, you can't trust anyone. Just because Sam

Morris left school it doesn't mean you're safe. You don't know Hippy Winter, I don't think you should be hanging out with him.'

'I know him well enough. I'm quite capable of choosing who I hang around with, so you can fuck off.' Gwen turned and stomped away.

'I'm sorry.' Matt caught up with her. 'I just want to be friends with you.'

Gwen stopped and turned to face him. 'What is all this about? Why would you want to be seen with me?'

'I like you. I've always liked you…'

The memory faded and Gwen was surprised to find Meadows still talking. She was relieved that no one noticed she'd zoned out.

'I've looked over the case notes and it appears that there were no sightings of Bethan on that day. I thought we could do a fresh appeal for witnesses. Perhaps a reconstruction. It could help jog some memories. Someone who didn't come forward at the time out of fear or protecting someone else may come forward now.'

'Are you out of your fucking mind?' Matt's jaw clenched, his nostrils flaring.

'Matt, please.' Gwen felt her skin prickle with shame.

'Well, what does he expect?' Matt cast Gwen a scathing look. 'Do you want the same thing that happened to you to happen to Ariana? Because that's what's going to happen if you allow him to stir it all up again.'

'Matt, I have no intention of putting either Ariana or Gwen in danger. Whether we do an appeal or not, whoever attacked Gwen all those years ago and put that letter in Ariana's bag is not going to hide away and see what happens,' Meadows said. 'It's better that we continue with our investigations while we have a chance of catching the person responsible.'

'Yeah, like your lot did such a good job last time,' Matt retorted.

Gwen could see that Meadows was struggling to keep his patience. She wanted to offer some reassurance that she agreed with him. But did she? What if Matt was right and she put Ariana in danger by continuing with this? She could feel her forehead tightening with the onset of a headache.

'This time there is a good chance that Gwen will remember who attacked her and Bethan. It's getting late, perhaps you could take some time to think things over. Meanwhile I promise that we will do all we can to ensure Ariana's safety.'

Gwen rose from the chair. 'I'll see you out.'

'I'll come and see you in a few days,' Meadows said as he stepped outside. 'Perhaps in the meantime you could come to the station with Ariana so we can eliminate your fingerprints.'

'That's not a problem. I'm sorry that Matt was rude to you. He's just worried about Ariana.'

'It's fine, you don't have to worry, I've had a lot worse.' He smiled then turned away.

* * *

Gwen closed the door and ran her hand through her hair. 'What a mess.' She sighed as she walked into the sitting room. Matt was slumped on the sofa, the remote control in his hand. She walked into the kitchen and closed the door. I didn't even offer them a drink, she thought as she noticed the unused cups. She switched on the kettle and put away the spare cups. The kitchen door opened and Ariana walked in.

'Why does Dad have to be so bloody rude?' She slumped down in the nearest chair.

'You were listening at the door,' Gwen teased.

'I just wanted to know what the police are going to do about the letter.'

'Listen, love, if you are worried then I can drive you to school and pick you up.'

'I'm not worried.' Ariana twirled a strand of hair around her finger. 'I think you should do the reconstruction. It might help you remember some more.'

Gwen poured two cups of tea and handed one to Ariana before sitting down. 'Whatever I decide, I want you to promise me you will be careful. Stay with your friends and if there's no one to catch the late bus with, call me. Just don't go with anyone, even if you think you know them well. Just me or Dad.'

'That's a bit extreme!'

'Not really, please, Ari, just until things calm down.'

'OK, if you will go ahead with the reconstruction.'

'Why are you so keen? Does it have anything to do with the young DC Edris?'

Ariana blushed. 'Hell yes, he was so hot I think I burst my ovaries.'

Gwen couldn't help laughing. 'He was kind of cute.'

'The other one isn't bad either. When he came to the hospital you called him Winter, why?'

'Because that's his name.'

'Winter Meadows?' Ariana laughed. 'Who the hell calls their child Winter?'

'It's not that bad. His family came from the commune.'

'Hippy Hill?'

'It's called Peace Valley. His younger brother was ill, asthma I think, so they moved here.'

'You seem to know a lot about him,' Ariana said, grinning.

'We all went to school together, your dad, Winter, and me. Only I was two years younger.'

'Did you shag him? And that's why Dad doesn't like him?'

'No, I didn't! He was nice to me after the attack. Everyone else treated me like a freak apart from your dad and Winter.'

'So, were he and Dad friends?'

'God no, your dad hated him.'

'Why?'

'I don't know, probably because he was different. Kids can be cruel sometimes. Poor Winter was bullied relentlessly.'

'By Dad?'

'Yes, he was a bit of a bully back then.'

'He still is.'

'Ariana!' Gwen scolded.

'But it's true. Don't think I don't know what goes on. I'm not a kid anymore.'

'I know, but he's your dad. Don't let village gossip fill your head. You know that Granddad died when I was eleven. I would have given anything to have a dad like my friends. No matter what, your dad loves you.'

'He has a funny way of showing it.' Ariana stood up. 'I'm going to my room, I've got homework to do.'

Gwen watched her daughter leave the kitchen. An image flashed across her mind.

She was stood in her childhood home, screaming at her mother.

'I hate you, I don't care if I never see you again.' Gwen concentrated hard on the memory. She could feel the anger boiling through her veins. Her mother was wearing a short-sleeved pink cotton shirt, her hair pinned up on top of her head. She held out her hand towards Gwen, her tear-filled eyes pleading.

'I'm sorry, love.'

The memory slipped away, leaving Gwen feeling frustrated. She couldn't remember ever speaking to her mother like that. She wondered if it was the day of the attack and that's why she didn't want to go home. But what were they arguing about?

Chapter Thirteen

Meadows sat at his computer typing an update for Lester. It was Monday morning, one week since Lester had agreed to re-open the case.

Not a lot to report. He scanned the document. *Some more flashbacks and the letter, better than nothing. At least it shows that the killer is still local and is aware of Gwen's recovered memory.*

He finished the email and pressed send, then turned to Edris. 'So what have we got so far?'

'Gwen and Ariana came in to give their prints. I've just received the report. No other prints were found.'

'Well, I wasn't expecting any. It also rules out the theory that one of the kids at school put it in there. It would look odd if they were wearing gloves at this time of year.'

'So that leaves someone outside of school.'

'Or a member of staff.' Meadows leaned back in his chair. 'I think you should go down to the school this morning. Speak to the headmaster and see what security measures they have in place. I'll go this afternoon and talk to Catrin Evans, Ariana was in her house last week. I want to know if she had any other visitors. She was also in the same year at school as Gwen and Bethan. Let it be seen that we're taking an interest in the school.'

'Shall I ask uniform to drive by at home time?'

'Good idea, maybe they could also set up a school visit. Give a talk on stranger danger. That should keep the kids alert to anyone out of the ordinary lurking around. I'm going to see Doreen Hopkins this morning, there's still a time gap from when Bethan left the house until Sam Morris left Gwen at the cattle grid. Assuming he was telling the truth and the girls didn't meet up until after four, where was Bethan for three hours? Someone must have seen her, or Doreen Hopkins was mistaken about the time she left the house.'

'I ran a check on Jack Hopkins. He died of a heart attack three years ago. There's nothing on him. Not even a speeding fine. So that rules him out.'

'OK, thanks.' Meadows stood and grabbed his jacket. 'I'll meet you back here this afternoon.'

* * *

Doreen Hopkins still lived at the same address. Meadows parked the car and took a few moments looking at the house. Blue paint was flaking around the dirty windows. A short path led to the front door with weed-covered concrete on either side.

Looks neglected, no husband to help with the upkeep. Probably lives alone. As he approached the house the door opened and a frail grey-haired woman peered out.

'Doreen Hopkins?'

She nodded.

'I'm DI Meadows. Thank you for agreeing to see me.' He smiled down at the tiny woman.

'You better come in.' She didn't return the smile, just turned and led the way silently to the sitting room.

Meadows' eyes wandered around the room: a tattered sofa with a faded throw sat in the centre, next to it a matching armchair with a large ginger cat curled into a ball on the seat. The coffee table was strewn with unopened letters marked with dark rings and ash that had spilled from an over-flowing ashtray. The walls caught Meadows' attention – every available space was covered with photographs of Bethan. Baby pictures, Bethan as a toddler, primary and secondary school pictures. Her short life had been catalogued and preserved on these four walls. Her face beamed from every direction.

'Please sit down.' Doreen sat on the edge of the sofa and took a cigarette from an opened packet. She lit it and inhaled deeply before letting the smoke snake out of her mouth. She looked around the walls. 'I know some think it odd that I keep so many photographs of Beth, but just because she was snatched away from me I refuse to act like she never existed. This way I keep her alive.' She took another drag on the cigarette as she continued to stare at the wall.

Meadows considered the woman that sat in front of him. He guessed her to be about sixty-five but grief had taken its toll and she looked closer to eighty. The pain etched deeply on her face pulled at his heart.

'Mrs Hopkins, I'm sorry to have to rake over the events surrounding your daughter's death after all this time. I don't know if you are aware that recently Gwen Thomas has experienced some recovery of her memory. In light of this we have re-opened the case.'

'Please call me Doreen.' She looked at the wall again and sighed. 'You don't have to apologise. I'll never have any peace until the monster that did this to my daughter and Gwen is caught and made to pay. I was thinking that I should go and see Gwen, poor girl. I guess it must be the same for her, not knowing what happened and the fear that the person responsible is out there.'

'I think it would be a good idea for you to go and see Gwen. I understand from her doctor that looking over old photographs and listening to music from that time period may help to fully recover her memory. Perhaps you could talk to her about Bethan, share some of your memories.'

'I'll try, but it's not easy. I see Gwen with her family and it brings home what Beth lost. What we all lost. She was our only child, I never got to see her grow up and have children of her own. Don't get me wrong, I'm so glad that Gwen survived but I can't help wishing that it wasn't my girl that died.' She ground the cigarette into the ashtray and took another from the packet.

Meadows could feel the smoke tickling the back of his throat and resisted the urge to cough. 'I know it is a long time ago but I would like to go over your statement.'

'It may be a long time ago but I've been over that day so many times it feels like it could've been yesterday.'

'You said in your statement that you didn't see Gwen that day, but Gwen now remembers calling at your house that morning.'

Doreen's brow wrinkled in concentration. 'Yes, she did call that morning, but I only saw her for a few moments.'

'Gwen said that Bethan was ill, but there is no mention of that in the statement.'

Doreen rubbed her hand over her face. Tears pooled in her eyes. 'Bethan wasn't ill. Those first weeks were so hard. I couldn't think straight. I know this is going to sound heartless but I didn't care about Gwen at the time. I couldn't even bring myself to visit her in the hospital. Bethan was gone and there was still hope for Gwen – it didn't seem fair.'

'Why would Gwen think that Bethan was ill that day?'

'Beth asked me to tell Gwen that she was ill, she didn't want to see her.'

'Didn't you find that odd?'

'Not really, you know what teenage girls are like, always having some falling out. Beth had seemed a bit down for a few days before, staying in her room playing music.'

Meadows wanted to ask about what he had seen on the post-mortem but it was unlikely Doreen would be able to shed any light on it and would only cause more upset.

'By all accounts the girls were inseparable and they were found together that day. Did Bethan give you any indication of where she was going?'

'No, it was a few hours after Gwen called that she came downstairs, she said she was going for a walk. Told me she wouldn't be long, kissed me on the cheek, and that was the last I time I saw her.'

'Bethan had a boyfriend at the time?'

Doreen's face darkened. 'Sam Morris.'

'Yes, from what I understand he was questioned but there was no evidence to suggest that he was responsible.'

'Just because there was no evidence doesn't mean he didn't do it.' Doreen's hand shook as she put the cigarette to her mouth.

'Why do you think that Sam Morris would have attacked Bethan?'

'I don't know, maybe he wanted more than she was willing to give. You know what boys are like at that age. Only one thing on their mind and they'd do anything to get it.'

Not all boys.

'Is there anyone else you can think of that would want to hurt the girls? Was there a boyfriend before Sam Morris?'

'No.' Doreen bristled. 'She wasn't that type of girl.'

'I'm just trying to build up a picture. Talk to everyone that knew the girls. Did you see anyone near the house when Bethan left?'

'No, I was in the kitchen.'

'Was her bedroom at the front or back of the house?'

'The front. Would you like to see?'

'Please.'

Doreen led the way to the staircase where they ascended under the watchful gaze of Bethan, smiling from pictures hung at various angles. Doreen stopped at a white-painted door and inhaled deeply before turning the handle. Meadows stepped inside and surveyed the room. The walls were painted a pale lilac with matching bedspread. A nightdress lay folded on the pillow surrounded by various soft toys. The mirrored dressing table was positioned against the wall with make-up, perfume bottles, and jewellery. All the surfaces were dust-free and a faint smell of polish hung in the air.

'I didn't have the heart to change anything in here. I put a lot of her things into the attic but I never use this room.' Doreen ran her hand over the bedspread.

Meadows walked across the room to the window and peered out. There was a clear view of the pavement on both sides of the road. He opened the latch and looked out; this gave a further view of the street, leading down towards Quarry Road.

If she had seen someone she knew outside she could have easily called out to them, or they could have waited outside the window and no one in the house would know that they had met.

Meadows closed the window.

'Thank you. I appreciate you talking to me.'

'You will come and tell me as soon as you make an arrest?'

'Of course.'

Meadows was glad to step outside into the daylight away from the oppressive sadness of the house. He stood and looked in both directions. The entrance to Quarry Road could be seen from where he stood.

If she headed straight to the footpath that would explain why there were no sightings. But what would she be doing up there for three hours alone? She had to have met someone.

He sat in his car for a few moments fighting a strong desire to visit Gwen. He felt his stomach fizzle at the thought. He started the engine and drove to his cottage in the next village. Inside, he made a snack then stood gazing out of the window as he drank his tea. He tried to focus his mind on 1999. The memories were fragmented.

If I'm going to ask people to think back that far I'm going to have to do it myself. The reconstruction is going to have to have some prompts.

He switched on his laptop and searched for music and news items from that time period. He wrote down a list: London nail bombings, Jill Dando murder, Tony Blair was Prime Minister, and it was the year of the Matrix, and pop bands S Club 7 and Westlife.

Meadows laughed out loud. 'Pop bands, I don't think so.' He searched through his playlist and selected AC/DC. *That's more like it.* After rolling a joint, he lit up, sat down in the armchair and closed his eyes. The lyrics for *Hells Bells* blasted out of the speakers. His thoughts turned to James, a young man who had joined the commune and introduced him to rock music. It was one of the things he missed the most when they had to leave. He'd spent hours singing along to James playing the guitar.

Dad hated this music, I could only play it when he was out of the house. He let his mind drift back to the past...

He was sitting in his bedroom, his CD player turned to full volume as he studied for the upcoming exams. It was late and he was cramming as much information as he could before his mother came up to insist he turn off the music and get some sleep. As the song came to an end he heard raised voices drifting up the stairs.

Great, Dad's pissed again.

He put down his text book and opened the bedroom door. His younger brother Rain was on the landing peering over the banister.

'Go back to bed.'

'No.' Rain looked defiant. 'He's been drinking again.'

'All the more reason to stay in your room.'

A crash followed by a scream sounded from below. Rain ran down the stairs, Winter followed, his heart thudding in his chest. In the kitchen he quickly took in the scene. A smashed plate on the floor, his father's face contorted with rage, his mother cowering by the sink.

'Win, take your brother upstairs.' His mother pleaded with her eyes.

'Rain, go upstairs now!' he ordered before stepping in front of his mother. He pulled back his shoulders and glared at his father. 'Why don't you leave her alone and go and sleep it off?'

Kern Meadows narrowed his eyes. 'Get back to your room, you moody little fucker, before I teach you a lesson.'

'Please, Win,' his mother begged as she stepped forward, eyes darting wildly between her husband and her son. 'Look after Rain, I'll be fine.'

Winter stood his ground. He could feel his body trembling, and clenched his fists. 'No, Dad, I think you better leave.'

Kern lurched forward before Winter had a chance to react. He could hear his mother's screams as he felt his father's fist impact his jaw, the metallic taste of blood filled his mouth as a second blow hit his stomach. As his muscles contracted he felt the air leave his body and he struggled to draw in a breath. He sank to his knees as his father continued to punch and kick him.

'Kern, stop!' he heard his mother scream.

A crack rent the air and Winter pulled his head up in time to see his mother crash to the floor. Rain stood, his eyes wide with shock.

'Run! Go and get help,' Winter shouted.

Rain looked from his brother to his mother then pulled a knife from the block and waved it at Kern. 'Get away from them,' he shouted.

'Rain, no!' Winter struggled to his feet, pain shot through his head and his body felt on fire.

'You threatening me, boy?' Kern laughed. 'You put that knife down now or you'll get a hiding you'll never forget.'

Rain lunged forward and as Kern held up his arm in defence, his son plunged the knife into it.

Kern yelped as blood spurted from the wound. Winter stood paralysed as Rain dropped the knife and ran. He watched his father take chase.

'Go after them,' his mother sobbed.

The song came to an end and Meadows felt his heart thudding as he brought himself back to the present.

Rain shouldn't have been the one to protect us, forced to use a knife on his own father. I should've been the one, if I was stronger back then I could have fought him. He stood and paced the room trying to disperse the feelings of anger and regret. *It wasn't long after that Bethan was murdered.*

He walked to the sink where he splashed cold water over his face, hoping to wash away the memory of his father.

Poor Gwen, the last thing I would want is flashbacks of the nineties sneaking up on me.

* * *

A cool breeze ruffled his hair as he drove with the car windows open. He was tempted to turn up the music but didn't want to appear pretentious. He pulled into the school car park and stood outside the car looking at the building. The old stone school still stood with its separate boys and girls entrances. A taller building had been erected in the late seventies, which Meadows remembered as the science block. A modern building had been added on after he'd left. It was a strange mix of old and new.

All around was silent and through the ground floor windows, Meadows could see pupils hunched over their desks as they scribbled the afternoon lesson. A feeling of apprehension hung over him like a dark cloud, threatening to rain down memories of his school days.

I hated this place.

He pulled his shoulders back and purposely walked towards the office, reminding himself that he was a grown-up and one of authority. He recognised Catrin Evans seated behind the reception desk. Her eyes lit up when she saw him and she tucked her red hair behind her ears before tilting her head to the side and smiling.

Meadows showed his badge and identified himself even though it was unnecessary.

'You're the second one today, I'm beginning to feel like a naughty girl.' Her laugh tinkled around the office.

'Is there somewhere we could go to talk in private?' He looked at the other two women in the office who were staring with curiosity.

'The staff room should be empty, we won't get disturbed in there.'

Meadows followed her up a flight of steps, averting his eyes from her legs. Once inside she shut the door and took a seat, crossing her legs. She made no effort to smooth down her skirt, which had risen up to reveal her thighs.

'So what can I do for you, Detective?' She curled a lock of hair around her finger.

Meadows took a seat opposite. 'As you are aware from the earlier visit by my colleague, we have re-opened the case into the murder of Bethan Hopkins and the attack on Gwen Thomas.'

'Yes, I'm aware, but I don't see how I can help.'

'You were friends with the girls.'

'Yes, when they chose to let me be part of their group. You know what it was like. I remember you. You think you had it hard, try being a redhead.'

Meadows smiled.

'If you could just tell me what you remember about Bethan. I'm trying to build up a picture of her personality.'

'She was popular with the boys, they all drooled over her and she knew it. She used to flirt to get what she wanted. All the boys wanted to go out with her and all the girls wanted to be her. If you were her friend you got to hang out with all the hot boys.'

'You mean like Gwen?'

'Well yes, Gwen wouldn't have raised an eyebrow on her own. I think she was jealous of Beth.'

'Why do you say that?'

'Beth had everything, her parents bought her all the clothes she wanted. She always dressed in the latest fashion and had all the chart music. Gwen was a little mousy by comparison. She didn't have a father and I guess not a lot of money. So she couldn't compete with Beth.'

Meadows felt a strong urge to defend Gwen. *It's not how I would've described her.* He gave Catrin a tight smile and continued.

'Gwen's uncle, David Collier, seemed to be a bit of a father figure to her. Did Gwen talk about him?'

'Not really, he used to come to parent evenings. Sometimes he would pick her up if she missed the bus. Why?'

'No reason, as I said I'm just trying to build a picture. You said a lot of boys were interested in Bethan. Anyone in particular?'

'They used to follow Matt Thomas and his gang around, but I don't think Matt was that interested. There wasn't anyone in particular, just any boy that took their fancy would get the attention.'

'What about after school?'

'I didn't see much of them outside school.'

'Boyfriends?'

'Beth was going out with Sam Morris at the time, as you know. I don't think Gwen had a boyfriend.'

'And before that?'

'Beth always had some boy on the go. I know I shouldn't say it but she was a bit of a slapper.'

'Gwen said that she called at your house the morning of the attack.'

'Did she? I suppose I must have been out. Saturday mornings usually meant helping my mother with the grocery shopping. I didn't know anything about it until the police called on the Sunday morning asking if I had seen the girls. It was me that told them about the quarry.'

'Did you ever go up to the shack with them?'

'Once or twice, we just sat around talking about boys and smoking.'

'I understand that you have a daughter the same age as Ariana.'

'Yes, Jessica and Ariana are good friends. Ariana comes around the house often.'

'Ariana said that she was at your house last Wednesday. Did you have any other visitors that evening?'

'Is this about the letter?' Catrin said. 'I know all about it, you should know you can't keep anything quiet around here.'

Meadows felt irritation crawl at his skin. 'Was there anyone else at the house last Wednesday evening?'

'No, just me, Jess, and Ariana.'

'Did you stay friends with Gwen when you left school?'

'Yes, we were friends when the girls were young but we had a falling out.'

'May I ask what about?'

Catrin blushed and smoothed down her skirt. 'It was about Matt. You know he has a reputation, he's had several affairs over the years. I told Gwen she should leave him, he obviously isn't happy with her.'

Meadows clenched his jaw. Catrin was starting to irritate him and he had a feeling there was more to the falling out than she was letting on. 'I see, so Gwen was upset by this?'

'Yes, we haven't spoken for years. So, tell me, is there a Mrs Meadows?'

Meadows stood up. 'I think that's all for now. If you remember anything that you think might be important, call the station and ask for DC Edris.'

There's no way she is having my number.

'OK, and in case you're interested, it is just me and Jess now.' She winked.

Meadows ignored the comment and left the staff room, more than happy to see himself out.

* * *

Back at the station he filled Edris in on the interviews.

'So what did you make of the redhead?' Edris asked, grinning.

'Don't even go there.'

'Well, you're single, I reckon you could be in there.'

'Not my type, but I bet she could teach you a few things.'

'Ugh, I've got more than enough experience with women, thanks.'

'So I've heard.'

Edris blushed. 'To be honest, she frightened the hell out of me. I was glad to get to the headmaster's office and that's saying something. Anyway, security's not bad there. You have to enter through the office. He agreed to uniform having a chat with the kids. Funny guy, though.'

'What do you mean?'

'Well, he appeared a little nervous when I first went in, then he remembered that I had been a pupil there and became all authoritarian, like I was still a kid.'

'Well, you are.' Meadows chuckled. 'He used to be my English teacher. Didn't like him very much back then. Anyway I have set up a meeting tomorrow morning at the television studio to discuss the reconstruction, they're going to put it out on the six o'clock news, Thursday. I'll call in to see Gwen after I've finished there. See what she's decided about taking part.'

'What're you going to do if she doesn't want to do it?'

'Go ahead anyway, Doreen Hopkins is keen on the idea. I've had another look at Sam Morris' statement, he claims that he saw the rugby boys coming back from the match at 5 p.m. but no one backed up his statement. According to the post-mortem report Bethan died between five and six. I want you to check that out. Go and see him in the morning.'

'You want me to go and see him?' Edris raised his eyebrows.

'Yes, he will recognise me and might think I have clouded judgement. It's better that he sees a fresh face. Go over his statement with him and tell him about the reconstruction. See what response you get.'

'OK great, I can handle that.' Edris stood up and put on his jacket. 'Fancy a pint?'

'No thanks, you go ahead. To be honest, I'm not one for socialising.'

'So I've heard.'

'Blackwell?'

'Yep.' Edris' face flushed.

'It's OK, I can imagine what he said. Go on, I'll see you tomorrow.'

* * *

Meadows typed up his notes from the interviews then drove to his mother's flat. He took the keys from his jacket pocket and let himself in the front door.

'Hi, Mum.'

The kitchen door opened and Fern Meadows appeared. 'I was just stewing some tea.'

'Nettle?'

'It's good for you, detox after all that crap you put in your body.'

Meadows took a seat at the kitchen table and watched his mother prepare the tea. Her long grey hair was braided and swung across her back as she moved. She wore a bright orange T-shirt over a long cotton skirt. Her feet as always were bare, with painted toenails.

'Have you heard from Rain?'

'Not in a while, you know what your brother is like, always trying to rescue people. The last postcard was from Cambodia.' She indicated the board on the wall which was pinned with various postcards from around the world.

'So tell me, what's troubling you?'

'Nothing, I just thought I would pop in and see you.' Meadows forced a smile.

'You can't fool me, Winney.' Fern ruffled his hair and placed a kiss on top of his head. 'You were always easy to read.' She returned to the pot and stirred vigorously.

Meadows knew her ways, she would stay silent until he spoke and he could never keep quiet for long. 'It's this case I'm working on. We've re-opened the case of the murder of Bethan Hopkins and the attack on Gwen Collier.'

'So I've heard, you know how gossip spreads.' She turned and looked at Meadows with a knowing smile. 'Ah, little Gwenny, that explains a lot. Have you seen her?'

'Yes, a few times.'

Fern filled two mugs and placed one in front of Meadows before taking a seat. 'Did it stir up all those old feelings?'

'Mum, please.' Meadows squirmed in his seat. 'There wasn't anything between Gwen and I.'

'Of course there was, and there could've been a lot more. I know how you felt about her. You used to light up whenever you spoke about her.'

'Well, that's all in the past now.'

'Is it?' Fern held his gaze. 'I know she married that Matt Thomas and has a couple of children.'

'Yes, and it's not a happy marriage by all accounts. He's allegedly had several affairs. I don't understand why she stays with him.'

'Women stay for all sorts of reasons and when children are involved it's hard.'

'Is that why you stayed with Dad?'

Fern flinched and lowered her eyes. 'That's different. Anyway, we were talking about you and Gwen.'

'Sorry, I didn't mean to upset you. This case just brings back so many bad memories.'

'I know.' She reached out and patted his hand. 'It wasn't an easy time for you and Rain. I still feel guilty that you had to bear witness to what went on between your father and me.' Fern sighed. 'Still, it's no use looking into the past, it will only make you bitter.'

'Sometimes we have to look back to get answers.'

'You know your father wasn't always that way, and there were a lot of good times.'

'I remember, things were different in the commune. He was happy there, then we moved and he was always angry. What happened to change him?'

'I don't know, it was a gradual change. He struggled to find work and he didn't fit in easily with village life. To be honest, I don't dwell on it, and I haven't thought about him in years.'

'Aren't you curious as to what happened to him?'

'No, what's done is done. Now, please, leave it alone.'

'OK.' He took a sip of his tea and tried not to grimace as the bitter liquid assaulted his taste buds.

'So what are you going to do about Gwen?' There was mischief in her eyes.

'There's nothing I can do. I will help her any way I can to recover her memory and find her attacker. It wouldn't be ethical or professional to do any more than that.'

'Is that all that's stopping you?'

Meadows sighed, he knew what was coming next.

'When was the last time you went out with a woman?'

'I haven't had the time, with the promotion and the move. Give me a chance.'

'You're not too busy for a bit of loving.' Fern winked. 'Don't leave it too long. If things are meant to be with Gwen then they will happen naturally, but you have to take the chance when it comes.'

'I will, but only when the case is closed. Then I can have a clear conscience with regards to work.'

'And what about Matt?'

'Well, if he doesn't cherish what he has then it's his own fault if he loses her.'

'That's the spirit, you need a bit of fight in you, and I want to see you happy. You know I worry about you.'

'I know, but I'm fine. Honestly.'

Meadows left his mother and drove home, thoughts of Gwen swirling around his head. He didn't want to see her unhappy but a greater part of him hoped that the rumours of Matt's affairs were true, and when the case was closed she would be free of the past and just maybe she would choose him this time.

Chapter Fourteen

Gwen hesitated near the entrance to the quarry path. A cold heavy feeling tugged at her stomach and kept her from stepping through the gate. It had been over a week since she walked the path, she had tried a few times to repeat the process but fear of what she might remember held her back. Part of her wanted to know the truth, but the vulnerable part wanted to hide away and not relive it all over again. Her worst fear was discovering her attacker was someone she knew and cared about.

She pushed the gate. Blue strained at his lead, desperate to get to the water that lay on the other side of the gate. Her chest constricted and she sucked in air as panic gripped her body. The ground moved beneath her feet, she bent forward as she tried to slow her breathing.

'I'm sorry, boy, I can't.' She turned and led him towards home.

As she walked through the village she tried to push thoughts of the attack to the back of her mind. She still felt light-headed from the panic attack and tried to think of something nice. An image of Meadows instantly made her smile. She knew he had been to see Doreen Hopkins the previous day and was disappointed he hadn't called in.

Anxiety gnawed her stomach, maybe Matt had put him off.

She tried to concentrate on the feel of the sun on her skin, willing it to melt away the dark mood that cloaked her body. Since seeing Meadows in the hospital she had found it difficult to concentrate. Her life now seemed pointless and missed opportunities came back to haunt her.

Her thoughts swirled around in her mind and she was oblivious to her surroundings as she approached the front door and pulled the keys from her pocket.

'Gwen.'

She spun around. 'Uncle David, you gave me a fright.'

'Sorry, love. Are you OK?' David smiled. 'You were off with the fairies.'

'I'm fine, come in.'

They walked into the kitchen. Gwen unhooked Blue from his lead and filled his water bowl before switching on the kettle.

'Have you been having a sort-out?' David indicated the cardboard box on the table.

'No, Doreen Hopkins brought that over yesterday. It's filled with Beth's things. I haven't worked up the courage to go through it yet.'

'Well, that's understandable. I can help you if you like.' He inched closer to the box.

Gwen looked at her uncle. Even though he was smiling, there was still an unease about him. She felt her skin prickle and had the sudden urge to ask him to leave. His hand was hovering close to the box. Why would he want to see what is inside? she thought. She tried to relax her face. 'So how are things with you?'

'Things are good, thanks. I just wanted to call in to see if you're OK and if you've had any more flashbacks.'

'Just a few.' She turned her back and warmed the pot before adding the tea. 'Nothing important though.' She turned and smiled. 'Mrs Hopkins was hoping that if I looked at Beth's things I would remember.'

'Poor woman. How is she?'

'She looks old and frail. She wants me to be part of the reconstruction. I think I should do it, I owe her that much.'

'You don't owe her anything.' David took a step towards her and placed his hand on her shoulder. 'You have been through enough.'

The flashback came suddenly…

She was running from the house, she could hear David shouting as he ran after her, feel him closing in. Tears blurred her vision as she reached the gate and yanked it open.

'Gwen, stop!' His hand grabbed her forearm and she was spun around.

'Let go of me!' she yelled, the fury bubbled up in her throat.

'Gwen, wait, we have to talk about this.' Anger reddened his face and he increased the pressure on her arm.

'You're hurting me.' She tried to wrestle free but his fingers dug into her flesh. 'I hate you!' She tried to prise his fingers from her arm but he was too strong. 'Let go or I'll scream the fucking place down!'

His face was so close she could feel his breath on her cheek. His eyes darkened.

'Don't you dare–'

Gwen blinked away the memory.

'Gwen, are you all right, love?'

She could feel the weight of David's hand on her shoulder. It made her feel uncomfortable. 'I'm fine, sorry, I just drift off to a world of my own sometimes.' She tried to force a smile as she saw concern crease his face.

'Here, let me finish the tea, you go and sit down. You're trembling.'

Gwen didn't argue, she took a seat and watched David pour the tea. Could he really have something to do with what happened?

'Here we go.' David placed a mug of tea in front of Gwen. 'Shall we see what's in the box?'

Gwen felt her body tense, she didn't want to open the box with him there. She picked up her tea and took a sip of the hot liquid hoping to chase away the chill that crawled over her back.

David seemed to take Gwen's silence as an indication that he should proceed to open the box. He pulled the tape back and opened the lid. The first item he pulled out was a T-shirt. He held it up for Gwen to see.

'Westlife, they were Beth's favourite group. She had posters of them covering her bedroom walls.' Gwen smiled. An image of Beth in a pair of jeans and the T-shirt filled her mind. She was laughing as she danced around the bedroom. Gwen felt her chest tighten as sharp pins penetrated her heart.

'I'm sorry, I can't do this now.'

'It's OK. Maybe I should leave you on your own. You can take your time going through the box.'

'Thanks. Finish your tea first though.'

David gulped down his tea and she followed him to the door. Meadows was pulling up in front of the house as David stepped over the threshold.

'Looks like you have another visitor.'

Gwen tried not to let the pleasure of seeing Meadows show on her face. 'Thanks for calling around.' She smiled at David who took the hint and turned away.

* * *

'I hope this is not an inconvenient time for you.' Meadows approached the house and smiled as his eyes locked with Gwen's.

'Not at all, come in. I've just made some tea.'

She could feel every nerve ending tingle as she poured the tea from the pot. She turned and saw Meadows fussing Blue, who wagged his tail as he lapped up the attention.

'I think you've made a friend there.' Gwen placed the mug on the table and took a seat.

Meadows peeled off his jacket and placed it on the back of the chair before sitting. He wore a light blue shirt which showed off the contours of his biceps.

Gwen squirmed in her seat.

'So, how've you been?' Meadows took a sip of tea.

'Good thanks.'

'I see your uncle has been checking up on you.'

'I guess he's just worried about me.' Gwen fiddled with the handle of her cup, the mention of David bought on another bout of anxiety.

'When I was here on Friday you asked Ariana if she had seen your uncle when she visited your mother. Why?' Meadows asked.

'Oh, it's nothing, really. It's just a feeling I had. When he came to the hospital he seemed edgy. He hovered at the bottom of the bed and looked like he was preparing to make a dash for it.' Gwen ran her hand through her hair.

'What else? It's important you tell me everything you can, no matter how trivial it seems.'

'Today when he was in the house he appeared keen to look over the things that Doreen Hopkins brought over.' She indicated the box. 'When he put his hand on my shoulder I had a flashback. He was chasing me, he grabbed hold of my arm tightly. I struggled and shouted but he wouldn't let go.'

Meadows expression darkened. 'Were you up the quarry in this flashback?'

'No, I was running from the house. I wasn't afraid, just angry. I really can't see that he would have anything to do with the attack. Why would he want to hurt me? He's had plenty of opportunities alone with me since.'

'Was he a father figure to you when you were younger?'

'I suppose he was. He was always around checking on me and Mum, doing odd jobs around the house.'

'You didn't mind?'

'No, why should I?' Gwen said.

'I'm just trying to build up a picture of your relationship with him. I spoke to Catrin Evans yesterday. She remembers that he used to attend parents' evenings and pick you up from school sometimes. She gave the impression that you weren't that fond of him.'

'Oh, did she?'

'From your reaction I guess you're not too happy with Catrin.' Meadows smiled. 'She mentioned that you had a falling out.'

'Did she tell you why?'

'Something about her wanting you to leave Matt.'

'So she didn't tell you that she was sleeping with him. That's why she wanted me to leave him, so he would move in with her.' Gwen felt her cheeks burn with humiliation.

'I'm sorry. I didn't mean to upset you.'

'Don't be, it's just the way things are. Look, I don't really want to talk about Matt and his women.'

'Right.' Meadows shifted in his chair. 'So, as far as you remember, you were comfortable with your uncle.'

'He didn't try anything, if that's what you mean. He wasn't like that. If he was some sort of pervert then I'm sure I would have remembered. I only lost a month or so of my memory.'

'Still, I think it might be worth questioning him again,' Meadows said.

'I don't know if that is such a good idea.'

'I'll wait until after the reconstruction. Have you given any more thought to the idea of being involved?'

'Yes, I'll help all I can. It tore at my heart to see Doreen Hopkins. She looked so old and frail. I doubt she ever got over losing Beth. I can't imagine what it feels like to lose a child.'

'I don't think it's something you ever get over, you just learn to live with it. In Doreen's case it's worse because she has no closure. Maybe if we catch the person responsible she will have some peace. I had a meeting with the film crew this morning. They have two actresses to take the part of you and Bethan, but it'd be good to get some shots of you walking along the footpath. Doreen Hopkins has kindly given me some photographs of Bethan, perhaps you could let me have some of you at that age.'

'I'll ask Mum to dig some out. That reminds me, I remembered having an argument with her. It must have been that day because I don't ever recall speaking to my mother like that. I was shouting and swearing.'

'Your mother said in her statement that there had been an argument that morning but she was vague. What was it about?'

'I don't know, I only remembered a bit of it. I doubt if it was important, but it must have been serious. She wasn't shouting back, just kept saying she was sorry.' Gwen sighed. 'So is there anything you can tell me about the original investigation? I take it you've looked at the files.'

Meadows took a sip of his tea and leaned towards Gwen. 'I thought we could walk up the quarry before filming. I can talk you through what was discovered. It could help jolt your memory if we're in the same place. The filming will start on Thursday.'

'That's only two days away.' Her stomach fluttered.

'I thought it would be better to do it sooner, while people are talking about it. I'll be with you the whole time.'

The fluttering in her stomach intensified at the thought of being with Meadows for the afternoon. She looked down at the table, afraid that he would see the ache in her eyes. 'It will be interesting to see the actresses taking part.'

'We've tried to keep them as close as possible to you and Bethan. They will be dressed in similar clothes to the ones you were wearing that day. I've been trying to build up a picture of Bethan. I do remember her from school but we never spoke. I get the impression that she was quite flirtatious.'

'I can imagine Catrin's description of us.'

'I'd rather hear it from you.'

'We were like any other teenagers with raging hormones, the only things we cared about was boys, music, and clothes, in that order. Bethan pushed the boundaries at school, sewed a hem on her skirt so it was higher than the ones the rest of us wore. She wore jewellery and make-up but for some reason managed to get away with it,' Gwen said.

'What about you?'

'Mum didn't like me to wear make-up. I used to put on mascara and lip gloss on the bus.' She smiled at the memory. 'Beth had an allowance so she could buy all the make-up and clothes she wanted. She always looked pretty.'

'What about boyfriends?'

'There was always a queue. All the boys were in love with her and she knew it. There was Sam, of course, and before that she went out with Gethin.'

'Did she ever mention anyone older?'

'She liked Mike Finch, you remember him, he was in the same year as you and hung around with Matt. I think she only went out with Sam to make him jealous.'

'So Sam wasn't the chosen one.' A smile played on Meadows' lips.

'No he wasn't, I wish I hadn't mentioned that to you now.' Gwen could feel the heat rising in her cheeks.

'So there was no one outside of school she talked about?' Meadows asked.

'No, why?'

'I think she may have been seeing someone older. Someone she had to keep secret.'

'I'm sure she would have told me. We told each other all our secrets.'

'There are some things she didn't share with you.'

'Such as?'

Meadows expression changed, he seemed to be wrestling with a decision.

Tension crackled the air and Gwen fiddled with the handle on the mug. 'What is it you are not telling me?'

'There was something in the post-mortem report that was never made public. Bethan was three months pregnant when she died. A DNA test showed that Sam was not the father of her unborn child.'

'Pregnant? No, she couldn't have been.' The information tore through Gwen's mind and cold fingers squeezed her chest. The air felt thin and she felt her skin prickle. An image of Beth lying on the shack floor filled her vision. Blood leaking from her head and seeping into the dirt. She imagined the child inside her stomach squirming as its lifeline was severed.

Gwen sucked in the air until her chest expanded, but still felt like there was no oxygen. Bile rose in her throat. Her stomach heaved as she stood, throwing back the chair as she bolted. She could hear Meadows calling out as she rushed into the bathroom just in time to empty her stomach. She sank to her knees as her vision blurred and numbness prickled her scalp.

Blue padded into the bathroom and nudged her with his cold nose. She reached out a hand and buried it in his fur.

'Gwen, are you OK?'

She looked up and saw Meadows standing in the doorway, concern creased his face.

'I'm fine.' She stood and rinsed her mouth before splashing cold water on her face. 'I'm sorry.' She turned to face him. 'I never knew. She didn't say anything. Poor

Beth, she must have been so frightened. Oh God!' She raised her hand to her mouth. 'That poor child.' She felt her legs buckle beneath her.

Meadows moved quickly and took a firm hold on her arm. 'Come on, I think you better sit down.'

A low growl rumbled around the bathroom as Blue challenged Meadows.

'It's OK, boy.' Gwen placed her hand on his head to soothe him. 'Sorry, he doesn't understand why I'm upset.' She felt the tears sting her eyes and bit down on her lip to try to stem the flow. 'I just keep seeing her lying on the floor of the shack and there is so much blood.'

She leaned against Meadows. Through the cotton of his shirt she could feel the heat of his skin and hear the steady rhythm of his heart. Sobs racked her body and she felt his arms drawing her closer. They stayed like that until Gwen felt control return to her mind and body.

'Feeling better?' Meadows pulled away.

Gwen could still feel his arms around her body, she wanted to bury her head in his chest and stay there. It felt safe. 'I'm OK now.' She wiped the tears from her face.

'I shouldn't have told you.'

'No, you were right to tell me. Just give me a few moments to compose myself.'

'I'll wait in the kitchen.' He gave her an encouraging smile and left the room.

Gwen looked in the bathroom mirror, and a pale face with swollen red eyes looked back. She washed her face and repaired her make-up before returning to the kitchen. Meadows was sat at the table, he looked up when she entered the room.

'Gwen, I'm worried about the effect all this is having on you. I could arrange for you to have some counselling.'

Gwen took a seat and ran her hand through her hair. 'I had enough victim support last time, thanks. Please don't worry about me, I really need to do this now, so don't hold back on me because you think I can't handle it.'

'I wouldn't dream of it.' The smile returned to Meadows' face. 'The filming will start at one, so I thought we could take a walk up the quarry about eleven.'

'That's good for me. I'll get those pictures for you by then.'

Meadows stood and put on his jacket. 'Thanks for agreeing to be part of the reconstruction, it will make a big difference.'

Gwen stood and followed him to the door where he turned and looked intently into her eyes. She held his gaze.

'Take care.' He turned and walked away leaving Gwen aching inside.

* * *

Meadows could still feel Gwen's tears on his shirt even though they had long since dried. The feel of her body as she clung to him lingered on his senses.

He pulled into the station car park and took a deep breath before leaving the car. Edris was sat at his desk and greeted Meadows with a smile when he entered the office.

'How did the meeting go?'

'Good, all set for Thursday and Gwen has agreed to take part. How did it go with Sam Morris?'

Edris spun his chair around to face Meadows. 'He's not what I expected. He looks older than his years for a start, I reckon he is or was a heavy drinker. Also a bit of a recluse. He never married and lived with his mother until she died a few years ago. He works at Dyffryn Du Motors as a mechanic but stays in the garage away from the customers. He was worried about the case being dragged up again. To be honest, though, I got the impression that he felt re-opening the case would clear his name.'

'But he was never charged.' Meadows plonked himself down in his chair.

'He says the village found him guilty anyway. Made his life hell.'

'Yes, I can see how that would happen. I wonder why he stayed.'

'I asked him that. He said he had nowhere to go and if he left people would assume it was because he was guilty. He had hoped that the police would find the killer and he could get on with his life. Instead he has had to live under a cloud of suspicion,' Edris said.

'Did you go over the original statement with him?'

'Yes, no change, which again makes me think he was telling the truth. It would be hard to remember a lie after all these years. He still maintains that he left Gwen alive and well at the cattle grid.'

'Did you ask him if he thought Bethan was seeing someone else?' Meadows asked.

'Yes, he said he was sure she was. He'd been surprised that she went out with him. It had been OK at first but then she stopped seeing him so often. He said he was supposed to meet up with her on the Friday before the attack but she never showed. He's also adamant that they didn't sleep together.'

'And he didn't have any idea who the other guy might be?'

'No, he thought maybe one of the rugby boys. He says he saw them coming back from a match that day about 5 p.m. But no one corroborated his story. I double-checked the statements.'

'OK, good work. Let's wait and see what comes out of the reconstruction. I don't think Sam Morris is our man but who knows? I could be wrong.' Meadows leaned back in his chair and ran his hands through his hair.

'Are you OK?' Edris asked.

'Yes. Why?'

'Oh I don't know, you seem a little stressed today. It can't be easy for you as you knew the girls.'

It's harder than you think and for an entirely different reason.

'It's not that, I just hope something comes out of the reconstruction otherwise we are in danger of Lester closing down the case. We are already running into the second week with nothing to report. If the case closes you will have to return to Blackwell.' Meadows laughed as he watched Edris' face fall.

It will be a shame, I'm actually beginning to like working with him.

Chapter Fifteen

Meadows stood in front of the bedroom mirror holding up different combinations of ties and shirts.

It's not for Gwen, I have to look good for the cameras.

'Who are you trying to fool?' he asked his reflection. He settled on a crisp white shirt and dark grey tie, ran a comb through his hair, then headed for Gwen's house.

Black clouds were gathering in the sky as he drove. He focused on the investigation, mulling over all that he knew and what he needed to do next.

He parked outside Gwen's house and stole a look in the mirror before climbing out of the car.

The front door opened and Gwen stepped out with Blue. Her hair had been straightened and she wore pale pink lipstick. Meadows' eyes travelled down her body; her petite figure was highlighted by a snug-fitting blue sundress.

'Hi, I hope you don't mind Blue coming with us. He'll howl if I leave him at home.'

'It shouldn't be a problem. I'll look after him when they're filming you, if he'll stay with me.'

'I'm sure he will, as long as he can see me he'll be fine. He is well behaved, you just have to be firm with him.' She turned and locked the door before taking a step towards Meadows. 'Is this OK?' She indicated the outfit she wore. 'I didn't know what to wear.'

You look beautiful.

'Yes, you look very nice. Maybe you should take a coat, in case it rains.'

Gwen looked up at the sky and shrugged. 'I'm sure it'll hold off, and besides it is sheltered once you get on the path.'

They walked through the village with Blue sniffing at gates and lampposts on the way.

'In Sam Morris' statement he said that he left you at the cattle grid at about 4 p.m. Do you think you would have walked across the mountain and picked up the footpath from there?'

'I don't think so. I never went to the quarry alone. It's kind of spooky up there.'

'Maybe you had arranged to meet someone or Bethan at the shack.'

'I can't see Beth waiting alone in the shack and, besides, she was ill that morning, so I wouldn't have been able to arrange a meeting. Neither of us had a mobile phone back then. I was going to get one for my sixteenth birthday.' She turned and smiled. 'Kids have them by six years old now.'

'So it's more likely that you walked back into the village and met Bethan before going to the quarry. It's a fair walk back down and doesn't leave a lot of time. You would have been just behind Sam, but it's not impossible. Doreen Hopkins said that Bethan wasn't ill that morning, she just didn't want to see you.'

'Oh, well, I can't think why not. We argued sometimes, I suppose, but if we weren't on speaking terms then I wouldn't have called for her that morning. It doesn't make sense.'

They reached the entrance to the quarry and Gwen hesitated by the gate.

'I'll be with you every step of the way.' Meadows opened the gate and placed his hand on the small of her back to guide her through.

Blue tugged on the lead as soon as he saw the water. 'Not now.' Gwen pulled him back. 'He likes to go swimming.'

'Why don't you let him go? We have plenty of time.'

Meadows watched as Gwen unhooked the leash and the big dog went bounding towards the stream. He leapt off the bank and landed with a splash before dipping his face to gulp down the water. Gwen and Meadows followed the dog and stood at the edge of the water watching.

'Why do you stay with him?' Meadows regretted the question as soon as it left his lips.

Gwen looked up at him. 'He married me. I don't think anyone else would have and there are the children to consider. I suppose I don't like the idea of being on my own for the rest of my life.'

'I don't think you would be on your own for long.'

Gwen laughed. 'Like I have a long queue of suitors lined up! It's not just the scars on my body, they run a lot deeper than that. Matt was the only one interested in me after it happened. Everyone else treated me like a freak.'

'Not everyone.'

'No, but you left...' Gwen turned away.

'You were already with Matt by then.'

'No, I wasn't.' She spun around and glared at him. 'Who told you that?'

Meadows clenched his jaw. *The lying bastard.*

'It was Matt, wasn't it? And you believed him.' Her eyes bored into his.

'It's in the past now. It doesn't matter.'

'It matters to me. I never understood why you left. I thought we were friends. I thought we were...'

'I'm sorry. If I'm honest, I would've left anyway. I had a place in university but I would have done things differently,' Meadows said.

'It's OK, it's not your fault.' She called Blue and he bounded over, dripping water in his wake. Gwen attached the lead and returned her attention to Meadows. 'So why don't you tell me about yourself? I'm at an unfair advantage, you know everything about me.'

'What do you want to know?'

'I don't see a wedding ring so I take it you didn't get married. Either that or you're divorced.'

'No, I didn't get married and I don't have any children. I was engaged, but we split up before I moved back. I guess we drifted apart.'

'I'm sorry.'

'Don't be. We parted on friendly terms. Moving back here has been a fresh start for me.'

'And then you ran into me and all my problems.' Gwen smiled.

'I'm glad I did. I did think of you after I left. Even thought of writing to you. Then Mum told me you married Matt and I guess I just moved on with my life. Come on, we better start walking or the film crew will be waiting for us.'

They walked until they reached the top of the steps where they paused to catch their breath.

'It's beautiful up here in the daylight.' Meadows looked around at the surrounding hills. In the distance he could see the wind turbines twirling in unison.

They walked further up the path and Meadows noticed the change in Gwen when they reached the shack. Her body was rigid and she twisted the lead around her hand.

'Shall we look inside?' he asked.

She nodded and he opened the door. He closely watched her reaction as her eyes darted around.

'There were more tools on the walls, your blood was found on an axe hanging about here.' He walked over to the wall and touched the empty space. He turned and saw Gwen put her hand to the back of her head, her eyes narrowed as she moved her hand in front of her face and examined her fingers.

'Blood,' she whispered, 'I'm bleeding.' The colour drained from her face.

Meadows stood still, not wanting to disturb the flashback. He watched her draw an unsteady breath then look around the shack until her eyes rested on the floor. She shook her head and stepped towards the door.

'I'm sorry I can't stay in here any longer.'

'It's OK, you're doing really well. What did you see?'

'Just blood on my hand. I could feel the numbness in the back of my head, then my vision started to blur, my legs felt weak. I could see Beth lying on the floor.' She hurried out of the shack.

'Don't try and fight the memories,' Meadows said as he followed her outside and back onto the path. 'This is where you were found.'

He leaned over the fence and pointed to the location he had seen in the photographs. The cliff face was jagged and he tried not to think about Gwen tumbling down, her broken body lying at the edge of the water.

Gwen stood next to him and peered over. 'There wasn't a fence then. It's a long way down, you would think I'd remember, but looking down there doesn't stir any memories.'

'I imagine you were unconscious by the time you reached the bottom. You might well have been unconscious when you went over.'

'You mean I was just thrown down there. Why? It would have been easier to leave me in the shack.'

'My theory is that you tried to escape.'

'And just left Beth?'

'No.' He turned and placed his hands on her shoulders. 'You didn't leave her to die. You had traces of Bethan's blood on your hands and clothes. You were trying to help her.' He looked into her eyes and saw the doubt. 'You must have been terrified but you didn't leave.

Whatever happened here I think you showed tremendous courage. You're stronger than you think.'

Gwen stepped back onto the path. She looked towards the direction from which they had come, then back up the path. He saw her eyes glaze as she stood rigid. Blue tugged at the lead, moving her arm like a puppet. Quietly Meadows stepped towards her. He heard her breath quicken, saw her cheeks flaring red. After a few moments her eyes refocused and she looked up the path.

'I came from this direction.' She pointed ahead. 'I was running from someone. I was so afraid he was going to catch me. I came to the shack to hide.' She bit her lip in concentration. 'So I did come from the mountain.'

'That's good. Come on, we will walk a little further up to see if you remember anything else. I'll ask the film crew to take shots from the cattle grid and across the mountain. Do you think you were on your own or was Bethan running with you?'

'No, I was definitely alone. I think I'd been running for a while because my chest was hurting and I was struggling to catch my breath. I could feel my heart beating against my ribs.' She walked as she spoke, all the while her eyes darted around as if searching for a trigger for her memory.

'It does make more sense for you to have come this way, we just have to work out how you met up with Bethan.'

'What if I didn't go to the shack but ran towards home? I could have met up with Beth. You did say that she was supposed to have gone out for a walk that day. I could have met her on the way to my house and told her about someone chasing me and then gone back up with her.'

'I suppose it's a possibility, but why on earth would you come back up here if you were afraid?' Meadows looked around.

It's very isolated. No one would have heard the girls scream.

'Beth wouldn't have been afraid. More likely she would have teased me. She would've wanted to look for herself, confront the person chasing me to show I made a mistake. I think she would've found the whole thing funny.'

'Then it would've had to have been someone you knew and not some random stranger.'

'I guess so, but who would have been up the mountain? It couldn't have been long after Sam left me at the cattle grid.'

'If he left you at the cattle grid,' Meadows said.

'You can't seriously believe that he's responsible for what happened. He had no reason to hurt me.'

'There was no evidence to tie him to the scene of the crime other than his coat, which he claims he gave to you. It doesn't mean that he is innocent.'

'He did give me his coat, I remembered that,' Gwen said.

'What if he found out that Bethan was pregnant? It would give him motive and you could've got in the way.'

'Sam wasn't like the rugby boys, he was a bit of a geek. I don't think he would have had the strength to fight the two of us.'

'OK. To be honest, I don't think Sam is our man but until someone comes forward to confirm his story I still have to treat him as a suspect.'

They reached the gate that led onto the mountain and stepped through. Once they were in the clearing they had a good view of the surrounding farmland. Fields had been sectioned off with dry stone walls penning in sheep ready to be shaved. The farmhouse lay nestled in the dip of the hill surrounded by outbuildings. Blue's ears pricked up as he caught the scent of sheep, he pulled at the lead, his eyes bright as he jumped around.

'No!' Gwen commanded. She led him to the brow of the hill where the road was visible in the distance winding its way up the mountain. She spun around then placed her hand on Meadows' arm.

'The barn! There was someone in the barn.'

Meadows followed her gaze. 'Is that another place you used to hang out?'

'No, I don't think we ever went into the barn, we stayed on the footpath or in the shack.'

'Come on, we may as well take a look now we are here.' Meadows led the way.

When they reached the barn Gwen became still. She stood, her eyes wide with trepidation. The wind had picked up, whipping her hair around her face. 'I can't go in there, I don't want to see it again.'

'What don't you want to see?' Meadows coaxed.

'I… I don't remember.' There was a tremor in her voice as she backed away.

'It's OK, we can come back another time. We should head back now.'

Once they were back on the footpath Gwen relaxed and was fully composed by the time they met up with the film crew. Meadows took his turn in front of the camera, outlining the history of the case and appealing for information. He was aware of Gwen standing to the side of the camera watching. He was itching to loosen his tie, he could feel the perspiration gathering on the back of his neck and his skin felt clammy. He focused his attention on the camera and tried not to let it wander to Gwen.

After several takes the actresses were brought in. A reconstruction of Gwen leaving the house and heading across the mountain was followed by Bethan walking towards the quarry. A crowd had gathered by the time it was Gwen's turn to be interviewed.

Meadows took hold of Blue's lead and watched Gwen answer the questions with confidence. He knew she must be nervous, but she didn't once hesitate or stutter. When the filming came to an end, Meadows handed the dog back to Gwen.

'You did really well.'

'I was shaking inside.'

'Me too,' Meadows said, grinning.

Gwen laughed.

'I'm serious, I don't even like having my photo taken.'

'Well, it didn't show and it will give the viewers some eye candy.'

'Well, if that's what the public want I should have got Edris to do the shoot.' He took off his tie and put it in his jacket pocket. 'They have all they need now so it should go out on the evening news tomorrow.'

'That soon?'

'Yes, it's only the local news. Do you think I would have got the part if it was national?'

'No, I think it would definitely have been DC Edris,' Gwen said, laughing.

They walked back to Gwen's house and Meadows was pleased to be invited in. As they sat drinking tea and talking in the kitchen the children arrived home from school. Ariana was first through the door. Her face fell when she noticed the absence of Edris but she quickly recovered and took a seat.

'So how did it go?'

'OK, I think,' Gwen said.

'Your mother was fantastic, you can see for yourself tomorrow.'

'I wanted to watch today,' Ariana complained.

'You would've put me off,' Gwen teased.

Alex sauntered into the kitchen and dumped his school bag on the floor before searching the cupboards. He took out a packet of biscuits and sat opposite Meadows.

'So do you think you're going to catch him this time?' Alex took a biscuit from the packet and stuffed it into his mouth whole.

Meadows studied the teenager.

He looks just like Matt at that age, I hope for Gwen's sake he doesn't have the same nature.

'I certainly hope so.'

'Good.' Another biscuit was jammed into his mouth. The front door slammed and Matt entered the kitchen.

He looked at each of them then sat next to Ariana. 'Well, this is very cosy.'

Meadows felt his body tense. 'Hello, Matt.'

'What are you doing here again?'

'We were filming today,' Gwen said, her face colouring.

'I know that. Why do you think I came home early from work? I thought you might need some support.' He glared at Meadows.

'You'll be pleased to know that it went well and hopefully we'll get a good response.'

Meadows stood.

I'd like to wipe that arrogant look off your face.

'I should be going, I'll let you know of any developments.' He smiled at Gwen.

'Bloody waste of time if you ask me,' Matt grumbled.

Gwen rose from the table. 'I'll see you out.'

Meadows followed her to the door. 'Thank you again for today. It made all the difference.'

'I'm glad I could help.'

Meadows climbed into the car and sat watching the house.

I suppose he'll give her a hard time now I've left.

He started the engine and pulled away, his fists curled tightly around the steering wheel as images of Matt loomed in his mind. He drove the short distance to the garage where Sam Morris worked.

He should be told about the reconstruction.

The garage owner led him to the workshop at the rear of the building, where a pair of oil-stained legs stuck out from beneath a car. A radio played in the background and Meadows could hear Sam humming away as he worked.

'Sam, sorry to disturb you at work. Is it OK to have a quick word?'

The trolley slid back and Meadows peered down at Sam.

Sam's grimy face was a map of lines and his overalls swamped his pitiful thin body. He looked rough, hardly recognisable as the boy Meadows knew at school.

Guarded eyes looked back at Meadows.

'Hi, Sam, I don't know if you will remember me. I'm Winter Meadows, we went to school together.'

Sam stood up and wiped his hands on a rag. 'Oh yeah, I remember you. You were one of the few people who didn't cross the road to avoid me.' A ghost of a smile played on his lips. 'What can I do for you?'

'I'm a detective now and I'm leading the investigation into the murder of Bethan Hopkins.'

'I see.' Sam sighed and his shoulders drooped.

'There's nothing to worry about. I just stopped by to let you know that we filmed the reconstruction today and it will be aired tomorrow evening.'

'I did hear about it. Got everyone riled up again.'

'I appreciate that it was a difficult time for you.'

'You have no idea.'

'Then enlighten me.'

'What's there to tell? I was with Gwen that day. I never denied it. I gave her my coat because it was raining but I swear I never touched them. Bethan's and Gwen's blood was all over the coat, that's what they told me. That doesn't mean I had anything to do with it, but no one believed me. I spent hours locked up in a cell but that was nothing compared to the interrogation. No one takes any notice if a suspect accidentally falls and gets a few cuts and bruises.' Sam glared at Meadows.

Overzealous DI wanting a confession.

'I'm sorry if you were treated badly back then.'

'If?' Sam gave a bitter laugh. 'After I was released I was scared to leave the house. Mud sticks and the whole village was convinced that I was guilty. Then threatening letters and dog shit were posted through the door. I swear it put my mother in an early grave. Why do you have to drag it all up again? It will be just like last time, I won't be able to come to work soon.'

Meadows felt sorry for Sam. He knew what it was like to be on the receiving end of prejudice but even that didn't compare to being accused of murder. 'You know things have changed now, technology and DNA profiling are far more advanced. There's a good chance that this time we will catch the person responsible. Would you be willing to give a DNA sample for elimination purposes? It would be a great help. We are re-testing all the evidence but as your DNA will be present on the coat it may have contaminated some of the other evidence.'

'I gave a sample at the time, didn't do much good then.'

'Like I said, things have changed since then, this is your chance to clear your name.'

'There's no way I am coming to the station. The minute I'm seen the gossip will start. There will be a witch hunt again.'

'You won't have to come in. I can send a plain-clothes officer to your home to take samples. It's a simple procedure.'

Sam nodded. 'As long as you don't use it against me.'

'Good.' Meadows smiled. 'Gwen remembers running from someone that day. Did you see anyone else near the mountain when you left her?'

'No, I told the police at the time and the officer that came the other day. I saw the rugby boys coming home from the match on Turnpike Road. I never understood why they denied seeing me, unless they had something to do with it.'

'We will be questioning them again. Is there anything else you remember from that day? Even if it seems insignificant to you. It might be important.'

'No, I wish there was. Gwen was upset that day but she didn't tell me why. She didn't want to go home even though it was raining. I guess that's a little odd.'

'Well, thank you for talking to me.'

'Just catch him this time, maybe then we can all have some peace.'

Meadows returned to his car.

Poor bugger, so many lives ruined. I'm not giving up even if Lester closes down the investigation.

Chapter Sixteen

Matt opened a bottle of beer and sat opposite Gwen, his eyes narrowed.

'You're spending quite a bit of time with Hippy Winter.'

The tension in the kitchen after Meadows left had sent Ariana and Alex scuttling to their bedrooms.

'Don't call him that.'

'Why not? That's what he is,' Matt sneered.

'He's Detective Inspector Meadows. I think he's done well for himself.'

'What's that supposed to mean?' Matt leant forward.

'Nothing.'

'No, really? I know exactly what you're implying. You think he's better than me.'

Gwen sighed. 'I didn't say that.'

'But you think it. Maybe if I'd had the chance to go to university I'd be in a titled position and not some poxy retail manager.'

Gwen picked up the cups and dumped them in the sink. There was no point in arguing with him when he was in this mood. She turned on the taps and watched the water flow into the sink.

'You stay away from him. Don't think I haven't noticed the way you look at him, it's pathetic! He's not to come into my house again. I don't want talk in the village.'

Gwen felt anger spike at her veins. She spun around and glared at Matt. 'How dare you! You've screwed every tart in the village, well, the ones who're desperate, and you aren't even discreet.'

Matt jumped up from his seat. 'You ungrateful little bitch, after all I've done for you.' He stepped closer until he was inches from her face. Blue jumped between them and growled but Matt ignored him. 'Do you think anyone else would have married you? I felt sorry for you. And so what if I need to run my hands over some soft skin now and again? Any other man would run a mile from those hideous scars. I stayed with you, gave you a home and family. You can't even hold down a job because of your fucked-up head. Even Hippy Winter ran away.'

Gwen ran her hand down her arm and felt the protrusion of the scar. She'd had skin grafts on her legs where chunks of flesh had been gouged out from the fall. Nothing could be done about the appearance of the thick scars from the operations. He's right, who would want me? she thought.

'Sometimes I wish I'd never married you,' she said.

'Leave if you really feel that way.'

She shoved past him, grabbed the box of Beth's possessions, and bolted upstairs to the bedroom.

'Bastard.' She felt the tears trickle down her cheeks and wiped them away with the back of her hand.

There was a soft knock on the door. 'Mum, are you OK?' Ariana opened the door then came in gingerly and perched on the bed.

'I'm fine, love. It's just been a difficult day. Lots of memories.'

'You don't have to make excuses for him. I don't know why you take that shit.'

'Do you want to look through the box with me?' Gwen desperately wanted to distract her daughter, she didn't have the energy to try to defend Matt.

'OK.' Ariana opened the box and took out a T-shirt. She looked at the picture of the band on the front. 'I guess you liked these guys,' she said, giggling.

Gwen managed a weak smile and put her hand into the box. She pulled out a jewellery case and opened the lid. Inside were pairs of gold and silver earrings and a charm bracelet.

'That's pretty,' Ariana commented.

'Yes, it is. She was given a new charm every birthday. She wore it a lot, it used to jangle on her wrist. She had loads of nice jewellery. Not cheap stuff like I used to wear.'

'Ooh, look at this.' Ariana held up a denim jacket with the fabric embroidered with roses at the hem.

'I loved that jacket. I was so jealous when she bought it.' Gwen took the jacket and ran her hand over the material.

'It's very nice,' Ariana said.

'Yes, I was saving up to buy it. The thing is, I don't think Beth really wanted it. She had a few denim jackets, then bought this one when I said I liked it. I only saw her wear it once. It's funny the things you get jealous of when you're young.'

Ariana had taken a stack of CDs out of the box and was looking at the covers. She held one up. 'Did you like these?'

'Yes, and Steps. I knew all the dance routines.'

'I can download all these and put them on my iPod for you to listen to if you like.'

'That'd be great. I'm sure it would help bring back some more memories.' Gwen dipped her hand into the box and pulled out an exercise book. 'Mr Ellis, Maths,' she read.

'He was there when you were in school?' Ariana's eyes widened.

'Yes, I guess he must be getting on now.'

'We call him the talking foreskin,' Ariana said, laughing.

'That's disgusting! Now I have an awful image stuck in my mind.' Gwen wrinkled her nose and pulled out another book. On the cover in neat handwriting Beth had written *Mr Epworth, English* with a heart drawn next to the name. Gwen closed her eyes; she could smell the classroom, taste the chalk in the air...

'Come on, try and make yourself look tempting, he'll be here in a minute.' Beth held out a lip gloss to Gwen. She was perched on the edge of the desk and was wriggling her skirt up to reveal her thighs.

Gwen didn't want to put on the lip gloss. The sun was shining through the window making the chalk dust dance through the air. It was stuffy in the classroom and she wanted to go home and change into a pair of shorts. The rest of the students had already left to catch the bus home.

'I don't know why you had to get us both into detention.' She stared at Beth, hoping her friend would get the message that she wasn't happy about playing this stupid game.

'There's no other way to get him on his own. He's so hot.' Beth sighed dramatically.

'No he's not. I think he's kind of creepy.'

Beth ignored the comment and pulled off her tie before loosening the buttons of her shirt. She pulled at the fabric, revealing her cleavage.

'You do know he touched Catrin's arse?' Beth ran her fingers through her hair, fanning it out over her shoulders.

'So she says.' So this is what it's all about, she can't stand the thought of Catrin getting more attention, Gwen thought, then put the top back on the lip gloss and handed it back to Beth.

'Well, I reckon he's definitely up for it.' Beth crossed her legs and watched the door. 'Aren't you going to take your tie off?'

'No,' Gwen folded her arms across her chest and leaned back in the chair.

The door opened and Mr Epworth walked in. He stopped and stared at Beth. 'Get off that desk and put your tie back on,' he ordered.

Beth slid off the desk. 'Sorry, sir,' she purred. 'It's hot in here.' She sashayed to the nearest desk.

Giles turned his back and started writing on the board. 'Gwen, I'm surprised at you,' he called over his shoulder. 'Defacing a desk, I thought you would have a little bit more respect for school property.'

Gwen didn't comment, but she could feel the heat burning her cheeks. *GC loves MT* had been carved into the desk. Gwen had taken the blame even though it was Beth's work. Beth had given backchat in Gwen's defence and had landed them both in detention. Gwen felt the anger stir in her stomach and clenched her fists.

Giles Epworth spun around. 'I'm not telling you again, put on your tie!' He glared at Beth. 'If I have to say it one more time you can spend the rest of the week in detention with the headmaster. I have better things to do with my time.'

Gwen glanced across at Beth and she could see the colour spread over her face. She grabbed her tie and tied it into a rough knot around her neck. Gwen suppressed a smile. About time someone turned her down, she thought.

'Start writing,' Epworth ordered before leaving the classroom.

'Maybe he only likes redheads,' Gwen said.

'Maybe he didn't want to show his true feelings in front of you,' Beth said. 'Next time I'll come on my own.'

'Mum are you OK?' Ariana touched Gwen's arm.

'Yes, I'm fine, love. I was just lost in thought.'

'So Epworth was your English teacher. What's with the heart? Please don't tell me you fancied him!'

'No, Beth had a bit of a crush on him. Come on, you can't tell me that there is not one teacher in the school that is attractive.'

'They're all gross, have you seen them? Old hairy geeks.'

Gwen forced a laugh, her mind still back in the classroom.

'If you're OK now I'll go back to my room.' Ariana placed the book back in the box and stood up.

'I'm fine, honestly. I had better make a start on dinner.' She watched Ariana leave the room then repacked the box. Gwen wondered if Beth had gone back on her own. Maybe she was seeing Epworth and that's why she kept being pregnant a secret, she thought.

Chapter Seventeen

Meadows sat back in his chair and listened in on Edris' conversation on the phone. They had worked the whole weekend taking calls from potential witnesses that had seen the reconstruction. A majority of these calls had only reinforced what they already knew. Only a few had added to the enquiry. Saturday evening had produced three calls claiming to have seen David Collier searching for Gwen at various times of the day and one from an ex-neighbour of Sue Collier's who claimed to have heard a heated argument involving Gwen, Sue, and David. One of the sightings was at 1.30 p.m.

Why didn't he report Gwen missing earlier? It was gone midnight before he rang the station. It's obvious that both Sue and David Collier thought that Gwen had run away. Did David find Gwen later that day? But what would be his motive? Could David be the man that Beth was seeing?

Meadows tapped his pen against his notes. He noticed that Edris had finished the call.

'Anything interesting?'

'That was a guy called Steven Powell, he says he saw Sam Morris at about 5 p.m. that afternoon. He's sure about the time because they had just finished a rugby match.'

'They?'

'Yes, he was with a group of boys.'

'That confirms Sam's story but why didn't he come forward at the time?'

Edris shrugged his shoulders. 'He didn't say.'

'OK, I think it's worth a visit.' The phone trilled on Meadows' desk and he snatched it up. 'DI Meadows.'

Silence on the other side.

'Hello.'

'Are you the detective in charge of the Bethan Hopkins case?'

'Yes, I am. Who am I speaking with?'

'I, erm… I don't want to give my name.'

'OK. Do you have some information relating to the case?'

'Yes. Giles Epworth was on the mountain that day.'

'You saw him?'

'Yes.'

'At what time was this?'

'It would've been about four, four-thirty.'

'Did you see Gwen Collier or Bethan Hopkins?'

'I saw Gwen.'

'Was Gwen with Giles Epworth?'

'Not exactly… Look, I don't really want to get involved with this.'

'I understand but I can assure you any information you give me will be confidential. Hello? Hello?'

The dial tone buzzed in Meadows' ear. 'Damn!' He replaced the receiver and recounted the conversation to Edris.

'If the caller saw Giles Epworth then he was also on the mountain. What was he doing up there?' Edris asked.

'Good question. Obviously something he shouldn't have been doing, else he would have given his name.'

'Or he could just have a grudge against Giles Epworth.'

'That's a possibility. I can think of many ex-students who would like to get their own back for unfair detentions.'

'Maybe there was more than one attacker? They could've been working together.'

'Good theory, Edris, but there's only one set of footprints unaccounted for at the scene and one DNA profile from the evidence found on Bethan's body, other than a trace from Sam Morris, likely to have come from his coat. I still think it's worth following up on Giles Epworth. Was there a statement from him in the original investigation?'

'No, I would have remembered the name, he was my headmaster.'

'OK, we'll interview him again tomorrow. Let's call it a day, you've been in all weekend. Don't you have anything better to do with your time? A girlfriend?'

'No... not anything serious, anyway.'

'Well, go home and get some rest. I'll pick you up in the morning. Blackwell and DS Paskin can man the phones tomorrow.'

Edris raised his eyebrows but didn't comment. Meadows smiled back; he knew Blackwell would cause a scene but he would have to back down once Meadows pulled rank. It wasn't something he did very often, he rarely thought of himself above others, but with Blackwell it was a different case. He smiled as he left the office.

* * *

Steven Powell lived in Ynys Melyn, a small village accessed by a bridge and with only one road leading in and back out. Meadows drove while Edris sat in the passenger seat looking at the scenery.

'It's like the Twilight Zone here, I bet people disappear like in the Bermuda Triangle.'

'It's not that bad,' Meadows said. 'It's got a pub and a post office. What more could you want?'

'A life.' Edris chuckled.

'Well, Steven Powell obviously chose to live here. He was originally from Bryn Melyn.'

'Bloody hell, do you know everyone that lives in this area?'

'No, but don't forget I grew up in Bryn Bach, and the majority of the people we'll interview in connection with this case I went to school with.'

'Can I ask you a personal question?'

'You can ask but I may not answer.'

'Fair enough. Was there anything between you and Gwen Thomas?'

What's the answer to that? There would have been if I had stayed and fought for her. I could have still gone to university and we would have found a way to work it out. I should have told her how I felt.

Meadows was aware that Edris was watching him, the silence in the car had grown uncomfortable.

'No, there wasn't anything between Gwen and me, we were friends, but if I'm honest I liked her very much. So, what about you? You were evasive yesterday when I asked if you had a girlfriend.'

'I'm not ready to settle down yet, there's a few I see now and again.'

'A few? You sound like the village tom,' Meadows said, laughing.

'I think "man whore" is the politically correct term,' Edris said. 'It's not like that, I don't make any promises. They're just friends with benefits.'

Meadows shook his head. 'I must be getting old.'

'Hey, don't knock it! It makes things less complicated.'

'I would think it made things more complicated. So that's what you get up to in the evenings.' Meadows glanced across at Edris who fidgeted in his seat.

'No.' Edris blushed. 'I'm not on the pull every night. I still live with my parents. When I get my own place things will be different.'

'Saints preserve us!'

'No, I don't mean it in that way. I'll get myself a regular girlfriend. It would be nice to come home to someone after a day's work, dinner on the table.'

'I think you should stop there, you're digging yourself a hole.' Meadows pulled the car up in front of a row of terraced houses.

'It's number nine,' Edris said.

'OK, you can take the lead, I'll just observe.'

'Oh, right.' Edris looked nervous as he straightened his tie.

'I'm supposed to be training you when we're on this case. I'll have to report your progress back to Lester.'

'Of course, but I only ever take notes when I work with Blackwell.'

'You've already interviewed Sam Morris and Epworth on your own. I would've thought by now you'd realise I work a little differently.'

'Yes, and I am grateful for the opportunity.'

'Good. Then let's get to it.'

As they approached the door it opened and a stocky man with a receding hairline stepped out. 'You must be the cops. You better come in before the neighbours start twitching their curtains. Nosy bastards around here.'

The sitting room was small with a worn leather sofa and two mismatched armchairs. Several empty lager cans were dumped on the coffee table. Meadows noticed a photograph next to the television of two young girls in school uniform. 'Your children?'

'Yeah, they don't live with me anymore. Split up with the missus a few years ago. She got the house and the kids. That's why I'm renting this dump.'

Meadows took a seat and leaned back while Edris perched on the edge of an armchair and took out his notebook. He nodded to Edris, indicating that he should begin the interview.

'When you called the station, you said you had seen Sam Morris at approximately 5 p.m. on the afternoon of the twentieth of June, 1999. Can you be certain of that?'

'Yeah, like I said on the phone, there was a match that day, it had been dry in the morning but rained during the game. We were all bloody stinking at the end of the game.'

'Did you speak to Sam Morris?'

'No, we weren't mates, he was one of those swots. He was walking down Turnpike Road.'

'You said you were with a group.'

'Yeah, me, Wayne Allen, Titch, that's Gary Lane, and Dai Roach.'

Edris wrote the names in his notebook then looked at Meadows, who nodded.

'Why didn't you come forward at the time?'

Steven squirmed in his seat. 'It's a bit embarrassing.' He rubbed his hand over his stubbly chin. 'The thing is, he was going out with Bethan at the time, don't know what she saw in him. If anyone was gonna go out with one of the hotties it was supposed to be from our gang. You know what it was like at that age. Anyway, Matt said Sam was guilty and deserved to get arrested so we should keep our mouths shut.'

'Matt Thomas?' Meadows, who had been quietly observing the interview, leaned forward in his chair. 'Matt was with you that day?'

'No, he had a knee injury so wasn't playing. It was later when we mentioned that we had seen Sam Morris and that we should go to the police that he persuaded us not to.'

'Persuaded you?'

'Matt Thomas had a way of getting you to do what he wanted. It was better to be on his side. You know what I mean.'

I know only too well.

Meadows sat back in his chair and let Edris continue with the questions.

'So do you think Matt Thomas was jealous of Sam? Did he fancy Bethan?'

'Who didn't? But she was two years younger than us. Matt was going out with Katie Pritchard at the time. Look, Sam was seen with Gwen that afternoon, everyone thought he did it.'

'So why come forward now?'

'I saw the reconstruction and thought, what if Sam didn't do it? You said on the TV that Sam left Gwen at four o'clock at the cattle grid.' He looked at Meadows. 'If I saw him at five then perhaps he didn't do it, he was heading home. What if the police wasted their time when they concentrated on Sam? I thought if I came forward this time it might help. I won't get in trouble, will I?'

'I shouldn't think so, but this could have saved time in the original investigation and spared Sam Morris years of living under a cloud of suspicion.'

Steven looked at the floor and shuffled his feet. 'I'm sorry. We were just kids.'

'Well, thank you for your time.' Meadows stood up. 'We will be talking to the others that were with you that day, in the meantime if you remember anything else that may be important please call the station.'

'So I guess we can cross Sam Morris off the suspect list,' Edris said as he slipped into the passenger seat.

'Check out the others in the group, see if they confirm Steven's story. I think we should pay a visit to Matt Thomas.'

Meadows smiled to himself as he started the engine. 'While we're up this way we'll call on Sue Collier. I want to go over her statement and see why she left it so long to report her daughter missing.'

* * *

138

Sue didn't seem surprised to see them. She busied herself in the kitchen making tea then brought in a tray and placed it on the sitting room table where Meadows and Edris were seated on a plush cream sofa. Edris eyed the biscuits that were set on a china plate.

'Sugar?' Sue asked.

'Two, please,' Edris said.

Meadows declined and watched Sue fill the teacups. She handed one to Edris. 'Help yourself to biscuits.' She moved the plate into the centre of the table, handed a cup to Meadows, then took a seat, smoothing down her skirt.

'So, what can I do for you, Detective?' she asked Meadows.

'We've had a good response to the reconstruction and are now following up new lines of enquiry.'

'It was very good, although it did bring everything back.'

'That's what we had hoped to achieve, that it would jog people's memories. In your statement you said there had been an argument between yourself and Gwen that morning. Could you tell me what the argument was about?'

'Oh, I don't really know.' Sue's hand fluttered at her neck. 'You know how teenagers are. I think she wanted to buy something, a new outfit, something like that.' Sue picked up her cup and sipped.

She's lying.

'Gwen remembers it being more than just a teenage disagreement, she says that she was very distressed.'

Sue fidgeted in her chair. 'She didn't tell me that she'd remembered that morning.'

'She recalls arguing with you but not what the disagreement was about.'

Sue visibly relaxed. 'I can't see why it would be so important.'

'Could you just talk me through that day, please?'

Sue put her hand to her temple as if to ward off the physical pain that came with the memory. 'Gwen was supposed to go shopping with Bethan that morning, I didn't expect her back until the afternoon. She must have come back while I was in the garden, I didn't hear her come in. Not long after she came downstairs, we had words, and she went out again. There's nothing more to tell.'

'David Collier was here that day?'

'Yes.' Sue coloured.

'Was he in the house when you and Gwen argued?'

'Yes.'

'And he went after Gwen when she left the house?'

Sue bristled. 'He only followed her to the gate then he came back inside.'

'What is your relationship with David?'

'He's my brother-in-law, he's taken care of me and Gwen since my husband died.' Sue glared at Meadows.

'Was he angry with Gwen that day?'

'No, what are you implying?'

'I'm not implying anything. He chased after Gwen that morning and when he caught up with her at the gate he tried to restrain her.'

'No, it wasn't like that.' Sue's temper flared. 'He wanted to make sure that she was OK. She was upset when she left the house. He wasn't angry with her and he came straight back into the house.'

'He went out looking for her later that afternoon. Several witnesses saw him.'

'He thought he could talk to her and calm things down, then bring her home so we could make up.'

'Did you often argue with Gwen?'

'No more than any other mother and teenage daughter.'

'It was David that made the call to report Gwen missing?'

'Yes, he stayed with me because I was so worried.'

'The call was logged at 12.15 a.m. You left it late, was that because you thought Gwen had run away?'

'Yes,' Sue said. Tears gathered in her eyes and she twisted her hands on her lap.

'It must have been a serious argument then,' Meadows said before draining his cup. He stood up and looked down at her. 'Thank you for your time today, I hope it wasn't too upsetting for you.'

Sue walked them to the door. 'David would never hurt Gwen.'

'I hope you're sure of that,' Meadows replied.

* * *

'What do you think?' Meadows asked Edris when they were seated in the car.

'I don't know. I don't think she would cover for David Collier if she thought he had hurt her daughter. Maybe she doesn't remember what they argued about that day.'

'Oh, I think she remembers. Every second of that day will be etched in her mind. I suspect her relationship with David is more than platonic and if you love someone that much then it's hard to think them capable of hurting someone. Perhaps the argument was between David and Gwen and that's why she won't tell us. She is definitely hiding something.'

'Are we going to see David Collier now?' Edris asked.

'No, I want you to arrange for him to come in to the station. It will be interesting to see how he reacts to a formal interview.'

'So, where now?'

'Let's go and see Matt Thomas, then we will call on Giles Epworth.'

It took them almost an hour to reach the supermarket where Matt worked as a manager. He appeared wearing a navy suit with a red striped shirt which strained at the buttons.

'Please come up to my office.' Matt gave a tight smile.

They walked up a flight of stairs in silence. Once in the office Matt closed the door and took a seat behind a desk.

Meadows noticed the absence of a family photograph and wondered how many staff meetings took place with the young female staff. He tried to push away the image. He pulled up a chair and sat opposite Matt.

'This better be important. I don't appreciate you coming into my workplace.' Matt's eyes narrowed.

'We interviewed one of your old school friends this morning.'

'Yeah, who's that?'

Meadows ignored the question. 'He told us that he saw Sam Morris at 5 p.m. on the day of the attack.'

'And what's that got to do with me?'

'He claims that you persuaded him not to come forward with the information at the time.'

Matt's face reddened and Meadows could see the tension in the other man's shoulders. 'Is that what he's telling you? Well, I can't be held responsible for what he saw or didn't see.'

'Why would you want him to hold back information that could have been helpful to the enquiry at the time?'

'Look, we were just kids. We all know that bastard is responsible for what happened and he got away with it. Loads of people saw him with Gwen that day and he was screwing Beth.'

'If our source is telling the truth – and we will be checking with the others in the group he was with that day – then it's not possible that Sam Morris attacked the girls. He was on Turnpike Road at 5 p.m. and has an alibi for later that evening. Were you seeing Bethan at the time? Is that why you were jealous of Sam Morris? Where were you that day?'

'How fucking dare you!' Matt jumped up from his seat and leaned across the desk. 'I could ask the same of you. You were always sniffing around Gwen.'

Meadows could feel Edris' curious look. 'I meant you weren't playing rugby that day, why not?' he said.

The colour drained from Matt's face and he sat down heavily in the chair. 'I had a knee injury so I stayed at home. Look, all of this has got me on edge. I'm worried about Gwen, you should never have dragged all this up. No good will come of it.'

'Wouldn't you like to see the person responsible caught?'

Matt huffed. 'If there's nothing else, I have to prepare for a meeting.'

'No, that will be all, for now,' Meadows said.

'I think you enjoyed that,' Edris said as they walked back to the car.

'The guy was an arsehole in school and he hasn't changed.'

'Interesting reaction when you asked him where he was the day of the attack.'

'Yes, I picked up on that too but I think it has more to do with his dislike for me than anything else. It's likely that he persuaded the others to keep quiet about Sam Morris for spite and no other reason. I just wanted the satisfaction of making him squirm. Still, I think you should have a dig around, see what you can find out about him.'

The phone vibrated in Meadows' pocket. He took it out and saw *Gwen* displayed on the screen.

Has Matt called her to complain already?

He answered the call and listened as Gwen recounted her memory of Epworth in the classroom. Meadows felt a surge of excitement. *First the sighting and now this.* He filled Edris in on the conversation as he drove.

'Wouldn't there have been other complaints if he's some sort of pervert?'

'Not necessarily. Most victims don't file complaints. Think about it: he's a person in authority. First a teacher, then a headmaster. There would be the fear of not being believed. There is also the possibility that if he only targets older girls, say fourteen or fifteen-year-olds and those girls have a crush on him, then they wouldn't see anything wrong if he took advantage of them.'

'So you think that Bethan Hopkins had a crush on him, he got her pregnant and panicked.'

'It's a possibility, Sam Morris was ruled out as being the father of the baby and from what Gwen just told me, Bethan certainly had a crush on Epworth. Let's see what he has to say for himself. If we hurry we may be able to catch him before he leaves the school.'

Chapter Eighteen

Giles Epworth took up his usual position at his office window to watch the pupils leaving school for the day. He spotted Ariana Thomas walking with Jessica Evans. They were soon joined by a group of boys. He could tell from their body language that there was a mutual attraction, you could almost see the testosterone in the air. Little sluts, just like their mothers at that age. Always hanging around the boys, teasing. Maybe I would have been better off in an all-boys school, he thought.

His eyes scanned the crowds, he knew most of the pupils by name and had a good memory of all those who had passed through the school during the time he had worked there.

He was about to turn away when he saw a car turn through the school gates and into the car park. Two figures emerged and as they drew nearer he felt his stomach clench.

He had watched the reconstruction, even though he had promised himself he wouldn't, he had been drawn to it like passers-by to a car crash. There was nothing in it to draw attention to him. The police didn't question him last time so he figured there was no reason for them to question him now – it was probably something to do with the school security. He watched the two men enter the building. He remembered Winter Meadows as he was at school at the same time as Bethan and Gwen. Moody boy, intelligent, but a bit of a loner, a misfit from a commune. Giles' lips twitched. Shouldn't have to worry about him, he thought. Tristan Edris was no threat either, cheeky little sod and a slut magnet.

He turned away from the window, his mind still in the past, swirling through all the pupils he had to reprimand over the years. They never should have made us give up the cane, yes, a good whack never did me any harm, he thought. An image of the cane swishing through the air and landing with a crack on bare flesh stirred him. Giles adjusted his trousers and sat behind his desk awaiting his visitors.

There was a sharp rap at the door, it opened and Catrin peered around.

'Visitors for you, Headmaster. DI Meadows and DC Edris.'

'Show them in.' He could see the gleam of excitement in her eyes and knew she'd be on the phone gossiping as soon as the door closed. He shuffled papers on his desk as the two men walked in, then looked up and smiled.

'Hello again, Tristan, and Detective Inspector Meadows. Your name sounds familiar. Were you also a pupil here?'

'Yes, many years ago.'

'So what can I do for you?' Giles sat back in his chair, hoping to give the impression that he felt relaxed in their company. 'Please sit down. Since Tristan's last visit we have been extra vigilant with security and the talk on personal safety from your colleague was very well received.'

Meadows smiled. 'That's good to hear. As you will be aware, a reconstruction was aired last Friday evening and

146

we've had a good response. We are currently following up new lines of enquiry.'

'Oh yes, I did hear about the reconstruction, but unfortunately I didn't get time to watch it.'

'A witness has come forward claiming to have seen you and Gwen Collier on the mountain that day.'

That's not possible, no one saw me, unless he came forward... No, he wouldn't, Giles thought. He could feel the perspiration gathering on his forehead. Meadows' eyes bored into him. 'Really? How bizarre. I'm sure there must be some mistake. I certainly would've remembered seeing Gwen that day.'

'Were you on the mountain that day?'

'To be honest, I don't recall. It's such a long time ago.' He could feel the familiar tightness in his chest.

'I appreciate that, but given the nature of the crime committed that day and the media coverage I would've thought that day would be fairly memorable. You were living in Bryn Melyn at the time?'

'Yes, I've lived there since 1990.'

'Do you often walk up the mountain?'

Giles glanced at Tristan who was scribbling notes. 'On occasion. I have a dog so I do a fair amount of walking. It gives me time to think. I also suffer from angina and the doctor recommended I take exercise.' He was aware that he was rambling and a pain tugged at his chest. He wanted to rub it with his hand but was afraid the gesture would be taken as nervousness.

'Did you have a dog in 1999?'

'Yes, a Westie called Theo.' He tried to force a smile. His mouth felt dry and he longed to reach into the drawer and take a gulp from the whisky bottle. Meadows' eyes were scrutinising his every gesture and Edris' pen was poised on the notepad.

'So it's possible that you were up the mountain that day?'

'Yes, I suppose so, but if I'd seen Gwen Collier I would have informed the police at the time.'

'How well did you know Bethan and Gwen?'

'I was teaching English at the time. I could check if I taught them, if you like.'

'You did teach them.'

'Right, well, a large number of pupils go through the school each year. You wouldn't expect me to remember every single one.'

'From information that we received it appears that the girls spent some time in detention with you.'

An image of Bethan sat on the desk in the classroom flashed across his mind. Nothing happened in the classroom, not with those two. This is Gwen's doing, bitch! He doesn't know what went on in detentions. He's just guessing, Giles thought.

'It's possible. Like I said, I've taught hundreds of pupils over the years and quite a few of them end up in detention. If I recall, you spent a fair amount of time outside my office, Tristan.'

Tristan looked across at Meadows, nodded, and gave a wry smile. Giles felt the grip on his chest loosen.

'Did you see Bethan and Gwen outside of school?'

'I live in the same village, so, yes, our paths crossed occasionally, but only an acknowledgement as I passed by.'

'Well, thank you for your time, Mr Epworth. We may need to come back once we've taken a formal statement from the witness that saw you and Gwen on the mountain that day.'

'Of course. As I said, it is a possibility. Out of interest, who was it who claimed to have seen me? It might help jog my memory.'

'I'm sorry we can't divulge that information.'

'I see, well, if there is nothing more I can do for you.' Giles rose from the chair.

The two men left the office and he let out a slow breath. The tightness in his chest drew his hand to the whisky bottle, he allowed himself a small sip then paced the office. There were only two people who saw him that day. Either Gwen had remembered or else he had come forward. Giles knew that if it was Gwen, the police would have taken him in. He needed to know where he lived now. As Catrin had slept her way through most of the valley, she was the best option, but he couldn't ask her outright.

Giles slumped down in his chair. He put his head in his hand as he tried to think of different ways he could get the information without raising suspicion. An idea came to him and he took a sheet of paper from his desk and wrote down five names. He smiled to himself then called in Catrin.

'The police have asked for my help with their enquiries. I need to know the whereabouts of these five former pupils. This is confidential, you understand. They're interviewing everyone that was in school the same time as Bethan and Gwen.'

Catrin took the paper and glanced at the names. 'This shouldn't be a problem, I know a couple of these guys.'

It was the response Giles had hoped to get. 'Just write down the addresses and get it to me as soon as possible.' He dismissed her with a wave of his hand.

He waited in his office for the next hour, knowing Catrin would be working to get him the information. He tried to concentrate on work but his mind was in turmoil. When he could stand the wait no longer he walked out of the office and forced a smile.

'I'll see you in the morning.'

'OK. I've managed to get two of the addresses for you and I'm working on the others.'

Giles tried not to show too much enthusiasm as he stepped closer to Catrin's desk and peered over her shoulder. He scanned the notes on her desk and felt a flutter in his chest.

'Good work.' He touched her briefly on the shoulder before leaving.

* * *

He had memorised the address that Catrin had written down and was pleased that his former pupil hadn't moved out of the area. As he drove nearer he felt a twinge of doubt. Should he show himself and confront him about going to the police? Giles shuddered. He could make things worse. He decided to just drive past the house, get a feel for the type of life he was living, check out what sort of car he drove.

The address was on a newly built estate. There was a large area of grass in the centre with a children's play park. Giles slowed down as he looked for the number. Very nice, he must be doing well, he thought. He parked a few doors down and sat in the car, watching in his rear-view mirror. Shouts from a playground drew his attention and he turned his head to watch the children. He wished now that he'd gone home and picked up the dog, he would have been able to walk around without arousing suspicion.

An ice cream van turned into the road, trilling a catchy melody. A group of children left the park, two of them ran into the house he was watching. A few moments later they emerged followed by a dark-haired woman who stood on the pavement watching them. He has a wife and kids. Good, I doubt he would want to explain to his wife what he was doing on the mountain that day, he thought as he started the engine and drove off. All he needed now was to know Gwen's weakness. He felt it was a good time to call Alex Thomas into his office.

Chapter Nineteen

'You do know that David has gone to the police station this morning to answer more questions?' Sue Collier sat at the kitchen table, her arms folded across her chest and her eyes fixed on Gwen.

Gwen ignored the accusation in her mother's voice. 'Yes, Mum, Detective Meadows mentioned that he wanted to talk to him.' She turned away and opened the dishwasher.

'So it's Detective Meadows now, very formal.' Sue huffed. 'I don't understand why you'd think that David would hurt you. Honestly, after all he's done for us. I don't know how I would've coped without him when your father died.'

Gwen took the dishes from the rack and placed them on the counter with a sigh. 'I didn't say that he attacked me.' She turned to look at her mother. 'Something happened that day with David. I know he chased me out of the house and grabbed my arm. Then after the attack he was never the same towards me.'

'Of course he wasn't the same. We thought we'd lost you. David took it really hard.'

Gwen moved a chair next to her mother and sat down. 'We argued that day, why won't you tell me what it was about?'

'It was nothing. Please, Gwen, can't you just leave things as they are?'

'I want to know what happened that day. I need to understand why someone wanted to kill me and Beth. Part of that is knowing every detail of that day so I can piece it all together.' Gwen placed her hand on top of her mother's and gave it a gentle squeeze. 'Please, Mum.'

Sue turned her head towards Gwen, tears moistened her eyes. 'I can't.'

Gwen stared at her mother, she remembered that she had been crying that morning. She took her hand from her mother's and rubbed her temples as she closed her eyes. She could see her bedroom walls. The posters tacked to the yellow paint. Mismatched furniture and flowery curtains. She was lying on the bed, frustration tensing her body...

Saturday ruined because Beth, for whatever reason, doesn't want to go shopping. Disappointment and anger made Gwen feel like crying.

She heard the front door open and sat up. Someone was in the house. She thought maybe Beth had decided to go after all. Whoever it was didn't call out. Gwen jumped off the bed and peered out the window. Her mother was still in the garden. She saw David creep towards her mother, he reached out his hand and squeezed her bottom. She saw her mother turn around and laugh. Why isn't she slapping his face? Pervert! she thought.

She watched, mesmerised, as David pulled her mother close and began to nuzzle her neck. Anger spiked Gwen's skin. Her mother was looking nervously around the garden as if afraid to be seen by the neighbours, then she wrestled him towards the back door, their laughter carrying up to the window.

Gwen crept downstairs and into the sitting room, she could hear them in the kitchen. She felt disgusted at the idea of her mother and uncle together in that way. She charged through the kitchen door and watched them guiltily pull apart.

'What's going on?' she shrieked.

'Gwen, love, I didn't know you were home.' Sue blushed as she smoothed back her hair. 'Uncle David has come around to cut the lawn.'

'I'm not fucking stupid!' Gwen could feel her breath quicken as her heart thudded in her chest.

'Don't talk to your mother like that,' David said.

Gwen ignored him and glared at her mother. 'How long has this been going on?'

'Nothing is going on.' Sue stepped forward.

'Maybe it's time she knew the truth,' David said.

Gwen's eyes snapped open, her mother sat staring at her cup on the table.

'What did I need to know?' Gwen demanded.

'What are you talking about?' Sue's face creased with confusion.

'David said I needed to know the truth that day. It's obvious you were seeing him and I can understand why you wouldn't want to tell me then, but it's more than that, isn't it?'

Sue stood up. 'Please, Gwen, I don't want to lose you again.' She started towards the kitchen door.

'Don't go.' Gwen followed. 'What do you mean lose me again? Please, Mum, just tell me.'

'Just drop it, Gwen.' Sue had reached the front door and opened it, and turned to face Gwen. 'You just have to trust me when I say that David would never hurt you.' She stepped out the door and closed it, before Gwen could say another word.

Gwen stomped back into the kitchen. Frustration pumped adrenalin through her body causing her muscles

153

to tense. She knew her mum was sleeping with David back then, maybe still was, but that didn't mean that he wouldn't have attacked her. Maybe he wanted me out of the way, she thought.

She finished emptying the dishwasher then grabbed Blue's lead. She needed to get out of the house. She called the dog then picked up Ariana's iPod and put it in her pocket.

As she headed towards the park the sky darkened with heavy black clouds. She remembered it had clouded over that afternoon, then the rain came as she was walking across the mountain. She was looking for somewhere to shelter. The barn. Gwen felt anxiety gnaw at her stomach as she tried to grasp the watery memory. The image of the barn faded as she entered the park. It was quiet, all the children were at school and the threat of rain had driven away anyone else that may have frequented the park at this time of day.

Gwen took the iPod from her pocket and placed the headphones into her ears. She scanned the playlist until she came across one labelled *Mum's old music* and hit play. Music filled the silence of the park. Gwen smiled as she was transported back to Beth's bedroom…

'What do you think?' Beth smoothed down the denim jacket and pranced in front of the mirror.

'It's alright.' Gwen sat on the bed with her legs folded and one arm supporting her weight as she observed Beth from behind.

'Alright? I think I look gorgeous.' She winked at herself then picked up a pair of gold hoop earrings. 'Not too sure if these go with it.'

Gwen rolled her eyes and picked up a magazine from the bedside table. She wasn't going to tell her she looked good in it. Beth had known she wanted that jacket. She'd been saving up for weeks. Jealousy scraped the inside of her stomach. She flipped the pages of the magazine without looking at the articles.

'What's the matter with you?' Beth had turned away from the mirror and was staring at Gwen, her lips pursed and one hand on her hip.

'Nothing.' Gwen tossed the magazine aside and swung her legs off the bed.

'You've been in a mood since you got here.'

'I just don't think this is a good idea.'

'Well, you can't back out now.' Beth's eyes narrowed. 'Come on' – she sat on the edge of the bed – 'it'll be fun.'

'Well, you do it then.' Gwen folded her arms across her chest.

'But he likes you, I've seen the way he looks at you.'

'It's disgusting. I don't want him touching me.'

'It's just this one time, you might even enjoy it.' Beth giggled. 'Look, you don't have to go all the way, just enough for me to take some photos. I'll be with you the whole time. Maybe he will fancy a threesome.'

Gwen felt her skin crawl. The idea of Epworth putting his hands on her made her feel nauseous. 'I can't do it.' Tears stung her eyes and she turned her head away.

'There's nothing to it; anyway, it's about time you got yourself laid. We'll go there tonight and pretend that we need help with our homework. I've watched his house, he lives alone. I've even got a bottle of wine in my bag. I'll let you wear my new jacket.' Beth took hold of Gwen's hand and pulled her to her feet. 'I'll do your hair and make-up, the dirty bugger won't be able to resist you.'

Laughter filled the bedroom…

'Gwen!'

Gwen looked up and saw Sam Morris staring at her. She pulled out her earplugs and looked around feeling disorientated. She didn't remember sitting down on the bench. She looked down, Blue was sat at her feet.

'Are you alright?'

She hadn't noticed the rain, now she felt a chill run through her body, her T-shirt was soaked and clung to her skin. Sam was glancing around nervously.

'I'm fine, thank you.'

'I didn't mean to startle you and I know you probably don't want to talk to me, but I saw you sitting here, staring at the floor. I just wanted to make sure that you were OK.'

Gwen studied his face. He looked different from how she remembered. His face had thinned and deep lines creased the skin around his eyes. Their paths hadn't crossed since the day of the attack. She guessed he was probably frightened to be seen anywhere near her.

'You didn't startle me, I was lost in thought, that's all.'

'I guess all the gossip since they showed the reconstruction on the TV has brought up some bad memories.'

'Just a few.' Gwen smiled.

Sam held out his hand for Blue to sniff then patted his head. 'Nice dog.'

'Thanks. Sam, I don't know if the police have told you, but I remember being with you that day. You gave me your coat because it had started to rain.'

'Yes, you were upset about something and didn't want to go home.'

'Did I tell you what I was upset about?'

'No.' Sam looked around again. 'No, you didn't tell me. I didn't hurt you or Bethan. You were my friend.'

'I know. I'm sorry I can't remember what happened that day but it's starting to come back to me now.'

'Good. Perhaps when you do remember everything we can both put the past behind us and move on. Anyway, it was good to see you. Take care.' Sam turned and walked away.

Gwen watched him exit the park through the gate. Her mind was still trying to process what she had remembered about Epworth. Had she gone to his house and seduced him? The thought brought on a wave of nausea. She didn't think she would have gone through with it. The very idea of it repulsed her back then, but she knew Beth could be very persuasive. She stood up and rubbed her arms.

'Come on, let's go home.'

She tugged on Blue's lead. I need to call Winter. I don't think Uncle David had anything to do with the attack on me and Beth, she thought.

Chapter Twenty

Meadows sat in Lester's office trying to resist the urge to loosen his tie. A beam of sunlight filtered through the window and cut across his chest making him feel uncomfortably warm. He sat back in his chair as he waited for Lester to finish his phone call.

'Sorry about that.' Lester placed the phone in its cradle and turned his slate grey eyes on Meadows. 'It's now been three weeks since you reopened the case. I was hoping for news of an arrest by this stage.'

'Yes, I'd hoped for the same. We've had a good response to the reconstruction and are following up some new leads. I feel that we're close to a breakthrough.'

Lester rubbed his chin and sat forward in his chair. 'What new leads?'

'David Collier, Gwen's uncle, is coming in today. There are gaps in his statement and definitely something he is not telling us. I believe Sue Collier, Gwen's mother, is covering for him. Gwen remembers being chased by her uncle that day. There is also Giles Epworth, headmaster at Dyffryn Du School. He was an English teacher at the time. We received an anonymous call stating that both Epworth and Gwen were on the mountain that day. We questioned him and he was very evasive about that day and his memories of the girls. Gwen remembers being in detention with him and Bethan flirting. She also intimated that he had made sexual advances to another girl.'

'This anonymous call, I take it you put out a trace?'

'Yes, the number was traced to a phone box. I'm hoping he will call again. We know that Bethan was pregnant, it would certainly give Epworth a motive if he was the father of the child.'

'What about Gwen?'

'Well, if it was Giles Epworth then it's likely that Gwen got in the way. I don't think that both girls were targeted. They just happened to be together that day. It seems more probable that Bethan was the intended victim. She had a reputation for being promiscuous, and there's the secret lover, the father of her unborn child. Sam Morris was tested, he wasn't the father but we're re-running the tests just to be certain.'

'So you are saying that you can't find anyone with a motive for attacking Gwen?'

'I still have to rule out the uncle. He was a father figure to Gwen after her father died. There's always the possibility that he viewed Gwen as more than just a niece.'

Lester narrowed his eyes. 'You think he may have been abusing the girls? Surely Gwen would have remembered something like that.'

'Not necessarily, she could have blocked the whole thing out. Her memory is returning in flashbacks. I don't think it will be long now before she fully recovers it.'

'OK, I'm going to trust your instincts on this one. Please do remember that this is a small operation, we don't have the resources you're used to. Forensic tests don't come cheap.' Lester sat back in his chair and gave Meadows a tight smile. 'You came here with an impeccable record and I cannot fault your work since you have been with us. I do however still have some concerns with regards to your interaction with the team. Perhaps it would be a good idea for you to socialise with them outside of work from time to time.'

Yeah, I can just imagine me and Blackwell having a heart to heart over a pint. Meadows nodded, he didn't trust himself to comment.

'Teamwork is important,' Lester continued. 'I know Blackwell can be a bit gruff at times but he is a good detective. Just give him a chance. How is Edris working out?'

'Good, he's very keen to learn.'

'Well, he's certainly been singing your praises. Blackwell on the other hand is not a happy man. I hear you've had him manning the phones.'

Meadows smiled. 'Edris and I were out interviewing potential witnesses.'

'It should be one of the sergeants out on interviews with you, but as you seem comfortable with Edris we'll leave it for now.'

'I would like him to see the case to its conclusion.'

'I agree.' Lester stood to indicate the meeting was over. 'Keep me updated.'

'Will do.' Meadows left the office and walked over to his desk where Edris was hovering.

'David Collier is downstairs. I put him in an interview room.'

'Right, well let's not keep him waiting. Do you want to sit in?'

Edris smiled. 'Hell yes, I want to see you in action.'

Meadows rolled his eyes. 'Next thing you'll be telling me is you want to play good cop, bad cop. Well, I am afraid you are just going to observe today.' He picked up the file with David Collier's statement and headed for the stairs.

David Collier was seated in the interview room, a cup of tea untouched on the table.

'Sorry to have kept you waiting.' Meadows sat and placed the file on the table. He saw Edris take a seat in the corner of the room and place his hands on his knees.

'I suppose these rooms are designed to make you feel nervous.' David Collier glanced around.

Meadows followed his gaze and tried to see it through the other man's eyes. There was a small window with frosted glass set high up in the wall; two fluorescent lights in the ceiling gave off a low buzz. The walls were painted beige with no pictures or notices.

'We've asked you to come in today to go over the statement you provided at the time of Gwen's attack. Before we begin, I would like to ask you if you would be happy to provide us with a voluntary DNA sample. It's just a swab of the inside of your cheek. Completely painless.' Meadows watched David pale. 'It would help eliminate you from our enquiries.'

'I see. So you would be just checking it against samples found at the scene?'

'Yes.'

And the paternity of Bethan's child. What else does he think we will be checking for? He's nervous about something. 'Does this concern you?'

'No, why should it? I have nothing to hide.' David folded his arms.

Meadows opened the file and read through the notes. He was aware of David fidgeting in the chair, he took his time before looking up.

'On the morning of the 20th of June 1999 you were in the home of Sue Collier.'

'Yes, I often called on Sue to help her out. I went around to cut the lawn.'

'There was an argument that morning between Gwen and her mother.'

'There was some sort of disagreement, yes.'

'Can you tell me the nature of this disagreement?'

'No, I don't recall, sorry.'

Yet you remember going to mow the lawn.

'You were angry with Gwen that morning.'

'No, why would I be angry with Gwen?'

'You chased after her and at the garden gate you grabbed her roughly by the arm.'

'I just wanted to make sure she was OK. She was upset when she left the house.'

'What is your relationship with Sue Collier?'

'She's my sister-in-law. We're friends.'

'Now there's a coincidence, she said exactly the same thing. Are you sure you're not more than friends?'

'Look, I don't see what this has to do with what happened to Gwen–'

'Did you know Bethan Hopkins?'

'Not well, sometimes she was at Sue's house with Gwen. I gave her a lift from school with Gwen on a few occasions.'

'You never married.'

'No.'

'No children?'

David hesitated long enough for Meadows to sense he was hiding something. 'No, I don't have any children.'

'You went looking for Gwen that afternoon.' Meadows could see Edris shift in his chair. There was a quizzical look on his face at the sudden change of direction with the questions.

'Yes, I was worried about her.'

'You were seen on several occasions throughout the day and as late as eight o'clock.'

'I told you, we were worried about her. It was raining and she didn't have a coat.'

'Did Gwen often run away?'

'No, not to my knowledge.'

'It must have been difficult for Gwen, losing her father then having you step in to take over.'

'It wasn't like that.' David reddened.

162

'Oh, really? It sounds like you were around the house often. Picking up Gwen from school, even attending parents' evenings.'

'I was there to support Sue, it wasn't easy for her bringing up Gwen alone.'

'It must have been quite an argument that day for Gwen to run off. Did she accuse you of something?'

'No! She argued with Sue.'

'Yet both you and Sue claim not to remember what the argument was about.' Meadows let the silence lengthen in the room. He watched David closely. Beads of perspiration had gathered on his forehead and his hands were folded and placed on the table, but his thumbs constantly rubbed together.

Meadows leaned forwards and locked eyes with David. 'I think you were angry with Gwen that day. You followed her up the quarry, maybe you argued some more. Was she screaming at you? Did she hit you? Was she upset about you and Sue or was it the fact that you liked younger girls? Did she find out about you and Bethan?'

'No! What sort of man do you think I am?' David stood up.

'Did she threaten to tell Sue?'

'I don't have to listen to this crap.' David turned and walked towards the door where Edris jumped to his feet.

'Sit down, Mr Collier,' Meadows ordered. 'You are of course here voluntarily but I could arrest you.'

David spun around. 'Arrest me? What for?' He clenched his fists, but it didn't disguise the tremor.

'Sit down,' Meadows repeated.

David sank into the chair.

'Did you follow Gwen up to the quarry that day? You probably didn't mean to hurt her, things got out of hand, you pushed her and she fell over the edge. Bethan was screaming and you were afraid, you had to stop her from telling what you had done. Is that how it happened?'

'No! I went out looking for her, and later Jack Hopkins called looking for Bethan. We assumed the girls were together, hiding somewhere. Then it got late, we were worried, Sue was in a state. That's when I decided to call the police and report Gwen missing. I thought your lot would be able to find her and bring her home.' David put his head in his hands.

'You can see how it looks. Gwen remembers running from someone that day. She would have known you were looking for her.'

David looked up, his eyes glistening. 'I would never hurt Gwen. I love her.'

Meadows felt a surge of anger, he lent in further. 'Love her?'

'Not like that!' A venomous look crossed David's face. 'Gwen is my daughter.' His shoulders slumped as he sighed.

'What?' Meadows took a few moments to process the information.

He can't be, Gwen's father died when she was ten years old.

'It's true. If you are going to take that DNA sample you can confirm it. That's what the argument was about that day. Gwen caught us together. We weren't doing anything, just having a cwtch. I wanted to tell Gwen the truth. Sue's marriage was never a happy one, my brother could be a right bastard at times. I tried to be a friend to Sue and I guess we fell in love. Sue got pregnant, she worked out quickly that it was mine, and if my brother suspected he didn't let on. Gwen idolised her father and Sue didn't want to spoil the image she had of him. I just wanted things out in the open, I wanted to be a father to Gwen and not just Uncle David.

'I told her that day; she was in such a rage when she left the house. I suppose it was too much for her to take in. We thought she would calm down and come home so we could talk it over. After the attack she had no recollection of the argument and we didn't want to risk upsetting her after what she had been through. We were just glad to have her back.'

'And you kept on seeing Sue in secret.'

'No, Sue broke it off after Gwen was found. She still feels guilty for what happened.'

'Why didn't you tell us this before?'

'We didn't want to risk Gwen finding out. She has been through so much. Please don't tell her. I want to do it myself.'

Meadows sighed. This certainly wasn't the way he expected the interview to go. He stood up and picked up the file. 'DC Edris will organise the DNA swab, you are free to go afterwards.' He left the interview room and returned to his desk.

Meadows started updating his notes. It was some time before he noticed the message placed on top of the files.

'When did this call come in?' He waved the note in the air.

Blackwell looked up from his desk. 'About an hour ago. She didn't leave a message, looks like she only wanted to talk to you,' he said with a smirk.

'Any other calls come in?'

'No.' Blackwell turned away.

Meadows picked up his phone and punched in Gwen's number, then changed his mind and ended the call.

Edris walked back into the office, plonked himself down in his chair and turned to Meadows. 'The DNA swab has been taken. Do you think he's telling the truth?'

'Yes, I think he is, or at least he believes he is, Gwen's father. It makes sense that they'd want to keep that information from her and I can understand their guilt over what happened.'

'So, what now?'

Meadows leaned back in his chair and put his hands behind his head. 'We give it a couple of days, see if that witness calls back about Epworth. Gwen called when we were interviewing Collier. I'm going to go up to see her shortly, I imagine she's remembered something else and wants to discuss it. Meanwhile I think you should continue looking into Matt's background and chase up the group that was with Steven Powell that day. David Collier was a long shot. Let's see what comes back from the DNA sample then we will have another crack at Epworth.'

* * *

When Gwen opened the door, Meadows could tell that she had been crying. Her eyes were red and swollen. When she stepped back to let him in he saw her take a quick glance in the mirror.

'If this is a bad time I can call back tomorrow.'

'No, it's fine, to be honest I need to get my act together before the kids come home. I'm not ready to explain to them why I am upset.' She led him into the sitting room and sat on the sofa.

'I got your message.' Meadows chose to sit in the armchair. 'I take it you've had a visit from your uncle.'

'Yes, Uncle Daddy and my mother just left.'

'I'm sorry, Gwen, it must have come as a bit of a shock.'

'I don't understand why they didn't tell me sooner. Again, I mean. I know I would have been upset as a teenager, but to leave it this long…' She ran her hands through her hair and sighed.

'I guess there was never the right time.'

'I feel so sorry for them both. They quite clearly love each other but didn't continue the relationship because of me. All those wasted years.' She looked wistfully at Meadows.

He felt a sharp tug at his heart, like an old wound opening up. 'Now there's a chance for them to start again.' *Maybe for us too.* A tingle of excitement rippled across his skin. 'Do you think they'll get back together?'

'I hope so. I'm not upset about them, or even about David being my father. I guess I've just had all the illusions about my dad shattered.'

'You shouldn't think that way. Whatever went on between your mother and David, your dad, well, he's still your dad, and from what you've told me he loved you very much.' Meadows felt like reaching out and holding her hand, but instead he leaned forward and smiled. 'So, what was it you wanted to tell me?'

'Giles Epworth. I remembered being in Beth's bedroom and we were dressing up and planning to go to his house.' Gwen's cheeks flared and she looked away. 'I'm sorry, this is really embarrassing.'

'Please don't be embarrassed. Did you have a crush on him? You wouldn't be the first to fall in love with a teacher.'

'No!' Gwen locked eyes with him. 'It wasn't like that. I thought he was creepy. Beth wanted to go to his house and get him to, well, you get the idea. She was going to take photos for evidence.'

'Blackmail?'

'I guess so. I don't know what you must think of me now. It looks like we wanted to trick him so he must have done something to upset us. Maybe he tried it on at school.'

'Do you remember going to his house?'

'No, only talking about it, but I remember not wanting to go through with it. Beth could be very persuasive.'

'Do you think it's possible that Epworth is the lover Beth kept secret?'

'I don't know. It didn't seem that way. She said that he fancied me, she was the one who was going to take the photos.' Gwen twirled a lock of hair around her finger.

'But it would make sense if Epworth was the one to have got her pregnant. Maybe she wanted to get back at him,' Meadows said.

'I'm sure she would've told me. I think I should go back up to the barn, I'm certain something happened there.'

'Wait until I can go with you. I don't think it is a good idea that you go alone.'

'Perhaps it's better that I do. I'll have Blue with me.' She reached down to stroke the dog who lay at her feet. 'I saw Sam Morris today. He looks so old and weary. I just want this over.'

'I have a feeling it soon will be.' Meadows stood up. 'I'd better go. Thanks for the information. I'll talk to Epworth again and let you know how I get on.'

Back at the station Meadows found Edris furiously tapping away at the keyboard. He took a seat and waited for him to finish his input. 'I think we should bring in Epworth. See what reaction we get when we ask for a voluntary DNA sample.'

'Shouldn't we wait to see if that witness calls back?'

'No.' Meadows filled Edris in on his conversation with Gwen.

'Well, that changes things. Why don't we just arrest him?' Edris said with a grin. 'I'd like to see the look on his face. You know, he used to make up excuses to come into the boys changing rooms after PE. I'm sure he was perving on us. You could feel his eyes creeping over your body.'

'I think young girls are more his thing, but who knows, he might swing both ways. Shame we don't have anything solid on him, we can't really justify an arrest. You got anything for me?'

'Not a lot. Wayne Allen, Gary Lane, and Dai Roach all confirm Steven Powell's story about seeing Sam Morris that day and Matt Thomas persuading them to keep quiet. Sam's mother vouched for him from six o'clock, so there wouldn't have been enough time for him to go to the quarry, attack the girls, and get home again for dinner. Unless his mother lied for him.'

'His mother died a year ago so we can't question her again. I think we should concentrate on Giles Epworth.'

'I've had a quick dig around on Matt Thomas. Nothing on him apart from the fact he likes to play around.'

'OK, you can go and see your favourite redhead again. See if she recalls Epworth being free with his hands when she was a schoolgirl. You're going to have to use your charm to get information: Epworth is her boss and she will be worried about her job. Meanwhile I'm going to ask Epworth to come in.' Meadows grabbed his jacket and headed for the school.

Chapter Twenty-one

Giles entered the police station and gave his name at the desk. He still didn't have a clear idea why he had been called in. He looked around the station and felt a twinge of anxiety. He wished now he'd called a solicitor but he'd been worried he'd look suspicious. He thought it best to come in alone.

He took a seat and tried to make his body relax; his shoulders felt knotted and the anxiety made him feel nauseous. It was half an hour before Meadows showed up. He led Giles to the interview room and placed a file on the table before taking a seat. Giles pulled the chair close to the table and clasped his hands together, placing them on his lap, before looking at Meadows. He doesn't have anything on me, he kept repeating to himself. He watched as Meadows slowly shuffled through the papers in the file. It was a trick Giles played himself with the students, let the silence fill the room and rack up the tension.

Meadows looked up from the file and smiled. 'Before we start, I would like to offer you the chance to give a voluntary DNA sample.'

Giles felt his stomach clench and had a sudden urge to ask for the toilet.

'Just for elimination purposes,' Meadows said.

'And what happens if I refuse?'

'You are quite within your right to do so, but it would be in your best interest to provide us with a sample.'

'I see. Does that mean that you are treating me as a suspect?' Giles crossed his legs beneath the table, hoping to ease the pressure in his bladder. 'I feel that I've been more than helpful with your enquiries. If there's something that you feel implicates me then please do get to the point. I'm a busy man.'

'Last time we met, you said that you had no contact with Bethan and Gwen outside of school. I now have a witness who claims the girls visited your house.'

An image of Bethan and Gwen standing at his front door flashed across his mind. Dressed like hookers, the pair of them, smiling and giggling, he thought. 'I did not have any contact with the girls outside of school, your witness must be mistaken, or maybe they called at my house when I was out.'

'Oh, I think they went to your house and you let them in. Were you having a relationship with Bethan Hopkins?'

'No, and I won't stand for these allegations.' Giles flexed his fingers.

'It wasn't an allegation, it was a question.'

Meadows' eyes bored into him. It felt as though he could see into his mind. The room felt airless and all of a sudden it appeared to shrink, the walls closed in around him.

'Would it be fair to say that you're friendly with your students?'

'I am the headmaster. It's not my job to be friendly.'

'So you don't give an encouraging pat on the shoulder or put a friendly arm around a student?'

'No. Look, I think I have answered all your questions. I have worked at the school for over thirty years and in all that time I have never had a complaint made against me. I will not have you tarnishing my reputation.' Giles stood up; his legs felt weak and he didn't know how much longer he could hold on to his bladder. He needed to get out.

Meadows stood. 'The DNA sample?'

'If you want me to come in again then I would appreciate you giving me some time to consult with my solicitor.'

'We'll be in touch.'

Giles rushed to the bathroom and relieved himself. He washed his hands and peered into the mirror. His reflection showed a pale face with a sheen of perspiration. He knew he looked guilty. He splashed some water on his face and patted it dry with a paper towel before leaving the station. He sat for a moment in his car. Pain rippled across his chest and his breath caught in his throat. It had to be Gwen again. She must have told the police that she had gone to his house. He put his hand to his chest and rubbed, but the pain didn't ease. He started the engine and drove towards home. He couldn't face going into school. He wished now that he'd given the DNA sample, they obviously thought this was about Bethan.

He felt his breathing return to normal and the grip on his chest loosen.

He was sure they didn't know. If he could find a way to keep Gwen quiet there was no chance of them finding out.

Chapter Twenty-two

Gwen packed a rucksack with a large bottle of water and a drinking bowl for Blue. She left a note to say she had gone up the mountain, just in case something went wrong, then left the house. It was a humid day, she hated days like this. It was OK to feel hot when the sun was shining, but days like this left the air clinging to her skin. She was wearing shorts and a vest, a rarity as she always felt conscious of the thick scars that ran down her arm and leg. She really didn't care who saw her – let them stare.

She held her head high as she walked up the hill towards the mountain. Meadows had phoned to tell her they had questioned Epworth again but as they had no evidence, they couldn't hold him and he refused to give a DNA sample. Unless the witness came forward again or she had another flashback, there wasn't a lot the police could do.

It was the phone call that drove her towards the mountain. She needed to remember, otherwise the case would be closed again and she'd never know what happened that day. At the cattle grid she paused and took a sip of water before filling Blue's bowl. Her eyes travelled over the rolling hills of the Black Mountain range with the pass winding its way upwards until it disappeared from sight. Usually she took the track down to the river but today she would need to go in the opposite direction. It was a route she had avoided since the attack. When Blue had lapped the last of the water, she repacked the bag then stepped onto the mountainside.

'Right, Sam left me here.' Blue turned his head to look at her before plodding on.

There was a gentle breeze and Gwen welcomed the cool air blowing on her face and lifting her hair. She walked past the farmland which was marked out by dry stone walls. A few sheep took umbrage to Blue but other than the odd bleat all was silent.

It was raining that day, I put on Sam's coat, she thought. She tried to force the memory but nothing would come. Uncle David had told me he was my father. I was angry, she recalled. She felt the tension in her body, then the images flooded her mind...

How could they? Sneaking around behind Dad's back. Poor Dad, I bet they were screwing when he lay in the hospital bed dying, she thought. Angry tears dripped down her face and mixed with the rain. She hadn't wanted to cry in front of Sam but now she was alone she didn't care. The rain became heavier, driving into her body and soaking her hair so that it clung to her head. She wasn't going home. She was going to hide up the mountain all night, let them worry. She pushed on against the wind. Sam's coat was holding off some of the rain but the thin material didn't offer any warmth. Anger was bubbling beneath her skin. Her mother had been crying when she walked out of the house, begging her to listen. Filthy slag! And Uncle David, how could he do that to his own brother? she thought. No amount of screaming or shouting could drive away the pain she felt gnawing at her stomach. She was never going home. She decided that she would stay with Beth, or she could if Beth would stop pissing about. She didn't know what she was playing at? She was supposed to be her friend. Beth should be there with her and if she wasn't with Sam last night, where was she? Well, she can go and fuck herself, they all can, she thought.

Gwen quickened her pace, the anger and the cold making her body tremble. She didn't know where she was going, she knew she could reach the shack from this direction and that would give her some shelter from the rain but the idea of being there alone brought more tears to her eyes. When she saw the barn she glanced back at the road, it was only just visible. It was a good place to hide out for a while, if she got scared in the dark she could get back to the road. There might even be some hay to lie on.

She hurried to the barn and stepped through the entrance. A small white dog appeared and jumped up on her legs, its tail wagging furiously. As she bent down to stroke its head she became aware of a low, guttural moaning. Curiosity overrode her fear and she stepped further into the barn. The sight that met her eyes made her gasp in shock and stumble backwards. A boy was kneeling on a bale of hay, naked from the waist down. His hands gripped the side of the bale as he was thrust forward, his teeth gritted.

Behind the boy Giles Epworth stood, trousers around his ankles, thrusting into the boy as he gripped him at the hips. His eyes were closed and he emitted a moan as his face glowed with ecstasy.

The boy squealed when he saw Gwen and Epworth's eyes snapped open. The three of them were momentarily paralysed, then Epworth pulled away from the boy. Gwen caught a glimpse of his erection before she turned and bolted from the barn. She ran towards the entrance of the quarry, the grass slipping beneath her feet as she pounded the ground. She could hear Epworth's shouts as he chased her. She turned briefly, then lost her footing. She fell forward and put out her hands to break the fall and yelped as she felt her left wrist absorb the impact with a crack.

'Gwen, come back!' Epworth was breathing heavily as he gained on her.

Gwen scrambled to her feet, ignoring the pain.

'Come back here, you little bitch!'

She ran into the copse of trees, then through the gate that led onto the path, she knew Epworth was close. Her chest hurt as she drew in the damp air. The pain from her wrist shot up her arm and her hand stung from the fall. Terror beat a rhythm through her body as she scanned the area for somewhere to hide. He'll kill me if he catches me. I can't run anymore, it's too far to get back to the village, she thought. Her legs felt heavy and weak as she jumped off the path and scrambled down the bank. It wasn't too steep at this end of the path but she still had to be careful; if she went down too far she would fall into the stream below. She crouched behind a tree and tried to hold her breath.

'Gwen! Gwen, where are you? I just want to talk to you.' Epworth had entered the quarry and was walking along the path.

Gwen pressed her body to the ground, she could smell the damp earth and feel the roots of the tree pressing into her skin. He walked past, calling out her name, she didn't dare move in case he came back...

A wet tongue lapped at the tears on her face. Gwen came back to the present, she had sunk to the floor and wrapped her hands around her knees. Blue nudged her hand and she moved it onto his body. The thick white fur running through her fingers calmed her breathing. She let her eyes travel around the barn. Now she knew what happened in the barn. I must have broken my wrist, she thought. The memory of the pain still lingered. She was convinced that Epworth must have come back, it was him, and she went back to school where he could watch her every day. A shiver ran through her body as she thought of Ariana and Alex, Epworth could get at them any time.

She took her mobile phone from her bag and fumbled with the button. When she managed to get through to the police station she was told that DI Meadows was out, and she ended the call without leaving a message. She tried his mobile but it went straight to voicemail. An eerie feeling crept over her body. Epworth could be lurking outside, waiting for her on the mountain. She tried to stop her imagination running wild. Epworth is in school, he's not following you, there is no one out there, she told herself.

She could feel her body trembling as she stepped outside of the barn and looked around. There was no one on the mountain and Epworth wouldn't harm the children when they were in school. She checked her watch, it was nearly time for them to come home. She hurried back to the road and walked briskly back into the village where she felt her fear ebb away.

Back inside the house she kept busy until she heard Ariana and Alex come through the front door. Now she was home, she wondered if it was a good idea to say something to them. They both ambled into the kitchen and started the daily raid of the cupboards.

'Good day at school?' Gwen forced a smile and hoped her voice didn't give away the anxiety she felt.

'It was OK apart from netball. We had to run around on the court for an hour while Mrs James sat on her fat arse and barked orders. It's too bloody hot to play netball.' Ariana plonked herself down on the nearest chair and gulped down a glass of squash. 'Then when I'm all sweaty I have to change back into my uniform for the rest of the day, it's disgusting. I don't see why we have to be made to look like skanky hoes for the rest of the day, we should have at least time for a shower.'

If Gwen hadn't been so preoccupied she would have laughed. 'I hated sport when I was in school, that sort of torture should be banned.'

'Well at least you got to go outside,' Alex complained. 'I've been stuck in study lessons all day. Even had to give up my lunch break, Epworth called me into his office.'

Gwen felt a chill run through her body. 'What did he want?'

'Talk about my expected grades in the exams. He says I'm slipping in maths so he's organised after-school tutorials to get me through my exams.'

'Like fuck you're staying after school with that pervert.'

'Mum!' Ariana's eyes were wide with shock at Gwen's outburst, it was a rarity that her mother used bad language. 'Why are you calling Mr Epworth a pervert?'

'I don't like him, he gives me the creeps. I don't want you or your brother anywhere near him.'

Alex was laughing. 'Does that mean I don't have to do extra study?'

'I haven't got a problem with you doing extra study, just not after school. I can help you with maths. What else did Epworth say?'

'Just asked how you are and how the investigation is going.'

'What did you say?'

'Nothing, I said you were OK. What's all this about?'

'Detective Meadows doesn't want us talking to anyone about the case.' She turned her back and started chopping vegetables, not wanting Ariana and Alex to see her distress. She knew there was nothing wrong with Alex's grades, Epworth was playing games. Wanting her to know that he can get to her children anytime. A shiver ran down her back. I have to speak to Meadows before the end of the day, she thought.

Gwen was in the kitchen when Matt came through the door. He opened the fridge, fished out a can of lager, and took it through to the sitting room. Gwen followed and watched as he plonked himself down on the sofa and picked up the remote control. She wondered what she'd seen in him all those years ago. Had she just been desperate to get married and have a family of her own? It hadn't always been bad but she doubted that he ever loved her.

She knew she should tell him about Epworth but any mention of the investigation would set him off. She couldn't be bothered with another argument. 'I thought I would go swimming after dinner. I haven't been for weeks.'

Matt looked away from the television. 'I think that's a good idea, get back to some sort of normality around here. I'll move my car, it's blocking you in.'

'Thanks.'

She packed her swimming bag and after they had eaten and she had cleared the dishes, she left the house. In the car she placed another call to the station but was told that DI Meadows wouldn't be back in until the morning. She couldn't wait until then. He'd told her that he'd moved into his mother's old house. She knew it was down the track that led to Bryn Bach farm.

She started the engine and turned right onto the main road, at the mini roundabout she took the turning on to Turnpike Road. There was a sharp S-bend in the road and she applied the brakes to take the corner. They felt spongy, so she took her foot off the pedal and pressed down again before turning the wheel. The road straightened out and into a steep decline, she applied the brakes again to slow the car but they had no effect on the speed. She pumped at the pedal, her hands gripping the steering wheel in panic as the car increased speed.

Ahead she could see the old stone bridge that crossed the river, after that she knew the road veered sharply to the right. There was no chance she could make the turn at the speed the car was travelling, she doubted she'd make it over the bridge. She'd hit head on into anyone coming the other way or hit the wall.

Adrenalin forced her options rapidly through her mind. She'd have to go off before the bridge. She was running out of road, she could see two old men standing on the bridge looking into the river. Please don't let me hit them, she thought. She hit the horn as she pulled hard on the steering wheel. As the front end of the car veered off the road the back end swung around and hit the stone wall. Metal crunched and she felt herself thrown sideways as the car spun. She continued to grip the wheel but had no control over the car. Time seemed to slow as the car hit the bank and the front end dipped forward. The car plunged towards the river as the airbag exploded and her head hit the back of the seat.

Chapter Twenty-three

The radio played in the background and a half-drunk cup of coffee sat on the table in Meadows' sitting room. He was sat in an armchair with a book held in his hand. He had been reading the same page over for the past twenty minutes and even though his eyes scanned over the words they didn't register. His thoughts were on Gwen and the case, he had worked solidly for the past three weeks and this was his first day off, but he couldn't relax. He had asked Edris to keep him informed of any developments then spent the day stripping the wallpaper from the bedroom. Every now and then he checked his phone to make sure he hadn't missed any calls. The mindless task had given him space to think. There was something about the case that he felt he was missing, over and over but nothing stood out. He sighed and lay the book on his lap.

He was about to reach for his secret stash of cannabis when a knock at the door stayed his hand. He ambled to the front door brushing off specks of paper that clung to his jeans. Edris stood on the doorstep, his hands in his pockets and a smile on his face.

'Sorry to bother you on your day off.'

'No worries, come in.'

Thank God I hadn't skinned up.

Edris followed him inside and stood looking around the sitting room.

'I haven't got around to redecorating yet. I've just made a start upstairs. To be honest DIY isn't my thing.'

'Well I'm sure it's going to look great when you've finished. I came around to tell you that Gwen has been involved in a car accident.'

Meadows felt his stomach clench. 'Is she OK?'

'I don't know all the details. Folland came up to see you, he thought you would want to know. Apparently she drove the car into the river at Bryn Melyn Bridge. There were no other cars involved. I came straight here.'

'Give me a sec to get changed and we'll go there and see what we can find out.' In the bedroom Meadows tried to calm his anxiety.

Please let her be alright.

He stripped off and after a quick wash put on a clean shirt and pair of trousers.

'OK, I'm ready, I'll drive,' he called as he hurried down the stairs.

When they arrived at the crash scene there was a group of spectators on the bridge, watching the car being pulled from the river. Meadows parked the car and approached the uniformed officer who stood watching over the proceedings.

'What happened?'

'The vehicle belongs to a Mrs Gwen Thomas. Looks like she lost control of the car. A couple of witnesses that were standing on the bridge at the time say that she was speeding down the hill. She sounded her horn before the car went off the road.'

'Is she badly injured?'

'She was conscious when she left in the ambulance. Badly shaken so I thought it best to wait until she's seen a doctor before questioning her. Do you mind me asking why CID are interested in a traffic accident?'

'She's part of an ongoing investigation.'

'Oh yeah, I thought I recognised the name. She's one of the quarry girls.'

'Yes, she is. I want this car checked out to see if it's been tampered with.'

'I'll get on to it.' The officer walked towards the tow truck and Meadows watched him give instructions to the driver.

'You don't think it was an accident, do you?' Edris asked.

'No, why would she be speeding down the hill? She's probably driven this road hundreds of times and would know you can't take the bridge at speed. If she sounded her horn before she went off the road she was obviously in trouble and was worried about the people on the bridge.'

Meadows walked to the end of the bridge and inspected the wall where the car had impacted. 'I don't think she lost control of the car. I think she knew she couldn't make the bridge and thought her best chance was to come off the road, but was going too fast to make the turn. Come on, let's go to the hospital and see what she can tell us.'

* * *

Gwen was sitting up in bed when Meadows and Edris arrived, and a large angry bruise shone on her forehead. Matt sat in a chair, his hair sticking up at various angles revealing patches of pink scalp.

'How are you feeling?' Meadows approached the bed.

'I'm OK, I think I had more of a shock than anything else. The doctor wants me to stay in overnight for observation. I'd rather go home,' Gwen said.

'It's probably better you stay in to be on the safe side. Are you up to answering some questions?'

'No she's bloody not!' Matt jumped up from the chair. 'I don't know what you are doing here. She already spoke to that copper before she left in the ambulance.'

'It's OK, Matt, I don't mind. Why don't you go and get a cup of tea?'

'I'll stay.' Matt plonked himself down in the chair and glared at Meadows.

'Can you tell us what happened?' Edris took out his notebook and pen.

'I'm not sure, it happened so quickly. I think the brakes on the car failed. It was OK when I left the house but when I started down Turnpike Road I tried to slow the car but the brakes felt odd. Then they stopped working. I could see some people on the bridge, I knew I was going too fast to make it across the bridge without hitting them and even if I managed to get across the bridge I wouldn't make the bend. I tried to pull the car off the road but I lost control.' Her voice quivered and she reached onto the bedside table for the glass of water.

'I'm having the car checked out to see if it's been tampered with.'

Gwen's eyes widened. 'You think someone is trying to kill me?'

'Don't be ridiculous.' Matt glared at Meadows. 'It is an old car.'

'Yes, but it's just passed its MOT.' A frown creased Gwen's forehead. 'I think it's Epworth.'

'Why do you think he would tamper with the car?'

'I was coming to see you when I crashed the car. I remembered what I had seen in the barn that day. I couldn't reach you at the station so I was hoping to catch you at home.'

'You said you were going swimming.' Matt's jaw clenched.

'I was, I just wanted to see Detective Meadows first.' She looked away from Matt.

'You didn't say anything to me.' Matt scowled.

Meadows sensed Gwen's unease, and Matt was obviously fighting to control his temper.

'What do you remember about the barn?'

'I was going to shelter there from the rain. Epworth was there with a young boy. They were having sex.' Gwen looked away.

'A boy?'

'Yes, about thirteen or fourteen years old.'

Meadows felt a flutter of excitement.

This could be the breakthrough we need. Epworth would want to keep that secret. What lengths would he go to?

'What happened then?'

'He saw me, he was angry and started shouting. I ran from the barn and he chased after me. I slipped and hurt my wrist.' Gwen rubbed her left wrist as if the memory brought back the pain. 'He was shouting for me to come back. I got up and ran to the quarry entrance and he followed me in. I hid behind a tree. I don't remember anything after that.'

Matt snorted and Meadows turned to look at him.

'You're not taking this seriously, are you?' Matt looked from Meadows to Edris. 'First she thinks it's her uncle and now the headmaster. Who's going to be next?' He turned to face Gwen. 'Your head is completely fucked up, I told you from the start that this investigation is stupid. You are making things worse and wasting their time.' He waved his arm, indicating the policemen.

Meadows could feel his anger threatening to erupt. He clenched his right fist tightly and put it behind his back to stop himself driving it into Matt's face. 'It is not a waste of time, and for your information everything Gwen has remembered so far has been corroborated. It's a fact that Gwen's left wrist was broken even though the rest of her injuries were on her right side and consistent with the fall. So yes, I am taking this seriously.' He turned his attention to Gwen. 'Do you know the boy that Epworth was with that day?'

Gwen's eyes were shining with tears and Meadows fought the urge to go closer to her. He knew Matt's words had stung her and she was struggling to keep her composure.

'No, I'm sorry, I don't know.' She took a sip of water, avoiding Meadows' eyes.

She knows, she just doesn't want to betray the boy to Matt. 'OK, I'll leave you to rest now.'

'Are you going to speak to Epworth?'

'I'll wait for the results on the car, but yes, we will be bringing him in for questioning.'

* * *

Meadows was in the office early the next morning, waiting for the results on the car. As soon as his phone rang he snatched it up. Edris hovered near the desk, his face showing his eagerness to hear the results.

'There is no doubt the brakes were cut,' Meadows informed Edris as he put down the phone.

'Do you think Epworth would go that far? It's a hell of a risk, he would've had to go close to the house and anyone could have seen him.'

'Well, someone cut them, and Epworth has motive. Gwen saw him having sex with an underage boy. That would be his career ruined. Gwen remembers him chasing her into the quarry so that puts him at the scene of the murder at the right time. He could've easily gone to her house during the night to cut the brakes, it's unlikely he would have been seen. He has good reason to silence Gwen.'

'And Bethan Hopkins, how does she fit into this?'

'Maybe she took a walk up the quarry footpath that day and met up with Gwen and Epworth. Doreen Hopkins said that Bethan was going out for a walk when she left the house.'

'So, are we going to bring him in?'

'I want to see Gwen first. I'm sure she knows the identity of the boy in the barn with Epworth. I'm betting he is our anonymous caller. If we can get his name then that'll be another witness against Epworth. I need you to get fingerprints from Matt and Alex and anyone else who may have been in Gwen's car. We already have Gwen's and Ariana's. If we can link Epworth to the car then we will have a stronger case against him. We'll also need a warrant to search his house and office at the school.'

'I'll get on to it, but to be honest I don't think he would be stupid enough to leave fingerprints on the car or have anything to incriminate him in his house.'

'He does appear very sure of himself, but he wouldn't have been expecting to see Gwen that day so wouldn't have been prepared. Maybe we will get lucky and be able to match his DNA to the crime scene.'

* * *

Meadows left Edris to apply for the warrant and headed for Gwen's house. The door opened as soon as he stepped out of the car and Blue bounded towards him, jumping up and placing his paws on his shoulders. Meadows was thrown off balance by the weight of the dog. He could hear Gwen giggling.

'Down, Blue!' Gwen ordered. 'Sorry, he's a bit overexcited today. I think he likes you.'

Meadows ruffled the dog's fur. 'It's OK. I don't mind, I wouldn't want to meet him when he was in a bad mood. So how are you feeling today?'

'A lot better, thanks.' Gwen led him into the kitchen and filled the kettle. 'Tea?'

'Please.' Meadows took a seat at the table and watched Gwen prepare the tea. Blue sat at his feet and placed his head on Meadows' knees, his bushy tail swept the floor.

'We had the results on the car this morning. I'm afraid the brakes were tampered with.' He watched as Gwen's body stiffened, she turned around to face him.

'Do you think Epworth is capable of doing something like that?'

'It wouldn't be difficult, he could have read it up online, these days you can learn how to make a bomb if you know where to look. After what you told me yesterday he certainly has motive to keep you quiet.'

'But he doesn't know that I've remembered what happened in the barn.'

'No, but you are still a threat to him, we've already questioned him twice so he is rattled.'

'Will you arrest him now?'

'Yes, but we could make a better case against him if you tell me the name of the boy you saw with Epworth. He could have witnessed what happened that day.'

Gwen chewed her bottom lip and turned away. She filled the cups from the teapot and stirred before answering. 'I'm sorry I couldn't tell you yesterday, Matt can be a bit of an arsehole sometimes and I didn't want him knowing and spreading it around.'

She picked up the cups and placed them on the table before taking a seat. 'It was Carl Perkins. He was in the year below me.'

'So he would have been about fourteen at the time.'

'At the most. I was so shocked at the time I couldn't take in what I was seeing, it's pretty sick. Epworth is a teacher. When you send your kids to school you expect them to be safe.'

'Well, I can assure you he won't be teaching again. If Carl Perkins will testify, the least we can have him on is intercourse with a minor.'

'Poor boy, can you imagine going into school every day after that? I bet he never felt safe.'

Meadows took a sip of tea then put his hand into his jacket pocket, pulled out a small electronic device, and laid it on the table.

'What's that?'

'It's a panic alarm. If you hit the button it will send a signal to the police station and they'll immediately dispatch a car. I want you to keep it with you at all times. Please don't tell anyone about it, not even your family.'

'But if you arrest Epworth why would I need it?'

'It's just to be on the safe side. I don't want to take any risks. Promise me you'll keep it on you at all times.'

Gwen picked it up and turned it over in her hand. 'OK.' She slipped it into her handbag. 'Thank you. I'm glad you came back.' She blushed but kept eye contact.

'So am I.' He reached across the table and touched her hand. Desire sent sparks through his body, making his skin tingle. 'I'd better go. Edris will call later to get fingerprints from Matt and Alex so we can eliminate them from the ones on the car.' He stood and drained the last of his tea. 'Please be careful, we still can't be one hundred percent certain that it was Epworth that cut the brakes on the car.'

'Well, I won't be driving anywhere soon and I will stick to the park and rugby pitch when I walk Blue.'

'Good.' Meadows resisted the urge to touch her again.

Back in the car he placed a call to Edris to look up Carl Perkins' address, then rested his head against the seat.

Would she leave Matt? If she didn't have the children, I think she would.

The phone trilled, jolting him from his thoughts. Edris gave him a home and work address for Carl Perkins. Meadows started the engine and headed for Bryn Mawr, figuring it more likely that Perkins would be in work.

He parked the car outside AJ Accountants and put on his jacket before entering the building. The secretary made a call then led him to an office at the back of the building.

Carl Perkins rose from his desk and shook Meadows' hand before sitting back down. Meadows looked him over; he was slim with a boyish face and soft hazel eyes.

'What can I do for you, Detective?' He smiled pleasantly.

Meadows recognised the gentle voice. 'As you must be aware, we have reopened the investigation into the murder of Bethan Hopkins and the brutal attack on Gwen Collier. I believe you made an anonymous phone call to the station claiming to have seen Giles Epworth on the mountain with Gwen Collier the day of the attack.'

Carl seemed to shrink in his chair. 'I, erm... I think you must be mistaken.'

'No, I don't think so.' Meadows leaned forward. 'Gwen remembers seeing you with Epworth in the barn that day. I understand how difficult this is for you. Please, Mr Perkins, your testimony could be vital to this case.'

'I'm sorry, I can't help you.' His eyes pleaded with Meadows. 'I have a wife and children.'

'I'm sure your wife would understand. What Epworth did was wrong, you were just a boy. Think of your own children. Would you want the same thing to happen to them?'

'You don't understand.' Carl's eyes misted over.

'Then help me understand. I am not here to judge you, I promise.'

Carl sighed, he stood up and walked to the window. 'I was a bit of a handful when I was in school.' He kept his back turned to Meadows. 'I got in a few scrapes and my grades were down. My father was a strict man and I rebelled, I just wanted to do anything I could to disappoint him. Epworth was kind to me, helped me with my homework and extra study. Then he started buying me gifts and giving me money. He made it seem like what we did was OK, it was like I owed him. I didn't like it but he sort of had a hold on me. I guess he was controlling. I didn't know how to get out of it, it's not like I could tell anyone what was happening, and who would believe me?'

'What happened on the mountain that day?'

'Epworth had arranged to meet me in the barn, he said it was safe there and as long as we arrived and left separately no one would find out. I don't know how long Gwen stood watching, I remember the look on her face, she was horrified. Epworth was furious, he was swearing and shouting as he chased her out of the barn.'

'Did you follow them?'

'No, I was too ashamed. I thought she was going to tell everyone at school. I ran back home and locked myself in my bedroom. Then I heard about the murder. At first I thought both of the girls were dead. I was terrified and stayed at home for a few days pretending to be ill. My father soon sent me back to school. I tried to avoid Epworth but he managed to get me in his classroom alone. He told me to keep my mouth shut about what happened.'

'Did he threaten you?'

'He didn't have to; he knew I wouldn't want anyone to know what we were doing that day. After that I stayed away from him and he didn't talk to me alone again. When I saw the appeal I wanted to come forward but even after all this time I'm ashamed.'

'You've got nothing to be ashamed about. Epworth groomed you. Would you be willing to make a statement?'

'I can't. Can you imagine what my life would be like? People talking about me and the effect it would have on my family. I don't think I could face anyone if it came out.'

'You're probably not the only boy that Epworth took advantage of. If you make a stand against him it may encourage others to come forward. We could make sure that he never gets a chance to do this to another boy. I can't promise you that your name won't come out, and if it goes to court you could be summoned as a witness. I will however do all in my power to protect your identity from the media. Please, will you just think about it?'

Meadows left Carl Perkins at his desk. He felt sorry for him and believed he would probably go home and confess everything to his wife.

Chapter Twenty-four

Giles Epworth stood in his kitchen chopping salad as a single potato revolved in the microwave. He placed the salad on the kitchen table then poured a large glass of red wine. He took a sip, savouring the bitter liquid on his tongue. The small dog fussed at his feet.

'You'll have food when I eat,' Giles snapped. 'I just want some peace. I've listened to Catrin prattle on all day about Gwen's car crash. She should've died, that would've been of more interest.' He felt a smile creep across his face.

The dog's ears pricked up and he scratched his paws against his master's legs. Giles shrugged him off and drank deeply from the glass. The microwave pinged and he set the already filled bowl of dog food on the floor before taking the potato and setting it on his plate with the salad. He topped up his glass before seating himself at the table. As he picked up his knife and fork someone knocked the door. He ignored it and sliced the potato, adding a generous amount of butter. The door sounded again, heavy insistent banging.

'This better be important.' He put down his cutlery and walked slowly to the door. He could see a tall, shadowy figure through the frosted glass. A sense of unease crept over his body as he turned the key and swung open the door.

'Giles Epworth, I have a warrant for your arrest and to search both your home and your office at the school.' Meadows thrust the paper at Giles.

Giles scanned the document. 'I don't understand, why would you want to search my house?' The paper shook in his hands. 'This is not convenient, I've just sat down to eat. You'll have to come back later.'

Meadows looked down at him. 'Please step aside and allow the officers to enter. DC Edris will take you to the station.'

Giles could feel his heart thudding against his ribs, he knew this would soon be followed by gripping pain. 'I need my medication.' He turned and hurried inside. He could hear Meadows close behind. He picked up his jacket and made sure his angina spray was in the pocket before turning to face Meadows.

'You're making a mistake, you can't just come into my home and look through my private things. This is outrageous!' He could see officers starting to file into the house while the dog yapped and growled.

'We have every right to search your property. Now, I would appreciate it if you would let my officers do their job. Either you can go with Detective Edris quietly or he can cuff you.' Meadows gave him a look of disgust.

'How long will I be at the station?'

'That depends.'

'What about my dog?'

'I'll call in an animal welfare officer. I assure you the dog will be well taken care of. Edris!'

Edris entered the room. His lips twitched and Giles guessed that the young officer was trying not to look smug.

'Read him his rights and take him in.' Meadows turned away.

The words washed over Giles as Edris read him his rights. He felt like he was in a nightmare; he pinched the skin on the back of his hand hoping to wake up.

'Come along, sir,' Edris said.

Giles stepped outside and saw that a small crowd had gathered across the road, even his next-door neighbour stood on the doorstep watching. He kept his eyes down as he hurried to the car. Edris opened the door and he slid into the back seat. He could feel all eyes upon him and hear the whispers. He glared at Edris, who had slipped into the driver's seat and was taking his time to start the engine. Giles was sure Edris was delaying on purpose, wanting to humiliate him.

The car pulled off and Giles let his head rest against the seat. He took slow breaths in and out. He focused on his breathing, trying to calm his anxiety as they travelled towards the station. Edris remained silent; occasionally Giles could see his eyes in the rear-view mirror looking at him. When the car pulled up in the station car park he felt a little calmer. He knew they didn't have anything on him and they wouldn't find anything in the house. He just needed to stay and cooperate. It would be alright.

Edris led him to the front desk where he was booked in by the custody sergeant. His pockets were emptied and the items signed for, he was then offered legal representation and a chance to view a copy of the police code of conduct but declined both. The only thing he was allowed to keep was his medication. Next, he was fingerprinted, photographed, and DNA swabs taken from the inside of his cheek. Edris stood and watched over the procedure. Giles sensed that the young officer gained some pleasure from having authority over his old headmaster. Finally he was put into a holding cell and the door locked.

He sat down on the bed and tried to quell the panic that fizzled through his veins. The room was small and felt airless. A faint smell of disinfectant lingered and Giles conjured up images of drunks and murderers, covered in blood and vomit, who had sat on the same bed. He could feel his shirt clinging to his back and longed to take a shower. His watch had been taken from him so he had no idea how long he had sat in the cell. Occasionally the flap in the door would open and a face would appear. Later he was brought a sandwich and tepid tea in a polystyrene cup.

'How much longer am I going to be locked in here?' he asked the young officer who brought the tray.

'Erm, I'm not sure. I'll see if I can find out.' He left, locking the door.

'Imbecile,' Giles muttered and bit into the sandwich. The crust was dry and the filling tasteless; he wasn't hungry but ate anyway to pass the time. The young officer didn't come back with the information.

Giles was lying on his back staring at the ceiling when Edris entered the cell. 'DI Meadows is ready for you now.'

'About time.' Giles swung his legs off the bed and followed Edris into the interview room where he took his seat.

Meadows was already sat at the table. He recorded the time and date together with the names of those present. His serious tone sent another wave of panic through Giles, who tried not to squirm in his seat. Meadows looked sternly at him.

'I understand you have waived your right to legal representation.'

'Yes. I have nothing to hide so it would be a waste of time and money to bring in my solicitor.' Giles fidgeted in his seat, the hard plastic was digging into his back and stress tensed his muscles. 'Now, can we get on with it? I think you've kept me here long enough. I would like to go home.'

'You're entitled to change your mind and request legal representation at any time during the interview.' Meadows gave him a tight smile.

'What were your movements last Wednesday?'

'Wednesday? I would have been in my office at the school from 8 a.m. I didn't leave until five-thirty that evening. I'm sure you can find plenty of witnesses to confirm this.'

'And after five-thirty?'

'I drove home, prepared and ate dinner, then took the dog for a walk. I got back about 8 p.m., watched some television then went to bed.'

'Is there anyone who can corroborate this?'

'No, as you are fully aware, I live alone.'

'Where did you walk the dog?'

'Around the park, then down Turnpike Road to the rugby pitch. I let him run around for a while then returned home.'

'Did you pass Gwen Thomas' house?'

'No.'

'And last Tuesday?'

'Much the same.'

'Are you sure you didn't go to Gwen Thomas' house? See her car in the driveway and take the opportunity to tamper with her brakes.'

'What?' Giles felt laughter bubble in his throat. It escaped his mouth and filled the interview room.

'Is there something that amuses you?' Meadows' eyes blazed.

'No.' Giles fought to control the hysteria that threatened to take over. 'No, I did not go to Gwen Thomas' house and I certainly did not tamper with her brakes. Why on earth would I do such a thing?'

'Well, it seems you have a secret, one that Gwen Thomas knew about. She had blocked it from her mind.' Meadows paused and leaned across the table. 'Until now.'

Cold sweat prickled the back of Giles' neck. 'I don't know what you're talking about.'

'I'm talking about what Gwen saw that day in the barn.'

Pain rippled across his chest, he put his hand against his ribs and pressed hard. He didn't want to hear it, everything would be ruined.

'She saw you performing a sexual act on an underage boy.' Meadows' lips curled.

'No, it's not true.' The pain gripped like a snake, coiling and squeezing until it constricted his breathing.

'Are you feeling unwell?' Meadows sat back in his chair and folded his arms.

Giles shook his head, he couldn't speak. He took the bottle from his jacket pocket and squirted the liquid under his tongue. He breathed in slowly as he waited for the medication to take effect. He heard the door open and close but didn't turn to look. A few moments later Edris entered the room and placed a plastic cup of water on the table. Giles picked it up and sipped slowly, and the grip on his chest loosened.

'Do you feel well enough to continue with the interview or would you rather be seen by a doctor?'

'Let's just get this over with. I can't imagine why Gwen would say those things. I'm sure she must be confused. You can't expect her memory to be reliable after the trauma she suffered and it being so long.'

'No, I suppose we can't.' Meadows smiled. 'But there's also Carl Perkins, who backs up her story.'

'He wouldn't!'

'Oh, why wouldn't he?'

'I mean he wouldn't say such things about me. I was good to that boy.'

'Yes, so I've heard. Bought him gifts and gave him money in exchange for sexual favours.'

'No, it wasn't like that. I loved him.' Giles slammed his fist on the table, the beat of his heart thrummed in his ears. 'You wouldn't understand that, would you? I've met your type before.'

'And what type is that?'

'Homophobes. That's what this is all about, isn't it?'

'I'm no homophobe, Mr Epworth, but I do detest paedophiles, and especially your type who use their position to abuse children.'

'No, I'm not like that.' Giles felt the bile rise in his throat. 'I told you, I loved him and he loved me.'

'And what about the others?'

'What others?'

'Did you think deleting the files from your computer would be enough? We have technicians that can retrieve those files and guess what we found?'

Giles felt shame crawl at his skin and put his head in his hand.

'Photographs, lots of them. Carl Perkins was only one among many schoolboys. It won't take us long to track them down.'

Giles kept his head down, he could feel his life being picked apart. He let the tears leak from his eyes.

'What happened that day when you caught up with Gwen? Did she threaten to tell everyone about you? Did Bethan turn up? Did she laugh at you? You had to keep them quiet, didn't you?'

'No!' Giles lifted his head. 'I didn't touch those little sluts.'

Meadows leaned in close, his eyes glinted dangerously. 'Little sluts, were they? We all know the type, coming into your classroom, skirts raised and buttons undone, revealing all that young skin. But it didn't do anything for you so they taunted you. That day was the last straw for you, you just snapped. Maybe you didn't intend to kill Bethan. Did you hit her when she laughed at you? Then Gwen was screaming, she tried to get away. You were frightened, you couldn't let her go. You had no choice, you had to push her down the ravine.'

'No! You can't just make things up. I didn't go anywhere near those two.'

'You chased Gwen that day.'

'Yes, I chased her out of the barn. I saw her fall and called out for her to wait. I just wanted to talk to her, beg her not to tell people what she had seen, but she got up and kept running. I followed her onto the quarry footpath then lost her. I called out then ran further down the path. I was frantic. I came to that old tool shack, I thought she might be hiding inside but as I got nearer I heard voices so I turned and ran back up the path.'

'Voices? So you're saying someone was with Gwen.'

'No, it wasn't Gwen, it was Bethan, and she was with a boy.'

'What boy?'

'I don't know. Can I go home now? I've told you everything I know.'

Meadows' eyes narrowed. 'No, you can't.'

'Then I want legal representation, you have no reason to keep me here.'

Meadows looked at his watch. 'We'll continue in the morning by which time we should have the fingerprint analysis results.' He called an end to the interview.

Giles was led back to the cell. He felt drained, he plonked himself down on the bed and wrapped his arms around his body. He rocked back and forth until finally he gave into exhaustion and curled into a ball.

* * *

Meadows sat at his desk nursing a hot cup of tea. He looked at Edris. 'Did you get the fingerprints from Matt and Alex Thomas?'

'Yes, and Sue Collier. I sent them off with Epworth's as soon as I booked him in.'

'Good, I take it you requested that Epworth's were checked against the ones taken from the original crime scene.'

The colour rose in Edris' cheeks. 'I'm sorry, I didn't put in the request for the fingerprints but I sent off Epworth's DNA.'

'That will take longer to process, we can only hold him until tomorrow afternoon.'

'I'll do it now.' Edris leapt from his seat.

Meadows turned to his computer and typed up a summary of the interview. When Edris returned he sat down next to him and spun his chair back and forth.

'So what now? Do we charge him?'

Meadows leaned back in his chair and rubbed his hand over his chin. 'We could charge him for sex with a minor but we really need Carl Perkins to make a statement. I'll call him in the morning. I think you should work on identifying the boys in the photographs we got from his computer, maybe one of them will be willing to testify.'

'What about the attack on Gwen and Bethan?'

'Let's see what we get back from the fingerprint analysis. If he was in the shack he would have left prints.'

'Imagine, all these years he has been at the school, it gives me the creeps. I wonder how they missed him in the first investigation.'

'They had no reason to suspect him, Gwen had no memory of what happened.'

'Yeah, I guess. Still, I think we'll be celebrating tomorrow. Lester is going to be well chuffed,' Edris said with a grin.

'Maybe.'

'You don't sound very convinced.' Edris stopped spinning the chair. 'What's troubling you? He admitted he was there and he had the motive.'

'Don't you think his behaviour was a bit odd during the interview? When I asked him about the brakes on Gwen's car he laughed. It was like he was relieved.'

'I don't follow.'

'Think of it from a different angle. If Epworth is not guilty of the murder then the only thing he would have been concerned about is us finding out about the boys. When I told him about Perkins I thought he was going to have a heart attack, yet he didn't appear that concerned when I questioned him about the attack on the girls. It was almost as though the worst had already happened.'

'He's a nutcase, and he's so full of himself that he doesn't think we have anything on him.'

'We don't have anything on him, all the evidence is circumstantial. He knows we could match his DNA to the scene yet after he admitted to being with Carl Perkins he thought he could go home. I don't think it occurred to him that we could charge him with murder, he's more concerned with protecting his reputation.'

'I reckon you're overthinking this. It's been a long day,' Edris said.

'Yeah, I guess you're right. You should go home, I have a feeling tomorrow is going to be a busy day. You can make a start on identifying the boys in the photographs on Epworth's computer; we can get him for that if nothing else.'

Meadows watched Edris leave the office then picked up the original case notes. He read through hoping that something would stand out and put his mind at ease.

Bethan was pregnant.

He leant back in his chair and put his hands behind his head.

Epworth is unlikely to be the father, he's not interested in girls. Suppose he's telling the truth and there was someone else in the shack that day. That someone could still be out there and trying to get to Gwen.

He closed the files and sighed. His eyes burned with tiredness and he could feel the onset of a headache. He switched off his computer and stopped to see the custody sergeant on the way out.

'Any problems?'

'No, your man is sleeping like a baby.'

'Good, the sooner he gets used to his new surroundings the better, because by the time I'm finished with him he is going to spend a very long time locked away.'

The custody sergeant grinned. 'That's what I like to hear, one less pervert on the streets.'

'See you in the morning.'

Meadows walked out into the night air. Only an empty house awaited him and he suddenly felt tired and lonely. *It would be nice if Gwen was at home waiting for me.* He felt a smile play on his lips. *Maybe one day.*

Chapter Twenty-five

Gwen awoke to the sun streaming through the window and casting a warm glow on the carpet. Matt was standing next to the bed staring down at her.

'Good morning.' He held out a cup of tea.

Gwen pulled herself upright and took the cup.

'Thanks, you're up early.'

'Yes, it's a beautiful day.'

Gwen sipped her tea, suspicious of Matt's good mood.

'I was thinking we should go out tonight to celebrate, the kids can go to your mother's. That way we can have the place to ourselves.' He perched on the edge of the bed and slipped his hand under the duvet.

'What are we celebrating?' Gwen wriggled away from his roaming hands.

'Epworth's arrest, of course. The whole village is buzzing. They took him in yesterday evening and he didn't come home. It's over, love.'

'I'll call Winter and see what is going on.'

Matt's lips curled. 'He won't be able to tell you anything that you don't already know.'

'No, I guess not.'

'Come on, I thought you wanted to have some closure? Well, now you know what happened that day.'

'Not everything, and I thought you didn't believe me. What was it you said? Oh yes, my head is completely fucked up.'

Matt reddened. 'I said I was sorry and I am trying to make an effort here. We can have a fresh start. You've no idea how hard it's been having this hang over my head for all these years.'

'Your head?'

'I mean over us, it's always been there. Now you can put it behind you.'

All of his affairs and unkind comments pricked at her mind. She tried to brush them off as she swung her legs out of bed.

'You're right, we should be celebrating, I'll give Mum a call, I'm sure the kids won't mind staying over.'

With a bit of luck he'll get so pissed he will fall asleep as soon as we get home, she thought.

Gwen showered, dressed, and made breakfast. As she sat eating toast in the kitchen Matt hovered nearby.

'Anywhere particular you want to go tonight?' he asked.

'No, you pick somewhere. Surprise me.' She tried to muster a smile.

'OK.' He took the frying pan out and poured in a generous amount of oil before setting it on the hob. 'I fancy a fry-up this morning.' He whistled as he took eggs and bacon from the fridge. 'Want some?'

'No, thanks. I'm going to take Blue up the river for a swim.'

'Good idea, no need for you to worry about being safe anymore. Right, I'll give the kids a shout, see if they want to join me for breakfast. It's about time the lazy buggers got out of bed.' He walked out of the kitchen and she heard him shout up the stairs.

Gwen gobbled down the rest of her toast then put a bottle of water into her bag before clipping on Blue's lead. She needed to get out of the house. Up on the mountain she welcomed the cool breeze ruffling her hair. The sky was cloudless and the mountain deserted, now alone she felt she had the space to let her thoughts free. Blue strained on the lead as soon as he saw the river. She let him go, and his tail swished through the air as he leapt into the water.

She let out a sigh as she settled on the bank. She wanted to feel different, like the weight of the past has been lifted but nothing had changed. She would only be completely free when she remembered the attack.

Doubts crept into her mind. What if Epworth didn't do it? What if I made a terrible mistake? she thought. She reached into her bag and felt for the panic alarm, then looked around. The mountain remained undisturbed. She tried to convince herself that Epworth was guilty. She had remembered him chasing her and the fear she felt as she hid behind the tree.

Blue scrambled onto the bank and shook his coat. Droplets of water landed on Gwen and soaked through her T-shirt, rousing her from her thoughts. She stood up, brushed the grass from her legs, and attached Blue to his lead. She walked slowly back into the village, she didn't feel like going home. Since Winter Meadows walked into the hospital that day she felt a change in her feelings towards Matt. Now she didn't know if she wanted to stay with him.

She walked past her home and headed to her mother's house. She found her mother lying on a lounger in the garden, a glass of juice in one hand and a book in the other.

'Hi, darling, what're you doing here?' Sue squinted through the sun.

'Just out walking Blue so I thought I would come and see you.'

'Let's go inside, it's getting hot out here.'

Sue poured a glass of juice and handed it to Gwen before filling a bowl of water and setting it on the floor. Blue gulped the water then lay down on the tiles, his head resting on his paws.

'I think you've worn him out,' Sue said.

'He's OK, he had a good swim in the river.'

'So where's Matt taking you tonight?'

'I don't know. To be honest I don't really feel like celebrating.'

'Well I can't say I blame you. To be honest the whole thing has left me feeling down. They were the worst days of my life and to think you went back to school and all the while he was there. He could have got to you anytime,' Sue said.

'It's not that, and I don't even remember the actual attack so there's a chance Epworth isn't guilty.'

'Well I'm sure the police must have something on him to have kept him at the station, maybe they matched his fingerprints to the scene.'

'Maybe.' Gwen picked up her juice and sipped.

'What's bothering you, love?'

'Why did you stay with Dad? It's obvious you love Uncle David.'

Sue shifted in her seat. 'Is that what's troubling you? Are you still upset about what happened between us?'

'No, honestly, Mum, I'm happy you have David, I think you deserve to be happy. I just want to know what went wrong between you and Dad.'

'Your father liked to have a good time and that didn't stop when we got married. He drank a lot and, well, I suppose, had a lot of lady friends. A bit like, erm, well, you get the picture.'

'You mean a bit like Matt?'

Sue blushed. 'Yes, I guess so, love. David was good to me and then something sparked between us. When I found out I was pregnant your father didn't question it, so

I let him think you were his. He was a good father even though he was a lousy husband.'

'Why didn't you leave him?'

'I couldn't, I had you. I used to think I would leave him when you were grown. Then he got sick and it wouldn't have been right for you to find out about David after your father died. It would've broken your heart.'

'I'm sorry, you must've been unhappy for a long time.'

'Are you unhappy?'

'Yes. I put up with Matt because I didn't think anyone else would want me, then there's the kids.'

'Oh, Gwenny.' Sue reached across the table and squeezed Gwen's hand. 'Can you not see how beautiful you are, even with your scars? I wish now I had the courage to speak up long ago. I so wanted to talk to you about Matt but felt like a hypocrite. He doesn't deserve you.'

'So you think I should leave him?'

'Only you can make that decision and you have to make it for yourself and nobody else. The children are old enough to understand. Ariana and Alex see the way Matt treats you, I don't think staying for their benefit is the answer.'

'Thanks, Mum. Maybe I'll get a chance to talk to him tonight.'

'Good, don't leave it too long. You're still young enough to start again.'

'It's not too late for you either, I think you and Uncle David deserve to be together. There's nothing to stop you now.'

'Perhaps, but I've denied him for so long I don't think he wants me in that way now.'

'Oh, I think you'll find he does! He's obviously crazy about you.' Gwen kissed her mother. 'Thanks for the chat. I'll call you tomorrow to let you know how this evening goes with Matt.'

* * *

After Ariana and Alex left the house to stay with their grandmother, Gwen washed her hair and picked out a mint green dress. She took her time getting ready, pinning up her hair and applying make-up. She checked her reflection in the bedroom mirror. The dress was pulled in at the waist and dropped to her ankles, covering the scars on her leg; her arms were bare so she took out a shawl and draped it around her shoulders. She smiled at her reflection.

Matt walked into the bedroom and slapped her playfully on the buttocks. 'You look nice.'

'Thank you.' She hadn't dressed for his benefit. Tonight she wanted to feel good about herself. 'Are you ready?'

'Yep.' Matt adjusted his tie in the mirror. 'Let's go.'

Matt had chosen an Italian restaurant in Swansea and ordered a taxi so they could both drink. Usually when they went out, which was a rarity, Gwen drove as Matt always complained about the taxi fares.

When they arrived at the restaurant Matt ordered a bottle of wine as soon as they were seated at the table, then picked up the menu.

Gwen glanced around the restaurant. Large murals depicting scenes from Italy decorated the walls. It would be nice to go there, she thought. An image of Meadows strolling through a vineyard entered her mind. The waiter appeared and poured the wine. Matt picked up the glass, sniffed, swirled the liquid, and took a sip before nodding his approval.

Gwen looked at the other diners. A young couple sat engrossed in each other while a group bantered as they ate their meal. She picked up the wine glass and drained it in one go. Nerves fizzled in her stomach. Now they were alone she didn't know how to bring up the subject of a separation.

'That's the spirit,' Matt said and refilled her glass.

They ordered their food and Gwen pulled her chair in closer to the table and leant forward so they wouldn't be overheard by the other diners.

'Are you happy?'

'What sort of question is that?' Matt's eyebrows furrowed.

'I mean with us.'

'Well, what do you think all this is about? I wouldn't be taking you out to dinner if I wasn't happy with you.'

'You must admit that things haven't been good between us for a while.'

'You haven't been easy to live with since all this business was brought back up, but things will be better now.'

'They weren't all that good before.' Gwen struggled to find the right words. She didn't want a scene at the restaurant so was reluctant to throw accusations about his affairs. Just now she would be happy to take the blame for their problems if it meant that she could get out of this loveless marriage.

'What are you getting at?' Matt's jaw clenched.

'I suppose I don't know why you married me in the first place. Was it out of pity?'

'No, of course not.' Matt sat back in his chair and folded his arms. 'Why are you doing this? I thought it'd be nice to go out but you seem intent on ruining the evening.'

'I'm sorry. I just want you to be honest with me.'

Matt drank his wine, refilled his glass, and called for the waiter to bring another bottle. Gwen waited for him to comment but he remained silent, she could feel the tension crackle in the air. The food arrived and she picked at the meat, pushing it around the plate. She didn't feel hungry and wished she had waited to talk to Matt at home.

'So how are things at work?' She forced a smile, hoping to soften his mood. It worked and he happily rambled on while she gave the occasional nod and smile. She let her mind wander, imagining what it would be like to be with Meadows. She felt the heat rise and spread through her body, tingling her skin. She squirmed in her chair and realised she hadn't been listening to Matt. She forced herself to concentrate. The conversation moved on to the children and Matt suggested they take a holiday once Alex had finished his exams.

'Are you ready to go?' Matt's face was flushed from the alcohol.

'Yes.' She drained the last of her wine as Matt called for the bill.

In the taxi his hands slid over her dress. She pushed him away, embarrassed in front of the driver.

'Wait until we get home,' Matt whispered in her ear.

The thought of sex with Matt made her skin crawl. I don't love him anymore, she thought. She leapt out of the taxi as soon as it pulled up outside of the house. Blue greeted her as she opened the front door.

'Hello, boy.' She put down her handbag and nuzzled his fur. 'I bet you want to go out.' She spun around when she heard Matt shut the door. 'I'm going to let him out.'

'Don't be too long.'

'Put the kettle on, please,' she called out as she headed for the back door. 'I fancy a cup of tea.'

She watched Blue dance around the garden. The night air seeped through her dress and she wrapped her shawl tightly around her shoulders. Blue sniffed at the shrubbery then bounded towards her. 'I thought you would stay out a bit longer,' she whispered. Reluctantly she walked back into the kitchen where Matt stood watching.

'I thought we would skip the tea. Come on, let's go to bed.'

'Yeah that's a good idea, I am quite tired now. It must be all that fresh air up the mountain today and the wine.' She faked a yawn.

Matt stepped forward and pulled her into his arms. 'That's OK, you can just lie there, and I'll do all the work.' He laughed as he pulled her closer, nuzzling her neck. His hands slipped down and grabbed her buttocks, squeezing hard.

Gwen squirmed. 'Not tonight, I told you I'm tired.'

'Don't be a spoilsport.' He tugged at the zip on her dress.

'Matt!' Gwen put her hands behind her back and struggled to pull his hands away. She felt her nails dig into his skin.

'Ouch, what did you do that for?' He pulled back his hand to inspect the skin.

'Sorry, I didn't mean to scratch you.' Gwen stared at the scratch on his hand and an image flashed before her eyes. Hands around Beth's throat, her fingernails clawing into the flesh. She shook her head, trying to clear her mind of the alcohol haze as she backed away from Matt.

'What is it?' he asked.

She bit her lip as she willed the image to return, closing her eyes and concentrating on the image of the hands...

Beth was struggling to breathe, her eyes bulged with terror as she tore at the hands squeezing her throat. He's going to kill her, she thought. Gwen flung open the door of the shack and threw herself at Beth. She dug her fingers beneath the hands and yanked.

'Let her go!' she screamed.

The hands let go of Beth's neck and Gwen spun around, coming face to face with Matt. His face was contorted with rage.

'What the fuck do you think you're doing?' Gwen shouted.

'Gwen, what's wrong with you?' Matt's voice chased away the image.

Gwen opened her eyes and gasped, she was back in the kitchen and Matt's hands were on her shoulders, shaking her body.

'You were there, you were strangling her.' Fear filled her chest and she could feel her heart beating wildly.

'What're you talking about?' Matt paled as his fingers dug into her shoulders.

'Get off me!' She shook him free and backed away. She needed to get to her handbag and hit the panic alarm, but she'd left it by the front door. She bolted through the kitchen door and into the hall, but before she reached her handbag, Matt caught her. He gripped her arm and spun her around, throwing her up against the wall.

'What the fuck's got into you?' he snarled.

'It was you! You killed Beth.'

'Listen to me, you don't know what you're talking about, you are confused.' He shook her violently.

Gwen struggled against his grip. Desperate, she lifted her leg and brought the heel of her shoe down hard on his foot.

'Argh! You stupid bitch!' Matt yelped. He slapped her hard, cracking her head against the wall. There was a growl and a flash of white as Blue leapt at Matt and sunk his teeth into his arm.

Matt howled and let go of Gwen as he tried to wrestle free from the dog, throwing punches with his free arm. Gwen heard Blue yelp as she reached for her bag.

'Call him off or I'll fucking kill him,' Matt shouted. Gwen turned and saw Matt smashing his fist into Blue's face.

'OK, stop hurting him. Blue, come here, it's OK, boy,' she coaxed.

Blue finally released Matt's arm but continued to bare his teeth. A low growl rumbled through his body and blood seeped into the fur around his mouth.

'It's OK,' she said, stroking his head.

'Put him outside.' Matt's arm was dripping blood, his eyes blazed. 'Do it or I'll get a knife and slit his fucking throat.'

Gwen coaxed Blue to the door. Tears blurred her vision as she opened the door and tried to coax the snarling dog outside.

She thought about making a run for it. She looked down at her shoes that were held in place by a thin strap around her ankle. There was no way she could outrun Matt. Her only chance was to get to the panic alarm.

'Don't even think about it,' Matt snarled as he stepped closer. He aimed a kick at Blue before pushing the door against him as he yanked Gwen inside. The sound of Blue's desperate howls came from the other side of the door.

Gwen dived for her handbag and put her hand inside, but Matt knocked her to the floor and grabbed a handful of her hair, snapping her head back.

'Going to call him, are you?' Matt ripped the bag from her hands, rummaged around inside and pulled out her mobile phone. He chucked the bag back at her and put the phone into his pocket.

'Why couldn't you leave it alone? I was afraid this would happen, in your fucked-up mind you only remember what you want to. You know I didn't kill Beth.'

Gwen managed to get her hand into her bag unnoticed. She felt around for the panic alarm and pressed the button. She had no idea how long it would take the police to respond. Her only option now was to keep him talking.

'I saw you, Matt.'

'You're confused. You saw Epworth kill Beth. If you go saying that you saw me strangle Beth, they'll put me away. Is that what you want? The kids will have no father and it'll all be your fault.' He bent over her and tugged at her arm. 'Come on, I think you need to calm down, take a few of your pills. You'll feel better in the morning.'

'No!' Gwen tried to wrestle free but he was too strong. He dragged her to the bottom of the stairs, she reached out and wrapped her arms around the banister.

'Please, Matt,' she begged.

'Just take your pills and forget about this. You haven't remembered everything, it's not what you think.'

Oh God, he's going to kill me. He'll make me swallow the bottle of pills and everyone will think I killed myself, she thought. She clung on tighter to the banister as Matt yanked at her arms. She could feel her muscles tearing as he pulled with all his weight. Her phone was ringing in Matt's pocket.

'That's the police trying to call me, if you don't let me answer they'll come to check on me,' she said.

'It's him, isn't it? You've been fucking him behind my back.' Matt grabbed a handful of her hair and yanked her head back. 'Do you think you can get rid of me? Have me put away so you can go running to him.'

'No,' Gwen whimpered.

'I'm not going to let that happen.' Matt drove her head into the banister.

Gwen put her hands to her head and curled into a ball. I need to hang on a bit longer, she thought as Matt aimed a kick at her ribs.

Chapter Twenty-six

Meadows leaned back in the armchair in his mother's sitting room and watched her pluck tobacco from a tin balanced on her knee.

'Were you about to go to bed?'

'No, love.' She rolled the tobacco up then licked the edge of the thin white paper. 'I don't often go to bed early these days, the pain keeps me awake so I stay up until I'm too tired to be bothered by it.' She lit up and inhaled deeply, blowing out a thick plume of smoke. 'So how come you're calling around at this time of night. Are you on duty?'

'Sort of, I've been waiting around all evening for some fingerprint results. I left Edris at the station. He didn't send them until late yesterday evening and it being the weekend, everything gets slowed down. It's not like London.'

'Is this to do with that Epworth man?' Distaste curled her lips.

'You know I'm not supposed to discuss cases.' Meadows smiled; he knew his mother was lonely and enjoyed discussing cases with him, anything he told her wouldn't go any further.

'Don't be daft, Winney, I'm your mother, besides everyone knows about it. And to think we left the safety of the commune and sent you to school with that pervert.'

Bloody Matt Thomas, I bet he's the one wagging his tongue.

'Rain was in the same class as some of the boys, do you think something could have happened to him?'

'Is that what's got you all worked up? Just because your brother is gay it doesn't mean that he would've let that man anywhere near him.'

'Yes, but he would've been vulnerable. You remember what he was like back then, he was so volatile, and that thing with Dad…'

Fern shifted in her chair and tucked a lock of hair behind her ear. 'It's just the way he was, he had a lot to deal with and people weren't so tolerant in those days. It must have been difficult for him and he had to hide his feelings. I'm sure he would've said something if that man tried anything.'

'I guess you're right. I can't help worrying about him.'

'You always were an overprotective brother. Anyway, Epworth will pay for what he's done so it isn't worth mentioning this to Rain. Are you going to charge him with the attack on Gwen and Bethan? There's been a lot of talk about that too. It's confusing for people. They don't know which crime he's been arrested for. Maybe you should make a statement.'

Meadows rolled his eyes. 'I can't make a statement in the middle of an investigation just to satisfy village gossips. We're still trying to trace the boys he may have interfered with. As for Gwen and Bethan, we have no physical evidence against him. That's why I am waiting to see if we get a match on his fingerprints and DNA.'

'You think he did it?'

'I don't know. It's odd, he admits to sending the threatening letter to Gwen but not cutting her brakes. I interviewed him again this morning, this time he had a solicitor. He still claims he lost Gwen in the quarry when he chased her and he hasn't wavered from his version. There's something I'm missing.'

'You have a gift for discerning the truth. Trust your instincts, it's never failed you before.'

'Perhaps, but I just can't think straight for some reason.'

'Oh, I think you know the reason. Maybe you don't want the investigation to come to an end.' Fern's eyes twinkled.

'Of course I do, why would you think that?'

'Because you won't have an excuse to see Gwen.'

Meadows sighed. 'There's that, but I won't let my feelings get in the way of my job. Anyway, who knows what will happen in the future? Besides, I don't know if I'm ready to start another relationship.'

'Nonsense. Don't be afraid to fall in love again. When this investigation is over, you go and tell Gwen how you feel. From what you tell me her husband is a right prick, she'd be a fool not to leave him and come to you.'

Meadows smiled. 'You certainly have a way with words.' His mobile phone trilled in his pocket. He took it out and saw Edris' name displayed. 'What have you got?'

'You better come in.' Edris' voice was tinged with excitement.

'I'm on my way.' He ended the call as he stood. 'I've got to go.' He bent over and placed a kiss on his mother's cheek. 'Stay away from the gossips.'

Meadows rushed to the station, where he found Edris hopping from foot to foot, a grin spread across his face.

'I take it you have good news for me.'

'Well, first I have to confess that I made a bit of a cock-up yesterday.'

'That's not what I was hoping to hear.'

'No, wait, it's good news.' Edris held up his hand. 'When you asked me to send off Epworth's fingerprints for analysis against the original crime scene, I sent off the lot.'

'The lot?'

'All the prints that I collected from the Thomas family for elimination, obviously Gwen's came back as a match but there was one other.' He pointed to the screen.

'Bloody hell.' Meadows felt his skin prickle. 'Are you sure, there's no mistake?'

'Yes, I double-checked. Matt Thomas' fingerprints are a match, and they were all over the shack.'

'I better warn Gwen.' Meadows took out his phone. He heard the dialling tone then it switched to voicemail. An uneasy feeling dropped like a stone in his stomach. 'We'll have to go up there, make sure everything is alright.'

'Maybe she's asleep, it's late.'

'I don't care. What if she had another flashback and remembered that Matt was at the shack? She could be in danger right now. If not then we'll bring him in anyway.'

They hurried down the stairs and were heading for the door when Folland called them back.

'I was just about to call you.' He walked towards Meadows. 'Gwen Thomas activated her panic alarm, I've sent a patrol car to check it out.'

'When did this happen?'

'Only a few minutes ago.'

Meadows ran for the car. He started the engine as Edris slid into the passenger seat and buckled his belt.

'Keep trying her number,' Meadows ordered as he swung the car out of the car park and accelerated. There was little traffic on the road but despite the speed he drove, he felt the precious minutes slipping away, minutes in which Gwen could be fighting for her life.

'Still no answer.' Edris took hold of the grab handle to stop himself sliding into Meadows as the car rounded a bend and the back wheel skidded on the road. As they turned onto Gwen's street they could see a police car outside her house, the blue lights illuminating the dark driveway.

'What are they waiting for?' Meadows yelled as he pulled up the car. Two uniformed officers hovered near the police car, one held a police radio to his mouth. Meadows jumped out of the car and ran towards the house.

'Sir, we can't get near the door,' the officer shouted. 'I've called for an animal control officer.'

Meadows swore under his breath as he saw Blue ramming his body against the door, emitting howls of distress.

'Blue! Come here, boy.' He approached the dog who growled and bared his teeth. 'It's OK.' He knelt down and offered his hand in a peaceful gesture. Blue stopped snarling and Meadows could see dried blood around his muzzle and down his chest; he couldn't tell if the dog was injured.

'Come on, boy, it's OK, no one's going to hurt you,' Meadows said as he slowly stood and approached Blue. The dog's tail hung between his legs and large blue eyes stared with distrust at Meadows. Meadows reached out and gently stroked Blue's head. 'Good boy, come on, let's go and find her.' He reached for the door handle and turned, and the door sprang open. Blue rushed past him and bounded up the stairs.

Meadows could hear screams as he followed Blue, he shouted for Edris as he rushed up the stairs. Ahead he saw Blue crash through the bedroom door, he caught a glimpse of Matt straddling Gwen, his hand forcing her mouth open. Blue leapt on to Matt, knocking him off balance, and Gwen tried to scramble away.

Matt struggled against the weight of the dog, grabbed Gwen's ankles, and pulled her towards him. Meadows lurched forward, grabbed Matt, and yanked him clear of Gwen. Matt scrambled to his feet, his eyes wild. He pulled back his arm and drove his fist into Meadows' face.

Meadows felt the impact as his head reeled back with a crack. Matt took another swing but Meadows was ready;

he ducked sideways and grabbed Matt's wrist before twisting his arm behind his back and forcing him against the wall.

'Edris, look for the kids,' Meadows shouted.

'They're with my mother,' Gwen croaked. She was still on the floor and her body trembled violently.

'Get off me.' Matt struggled. 'You have no right breaking into my house and attacking me.'

'We received a distress call from your wife. You didn't know she carried a panic alarm, did you?' Meadows said. He could feel the adrenalin pumping through his body and struggled against the urge to smash his fists into Matt. Edris handed him the cuffs and he clamped them onto Matt's wrists before spinning him around. 'Don't move.' He turned to Edris. 'You'd better call for an ambulance.'

Blue stood in front of Matt, his hackles raised and teeth bared. 'Good boy.' Meadows patted the dog before turning to kneel beside Gwen. His eyes studied her face. Her lip was split and blood trickled down the side of her mouth; her hair was a wild tangle and imprints from Matt's fingers could be seen on her face where he'd tried to hold her still. His eyes travelled down her body; her dress was torn and spattered with blood, and one shoe was missing. Pills dotted the floor around where she sat.

'Are you OK?' He touched her arm gently.

'Yes, I think so.' Her voice trembled and tears leaked from her eyes.

'Just stay where you are, an ambulance is on its way.'

'I don't want to go to hospital, I'm not hurt.'

'Well, let's just get you checked out.'

'I'm the one who's fucking hurt,' Matt bellowed as he lunged towards Meadows.

Edris stuck out his foot and Matt crashed to the ground, landing with a grunt.

'Oops,' Edris said with a smirk.

'I told you not to move,' Meadows said.

'Bastards!' Matt wriggled on the floor.

Meadows turned and saw the two uniformed officers stood in the bedroom doorway. 'Get him out of here. You better get his arm checked out, then lock him up.'

'What for? This is between me and Gwen.' Matt was hauled to his feet.

Meadows stood and moved within inches of Matt's face. 'Matthew Thomas, I am arresting you on suspicion of the murder of Bethan Hopkins and the attempted murder of Gwen Collier on the 20th of June, 1999.'

'What? No! Gwen, tell them it isn't true.'

Gwen shook her head, tears tracking down her face.

'I am also arresting you for the attempted murder of your wife, for tampering with the brakes on her car with intent to cause injury or death.'

Matt screamed and shouted abuse as he was led away. The paramedics arrived and checked Gwen as Blue sat at her side, his head resting on her lap. She refused to go in the ambulance and they were satisfied that her injuries were only superficial. Then she sat on the bed and watched as Meadows snapped on latex gloves and collected the pills that had spilt from the bottle.

'Tranquilizers, did he really think he'd get away with forcing you to take these?' Meadows shook his head.

'He said he wanted me to forget.'

'I'm sorry, Gwen, I didn't suspect Matt.'

'It's OK, you had no reason to think he was involved. I married him and I didn't have a clue. Why do you think he did that? I mean, marry me?'

'I don't know. I suspect he wanted to be close in case you remembered.'

'So he could keep me quiet.' Gwen wrapped her arms around her body.

'Come on, Edris should have made a cup of tea by now.'

'Just give me a few moments.'

Meadows found Edris in the kitchen. 'See if you can find some brandy to put into that tea. She's still shaken up, I wish she would go to the hospital.'

They sat in the sitting room, Gwen wrapped in a fluffy towelling robe on the sofa with Blue sat at her side. Edris and Meadows took the armchairs.

'Is there someone who can come and stay with you?' Meadows asked. 'I don't think you should be alone.'

'No, there isn't anyone. I don't want to alarm my mother or the kids.' She cradled her cup, her hands trembling. 'I'll be OK, honest. I'll call my mother in the morning. I want to take Blue to the vet to make sure he's OK. He tried so hard to help me. Matt kept punching him but he didn't let go.' She sank her hand into the dog's fur. 'Matt threatened to kill him if I didn't put him outside. Poor Blue, he didn't understand what was going on and why I put him outside. I could hear him howling and bashing the door.'

'He's quite the hero,' Meadows said. 'Do you feel up to telling us what happened tonight?'

'I remembered Matt strangling Beth. I went into the shack and pulled his hands away. I should have kept quiet about what I remembered but I guess I was so shocked I wasn't thinking straight. Then I tried to get to the panic alarm, I'd left it in my bag by the front door. Matt came after me, that's when Blue bit him.'

'What else do you remember about being in the shack?'

'Nothing after that.'

'Did Matt say why he had attacked Bethan?'

'No, he denied killing her. He wanted me to take the pills, said I needed to calm down. I think he was going to get me to take an overdose.' She wiped away her tears with the back of her hand.

'OK, I think it's best you try to get some rest now. We'll take a formal statement from you tomorrow, there's no hurry. You can come to the station when you're feeling better.'

'What will happen to Matt?'

'We'll question him in the morning, we've already matched his fingerprints to the ones taken from the shack. I'm fairly certain we have enough to charge him.'

'So you will keep him at the station. You won't let him out, will you?'

'No, once he's charged he'll have to appear in court, and we will recommend that he is not granted bail. It's likely he will be remanded in custody until the trial. Try not to worry, you're safe now.'

'Thank you.'

Meadows stood up. He felt reluctant to leave Gwen on her own, and if it hadn't been for Edris he would have stayed with her. 'I'll see you tomorrow.'

He dropped Edris at home before returning to the cottage. He sat in the darkness, his body felt heavy and his jaw ached from where Matt had hit him, but his mind was still turning over the events of the evening and he wanted to calm his thoughts before going to bed.

He let his imagination wander and felt his body relax and his eyes grew heavy as images of Gwen filled his mind.

Chapter Twenty-seven

Meadows awoke feeling cold and stiff. He checked his watch; he had only slept for a couple of hours in the chair but his neck was sore and he groaned as he stood and stretched. In the shower he turned up the heat and let the jets of water ease his aching muscles. He felt tempted to let Matt stew in the cell for the day but was eager to face him. There were still questions that needed answering and on top of that he still had to deal with Epworth.

He took his time dressing and drank a strong black coffee before leaving the house. The caffeine awakened his senses and by the time he reached the station he felt alert.

Blackwell looked up from his desk when Meadows walked in. 'You've been a busy boy, two suspects in custody. Having a few problems making up your mind who did it?' He chuckled.

'No, I actually solved two crimes at the same time, not a bad week's work. There's plenty to do on the Epworth case, you can give Edris a hand if you're bored.'

Blackwell scowled and turned his head away.

'Paskin, can I have a word?' Meadows called across the office.

A pretty, slim brunette walked over to his desk, a pleasant smile on her face. 'What can I do for you, sir?'

'Gwen Thomas is coming in to make a statement today. I have a feeling I'll be tied up in interviews most of the day and I think it would be good to have a woman officer take her statement.'

'OK.'

'Good, I'll get Folland to let you know when she comes in.'

Edris walked into the office yawning. He smiled at Meadows.

'Good time last night, was it?' Blackwell sniggered. Edris ignored him and walked up to Meadows' desk.

'Sorry I'm late.'

'That's OK, I didn't expect you in until later. You're owed a fair amount of overtime.'

'No problem, I'll take a few days off when we've tied up all the loose ends. You were right about Epworth, he didn't do it and I was all ready to charge him.'

'We'll still be charging him, just with a different crime. You've done well, if it wasn't for you we wouldn't have had the match with Matt's fingerprints and we could've been looking at another murder this morning.'

'Well, I doubt Matt Thomas is going to be too happy about that. He didn't want to give his prints in the first place, and I had to assure him that they were only for elimination purposes.'

'Well, they were,' Meadows said. 'Give me an hour to update the case notes and email Lester, then we'll interview Matt. He should have had enough time to cool off.'

When Meadows and Edris entered the interview room they found Matt sat next to the duty solicitor, a slender man in a dark double-breasted suit. His face displayed displeasure, and Meadows assumed that he wasn't too pleased to be sat in the police station instead of at home eating his Sunday roast.

Meadows took a seat and surveyed Matt. His bandaged arm poked out from beneath a sling, his clothes were rumpled, and stubble covered his chin. He stared at Meadows with dark circled eyes.

Well, he can hardly call his wife to bring him a change of clothes. He recited the time and date together with the names of those present for the benefit of the recorder before conjuring a pleasant smile.

'How is your arm?'

'How do you think it is?' Matt scowled. 'I have five stitches, not to mention the damage you did when you cuffed me.'

'We had no option but to restrain you. I'm sure if you want to make a formal complaint your solicitor will help you with the procedure.'

'You're damn right I want to make a formal complaint. You've been screwing my wife and the two of you have concocted a story to set me up.'

Meadows felt his temper flare. 'I can assure you my relationship with your wife has been strictly professional, so unless you have any evidence to the contrary I suggest you refrain from making such wild allegations.' Meadows opened a file and took out a copy of the fingerprint analysis.

'Would you like to explain how your fingerprints came to be all over the crime scene?'

'I don't know what you're talking about.'

'I'm talking about the shack where the body of Bethan Hopkins was discovered.'

Matt leaned in close to the solicitor and whispered.

'My client was under the impression that he consented to his fingerprints being taken for the purpose of elimination from his wife's car.'

'Yes, that is correct. However, all the fingerprints taken during the course of this investigation were automatically checked against the original crime scene.'

Meadows glimpsed Edris shift in his seat before returning his attention to the solicitor. 'Whatever the reason the prints were taken for doesn't detract from the fact that they were a match to those found at the crime scene. We also took DNA samples from your client last night, and we are awaiting the results. Scrapings were taken from under Bethan Hopkins' fingernails. Gwen Thomas states she saw your client strangle Bethan and she scratched at his hands whilst fighting for her life.' He paused and watched Matt's face pale. 'It's only a matter of time before we get the results back, that together with the fingerprints places your client in the shack on the day of the murder.'

'You bastard, you're enjoying this,' Matt hissed.

Meadows ignored the comment. 'What was the nature of your relationship with Bethan?'

'As you well know we went to school together.'

'Were you having a sexual relationship with her?'

'No.'

'Did you know that Bethan was pregnant at the time of her murder? The DNA test will show if you were the father.' Meadows leaned across the table. 'Why prolong this, don't you think it's time Bethan's mother knew the truth? And what about Gwen?'

'Don't talk to me about Gwen!'

'Just tell us what happened, Matt. It's over, there's no point in lying.'

Meadows placed a picture of Bethan on the table and pushed it towards Matt; he saw the solicitor take a peek and turn away in disgust. 'See the bruises around her neck? Details of these were not revealed to the press. How would Gwen know about these marks if she didn't see you do it?'

'Alright, yes, I was having sex with Bethan. We'd been seeing each other for a few months, but I didn't kill her.'

'You were with Bethan that day?'

227

'I saw her on the Friday night. We didn't talk for long, and she was in a funny mood. She told me to meet her at the shack on Saturday afternoon. I was supposed to be watching the game that day, I'd injured my knee so I couldn't play. I thought I'd be on for a bit of fun, so I decided to bail on the game and go to the shack. It started to rain and I was soaked when I got there, she was waiting inside.'

'You had sex?'

'Yes. Afterwards she told me she was pregnant and asked what I was going to do about it. I told her I didn't believe it was mine. You know what she was like, she'd screwed her way through half of the rugby team. She started getting hysterical, screaming that I'd ruined her life and I had to go with her to tell her parents. I freaked, her dad was really strict and I wasn't about to be saddled with a baby. I told her she could do what she wanted but she wasn't going to ruin my life. I called her a slut. She started hitting me and trying to scratch my face. I lost it for a minute, I put my hands around her throat. I wouldn't have killed her, I was just trying to frighten her, get her to back off. She clawed at my hands and drew blood. Gwen came in at that moment, she yanked my hands away as she screamed at me. Then I left.'

'You left? Just walked away?'

'Yes.'

'Well, excuse me if I find that a little hard to believe.' Meadows pushed the photograph of Bethan closer to Matt. He took another photograph and placed it on the table; it showed Gwen lying at the bottom of the ravine.

'Look again, Matt, is that what you call frightening someone? I'm sure those girls were terrified. The bruises on Bethan's throat show your intent. I think if Gwen hadn't come into the shack you would've kept squeezing until you killed her.'

'No!' Matt turned his head away from the photos. 'I was angry. I didn't mean to hurt her and I certainly didn't kill her. They were both alive when I left the shack.' Matt rubbed his hands over his face. 'What sort of animal do you think I am?'

The worst kind. Meadows sat back in his seat. 'I get that you were angry. You were young, just having some fun, and there's Bethan telling you she's pregnant and expecting you to take responsibility. What really happened? Did you hit Gwen? We know she sustained a head injury from the tools hanging on the wall, did she fall backwards? There must've been a lot of blood. Then Bethan started screaming, you had to keep her quiet. You panicked, it's understandable.'

'No! No! For fuck's sake, I told you, they were both alive when I left them. Don't you think someone would've noticed if I was walking around the village covered in blood?'

'You could've easily cleaned yourself in the stream, got rid of your clothes when you got home. It's not like we can search your home for the clothes you were wearing that day.'

Matt's face twisted with anger. 'You're trying to set me up. You know that Epworth was after Gwen that day, you have him locked up. He must have found the girls after I left.'

'Funny how there's no trace of Epworth in the shack yet your prints are all over the scene. You admit to getting Bethan pregnant and putting your hands around her throat. It doesn't look good.'

'I've already explained all that, I was there so of course my bloody fingerprints are going to be all over the shack, that doesn't mean I killed Bethan.'

'You went to great lengths to hide the fact you'd been there that day, even persuading your friends to withhold information about Sam Morris.'

Matt shuffled in his seat. 'I shouldn't have done that but I was afraid. If anyone knew I was there I would've been accused of Bethan's murder, no one would believe that I didn't kill her. I thought if Sam Morris was the main suspect there would be no questions asked.'

'So you were willing for an innocent man to go to prison in your place?'

'No, I didn't know about Epworth back then. Sam was with Gwen that day so he could've done it. Look, I was young and scared. What would you have done?'

'You could have come forward and given the police the information.'

'Yeah and get sent down for something I didn't do.'

'So you stayed around and married Gwen. Why did you do that?'

Matt scowled. 'So you couldn't have her.'

Meadows laughed. 'Do you expect me to believe that?'

'Yeah, well, that was a bonus. At first I wanted to stay close to her, see if her memory started to come back. I did fall in love with her despite the scars. Do you think I would have stayed with her all this time if I didn't love her?'

'Yet a week ago you tried to kill her by cutting the brakes on her car.'

'No, I just wanted to frighten her.'

The solicitor put a warning hand on Matt's arm and whispered in his ear.

'I think it's a little late for a "no comment" stand.' Meadows glared at the solicitor. 'You cut the brakes to keep her quiet, you knew she was close to remembering what happened that day.'

'I just wanted her to stop with the investigation. She was supposed to go swimming, she should never have been driving down Turnpike Road. If she had gone the way she was supposed to she wouldn't have been in any danger. There are no hills in that direction.'

'It didn't work, though. She still remembered you strangling Bethan so you had to try again to silence her. This time with a bottle of pills.'

'No, this is what I was afraid of all along, that she would only remember part of what happened and jump to the wrong conclusion. I couldn't let her run to you. I wanted her to take a couple of pills so she would calm down and I could reason with her. I wanted her to wait until she remembered everything but she became hysterical. I wasn't trying to kill her.'

The solicitor looked at his watch and sighed. 'Are you going to charge my client? So far all you have is fingerprints from a twenty-year-old crime scene for which he has given a reasonable explanation.'

'Missing out on your Sunday dinner, are you? As you are aware, I can hold your client for another twenty-four hours before I charge him. I'll await the results from the DNA analysis but this is just a formality. Meanwhile your client can take some time to consider his position.'

'Oh, fuck off, you pompous dickhead.' Matt stood abruptly, knocking his chair to the floor.

Edris stepped forward poised to restrain him.

'You're going to look like a right prick when the truth comes out,' Matt snarled.

* * *

Matt was led back to the cell as Edris and Meadows headed for the canteen. Most of the officers working the weekend had already eaten so they had a choice of tables. They each picked up a tray of food and sat at the back of the room where they wouldn't be overheard by the staff.

'Do you think it's possible that Epworth could have come across the girls after Matt left?' Edris asked as he forked a potato.

'Don't go there.' Meadows sighed. 'I think it's unlikely but Matt could use it in his defence. It'll cast doubt on the case even though there is no evidence of Epworth having been in the shack. The best chance we have is that Gwen remembers the actual attack.'

'Do you think she will?'

'She's close, it's just a matter of how long it will take. In the meantime I think we should charge Epworth with sexual assault. That will keep him locked up for a while. When the press get hold of it I doubt even he would want to apply for bail. We have Matt on attempted murder, he admitted cutting the brakes. Let's give it another day to see what develops, I would rather be charging him with murder. We'll interview him again in the morning, see if he wants to change his story.'

Paskin had left the office for the day by the time Edris and Meadows returned to their desks but she had left a copy of Gwen's statement. Meadows read through it and handed it to Edris.

'It doesn't tell us anything that we don't already know.' Edris placed the statement on Meadows' desk.

'I didn't expect to see anything new but from this it's quite clear that she thought Matt intended to kill her.' He plonked himself down in his chair. 'You get off home, you've had a long weekend. Have a good rest and I'll see you in the morning.'

'What about you?'

'I won't stay much longer, I just want to update the files.'

'OK, I'll see you tomorrow.' Edris put on his jacket and left Meadows at his desk.

Meadows sighed as his fingers flew over the keyboard. He was glad to be alone; he wanted time to think without Edris' input, which only seemed to complicate the case. The euphoria he usually felt when a case was solved and the perpetrator in custody was missing. Doubts niggled his mind like gnats on a warm summer's evening; no matter how many times you swatted them away, they came back to nip at your skin.

When he arrived home, he moved his stereo to the bedroom he slept in as a teenager. There was a single bed pushed up against the wall, covered with a green blanket. He had stripped off the old wallpaper but when he turned on the music and lay on the bed he could picture it as it had been. The sounds of Black Sabbath filled the room and vibrated through his body, he closed his eyes and let his mind drift back in time...

The bus pulled up in front of the school gates and Winter jumped off with Rain, hoping to get ahead of the crowd. Matt soon caught up to them and shoved him in the back.

'Oops, I didn't see you.' The group of boys around him laughed.

'Fuck off.' Rain clenched his fists.

'What did you say?' Matt grabbed the front of Rain's jumper and twisted it as he pulled him close. 'I think you need to learn some manners, hippy boy.'

'Leave him alone.' Winter grabbed Matt's wrist and yanked his hand free of Rain's jumper.

Bethan sidled up to the group. 'I love the smell of angry boys in the morning.' She winked at Matt. 'I hope you're going to take your shirt off before you fight.'

Winter caught sight of Gwen, her eyes narrowed at Bethan. 'Come on, we'll be late for reg.' She stepped forward, positioning herself between Matt and Winter and tugged on Bethan's arm. 'You two should go.' She looked from Rain to Winter. 'Epworth is looking out of the window.'

'Come on.' Winter turned to Rain and they walked away. He could hear the girls talking as they walked behind.

'You're such a spoilsport,' Bethan whined. 'I think you have a thing for Hippy Winter. You should ask him out, I bet he fucks like a wild boar. Yeah, a dirty beast, do you think they wash?'

'Shut up,' Gwen said. 'You can be a real bitch sometimes.'

Meadows opened his eyes. He could still feel the humiliation of that day, hear Bethan's words burn his skin.

I wonder how many people she pissed off. She had a reputation with the boys. What if the DNA test results come back negative? Anyone could be the father of her baby. Meadows sat up and rubbed his hands through his hair. *It doesn't matter, Matt's prints are still a match and there's little doubt that the scrapings under Bethan's fingernail will be a match.* He tried to shrug off the feelings of doubt that unsettled his stomach and set his nerves tingling. *I have the right man.*

Chapter Twenty-eight

Meadows was dreaming. His body thrashing and twisting the sheets as images of Matt strangling Bethan tormented his mind. Bethan's face morphed into Gwen and Matt laughed as she struggled to breathe. Meadows pulled on Matt's arm, his fingers digging into the flesh.

'What do you think you're doing? I was trying to stop her,' Matt shouted.

Gwen ran from the shack and Meadows chased her. 'Stop!' he yelled but no sound came from his mouth.

Gwen turned and looked at him. 'You were supposed to help me.' She turned away and leapt off the edge of the ravine.

'No!' Meadows woke himself shouting. Perspiration covered his body and his tongue was dry and swollen. He took a sip of water from the glass on the bedside table then lay staring up at the ceiling waiting for his heartbeat to slow.

He jumped out of bed, showered, and dressed before heading for the station. It was still early so he had the luxury of sitting at his desk alone. Fragments from his dream kept intruding on his thoughts.

I'm sure I'm missing something.

He picked up the photographs and flicked through them until he came to the one of Gwen lying at the bottom of the ravine, her hand trailing in the water.

There were no scrapings under her nails. They could have been washed away by the water but surely she would have fought with both hands. Bruising to her cheek but that could have come from the fall.

'You're in early.'

Meadows looked up from the photograph and saw Edris standing at his side. 'So are you,' he said.

'Yeah, I wanted to have a head start as well as being here when the DNA results come in. Have you found anything of interest?' Edris indicated the photo.

'Not sure. According to the reports, Bethan had blood from Gwen on her clothing, hair, and hands as well as the unknown DNA under her fingernails. From that we can assume that she was still alive when Gwen was thrown up against the wall.'

'Unless she went to Bethan after she hit her head to try to help her.'

'Then you would only see a splatter of blood, this is more widespread. Gwen's blood was also found on the floor but the only DNA found on Gwen was Bethan's and Sam Morris', which came from the coat she was wearing. Here, take a look at the footprint.' Meadows handed Edris a photo.

Edris scrutinised the photo. 'What am I looking at?'

'There are clear prints outside the shack. The unidentified print is the right size for Matt, only we have no chance of matching it to his shoes. It doesn't matter as he admits to being there. Bethan was in the shack before it started raining.'

'What are you getting at?'

'I don't know.' Meadows sighed. 'Gwen would also have tried to grab the attacker to save herself but there were no DNA samples under her nails.'

'She could have grabbed onto clothing, or been unconscious and was thrown over.'

'She went over backwards.'

'So what do you think happened?'

'I don't know but something doesn't add up. If you take Epworth and Matt out of the picture, what are you left with?'

'You think Matt Thomas is telling the truth?'

'It's a possibility.' The scenario running through Meadows' mind made him feel nauseous. He didn't want to share it with Edris, didn't want to make it real. 'I'm going to see Gwen. If the DNA results come back, give me a call.' He stood and glanced one more time at the photograph before leaving the station.

He drove slowly. Now that he had Matt in custody he didn't know how he would react when he saw Gwen, didn't know if he had the strength to fight his feelings.

I have to keep it professional at least until the trial is over.

Beneath these feelings lay an anxiety that gnawed at his stomach, a feeling of foreboding that he couldn't shake.

He pulled up in front of Gwen's house, expecting her to appear at the door. The door remained closed. He waited a few moments to clear his mind before getting out of the car and knocking on the door. Images of Blue, blood covering his mouth, filled his mind as he remembered the last time he had been in the house.

There was no answer to his knocking so he walked around the back and peered through the window. The house was quiet with no sign of Gwen or Blue.

Probably out walking.

He drove to the quarry; he had a sense that she would be at the shack trying to slot together the last pieces missing from her memory.

He got out of the car and put on his jacket. There was a gentle breeze blowing the fluffy clouds across the sky, they covered the sun blocking out the warmth. He walked through the gates, part of him expecting to see Gwen sat on the bank watching Blue splash around in the water. There was no one there, the water tumbled over the rocks and the breeze rustled the trees filling the silence. He walked further in, the eerie atmosphere making him quicken his pace as pieces of the puzzle slotted together and the scene played through his mind.

It would be better if she doesn't remember. I don't want to do this.

Icy fear coiled around his body as he reached the steps and hurried on.

* * *

Gwen stood outside the barn with her eyes shut as she tried to will the memories to surface. All she could see was the look of horror on her children's faces as she sat them down to explain why their father had been arrested. She felt she owed it to them to remember. She had to be sure it was Matt. There is only one piece of the puzzle missing.

She opened her eyes and stepped into the barn, Blue followed at her heels. An image of Epworth and Carl Perkins danced before her eyes. The shock on Epworth's face, then the anger. She took a deep breath and left the barn. I was running from Epworth, she thought. She retraced her footsteps to the place where she fell and felt the pain in her wrist from the memory. She had been so very angry, Uncle David's revelation, Bethan lying about being ill. She clenched her fist as she walked towards the quarry. She could feel the fear and anger rising in her body.

She entered the quarry and stopped next to the trees that had shielded her from Epworth. She hadn't known what to do. Epworth had gone back to the mountain so it wasn't safe to go that way. She couldn't go home and face her mum and Uncle David. Epworth could have walked back to the village and be waiting at the gate to the footpath. As she continued along the path, the memories became vivid until she was no longer observing from a distance but reliving each moment...

She could see the shack up ahead. I can hide out there for a while, she thought. Her wrist throbbed, making her feel nauseous. She cradled it in her arm and looked down, she could see the swelling spreading to her hand. As she neared the shack she heard raised voices. She crept to the door and peered through the gap. Matt stood rigid, his face flushed and fists clenched at his side.

'Please, Matt, I'm scared,' Beth was saying.

Gwen forgot the pain in her wrist and pressed her face against the gap.

'This is nothing to do with me. Do you think I'm going to let a little slut like you ruin my life?' Matt sneered. 'You've screwed most of the rugby team so the baby could be from any one of them.'

Gwen gasped. Baby? No, Beth would've told her. Her confusion gave way to anger. She'd been with Matt. The bitch.

A crack rent the air as Beth's hand collided with Matt's cheek. 'Don't think you are going to get away with dumping me now. I'm going to tell my father you got me drunk and took advantage of me.' Beth's face contorted with rage as she lunged at Matt and pummelled him with her fists.

'Get off me, you crazy bitch!' Matt tried to fend off her blows as she continued to punch and kick. He put his hands around her throat and squeezed until she stopped fighting.

Gwen was mesmerized as she watched Beth crawling at Matt's hands as she struggled to breathe, her eyes bulging. He's actually going to kill her, she thought. She flung open the door and grabbed Matt's wrist.

'Let her go!' she screeched at Matt.

Matt looked stunned. Gwen wasn't sure if it was from her sudden appearance or that he realised what he was doing but he dropped his hands to his side.

Gwen looked at Beth, who was bent double gasping for breath, her body shaking violently.

'What the fuck do you think you're doing?' Gwen turned on Matt.

Matt looked from Beth to Gwen. 'I should've known you wouldn't be far away, you're just like her. Pair of scheming bitches.' He turned and stormed out of the shack.

Beth's breathing returned to normal. She straightened up and smiled as she rubbed her throat. 'It's just as well you came in. Were you following me?'

Gwen couldn't believe that Beth was acting like nothing had happened and she'd been shagging Matt behind her back. Gwen felt the anger burn through her body.

'Bastard!' Beth ran her fingers through her hair. 'We'll get him. I'll tell my father he raped me and that I was too ashamed to tell anyone. I'll say I went to your house after and you helped me, gave me fresh clothes. Are you listening to me?'

'No, you're off your fucking head. I'm not lying for you.'

'Some friend you are.'

'Friend!' Gwen felt her body tremble with fury. 'You've been screwing Matt! He's supposed to be mine. You're a selfish bitch, you don't care who you hurt to get your own way. You've never been my friend, you just used me.'

'Is that what you're upset about?' Beth laughed. 'You've been dreaming after Matt for the past two years. If you would've been less of a prude and opened your legs maybe he would have been interested. Anyway, I thought you were after dirty Hippy Winter.'

'Don't call him that. If anyone's dirty, it's you. You're nothing but a filthy whore!'

'So you do like him.' Beth stepped closer. 'My father says we shouldn't let his family live in the village. He says it'll encourage more to come. Dirty hippies running wild, stealing. Is that what turns you on, a bit of rough?'

Gwen drew her hand back and slapped Beth hard across the face. She felt the sting on the palm of her hand.

'Bitch!' Beth lunged at Gwen and shoved her up against the wall.

Gwen felt a sickening thud as the back of her head impacted the axe hanging from the wall. She put her hand to her head. She could feel a gash and her stomach lurched. 'Look what you've done!' She showed her blood-covered hand to Beth.

'Serves you right, you hit me first.' Beth's laughter filled the shack.

Gwen felt the blood drip onto her neck and fought against the dizziness. Uncle David, Epworth, Beth, she hated them all. She threw her body against Beth, knocking her to the floor.

Beth rolled over until she straddled Gwen. She gripped a handful of her hair and repeatedly smashed her head against the floor. Gwen put her hands up and tried to scratch at Beth's eyes but Beth grabbed her injured wrist and began to twist.

Gwen yelped and felt around the floor with her free hand. When her hand met with a stone she grabbed it and with all her strength brought it crashing against Beth's head. Beth's grip loosened on her wrist and she toppled over. Gwen twisted her body until she was leaning over Beth.

'I hate you!' She smashed the stone against Beth's head again and again.

There was silence in the shack; Beth lay still with her eyes staring.

'Beth?' Gwen shook her. 'Beth, oh no, Beth, say something!' Gwen got to her feet and looked down at Beth. Her skirt was bunched up, revealing her thighs, while her top was smeared with blood. She felt bile rise in her throat as she saw the blood leaking from Beth's head and soaking into the ground.

I need to get some help, she thought. She backed out of the shack and onto the path, she couldn't tear her eyes away from Beth's lifeless figure. She could feel her body shake as she continued to back away. Her vision blurred as dizziness overwhelmed her. She felt her foot slip, and her body tilted backwards; the stone she held in her hand fell from her grasp and clattered against the cliff face before falling into the depths below.

I'm going to die, she thought. She could see the leaden grey clouds drifting across the sky as drops of rain fell on her face. There was no sound other than her heartbeat ringing in her ears as adrenalin pumped through her body, kicking her brain into survival mode. She flailed her arms, trying to grasp at anything that would stop her falling, but only air swished through her fingers.

Time slowed as gravity pulled her down; she was falling, the air whistling through her hair. Fear froze her thoughts. She closed her eyes and waited for the impact.

* * *

As Meadows approached the shack he saw Gwen standing by the railing staring down into the ravine. Blue lay at her feet.

'Gwen.'

She turned and stared at him as if he was an apparition.

Pain filled her eyes. Blue stood up and wagged his tail.

'I came up here because I wanted to remember everything that happened that day. For once I wasn't afraid.' Her voice was distant, she appeared to be lost between the past and present. 'It must have only taken a few seconds for me to fall over yet it seemed like a lifetime.'

'Do you remember what happened?' Meadows stepped closer.

'Yes.' She shrank back from him. 'You know, don't you?'

'There was only one set of footprints at the edge of the ravine. Yours. Your blood was in Bethan's hair and over her clothes as well as the floor. I've heard enough about Bethan over the last few weeks to know that she could be thoughtless and selfish. Then there was Matt, he was supposed to be yours. Everyone has a breaking point, a moment of madness. First you find out that your uncle is your father, then seeing Epworth with Carl Perkins, and to top it off Bethan is with Matt. You must've been in a lot of pain from your broken wrist.' He wanted to give her an out, some sort of justification.

'I was so angry that day, it felt like everything had gone wrong and my world was tumbling down and crushing me. I killed her. There's no excuse for what I did. I'm so sorry.' She sank to her knees and buried her face in Blue's fur. 'I honestly didn't remember. All these years I have been afraid that there was someone out there responsible and the only person I should've been afraid of is myself.' Sobs shook her body as she clung onto the dog.

Meadows knelt down beside her and placed his hand gently on her shoulder. He wanted to offer some comfort, tell her that everything would be OK, but he knew it would be pointless, just empty words. It wasn't OK and he was going to have to take her to the station and charge her with murder.

'Come on.' He pulled her gently to her feet.

She stood facing him. 'How could I have done such a thing? What's going to happen to me? What about my children?'

Meadows pulled her into his arms and stroked her hair as she clung to him.

'I'm so sorry, Gwen.'

She looked up at him, her eyes searching his. She placed her hand against his face and he didn't resist when she placed her lips on his mouth. He felt the warmth of her mouth, tasted the salt of her tears as he allowed himself this moment when nothing mattered but the two of them and what might have been. Reluctantly he pulled away, took her hands from around his neck, and held them for a moment before letting go.

'Please let me take Blue to my mother and let me explain to her, I want her to hear it from me.'

They walked back to the village in silence. Sue Collier's welcoming smile soon disappeared when she saw the devastation on her daughter's face. Meadows stood in the kitchen while Gwen sat her mother down in the sitting room and knelt at her side. He observed them through the doorway, listening as Gwen went through the events of that day. He saw Sue crumple and Gwen fold her mother in her arms. He felt like crying watching the two of them.

I could walk away, she's not a danger to anyone else, but then Matt would likely go to prison for murder. Can I live with that?

As much as he disliked Matt Thomas, his conscience won over. He stepped into the sitting room. Gwen looked up and nodded.

'Mum, I have to go now.' She untangled her arms from her mother's grasp and stood up. 'Please look after the kids for me, you're going to have to tell them what happened. Tell them I'm sorry and I love them.' She hugged Blue and handed the lead to her mother.

As they left the house they could hear Blue's whining mixed with Sue's howls of despair.

Chapter Twenty-nine

The light was fading outside the office as Meadows sat at his computer typing up the final chapter of the case. He felt numb. The interview with Gwen was just a formality; she didn't want legal representation, just wanted to make her confession and take the consequences. Meadows couldn't bear to hear the story again so he let Edris and Paskin conduct the interview. Now Gwen sat in a cell beneath the office. Tomorrow she would be moved. Meadows had been tempted to go and see her but couldn't stand the thought of seeing her locked up.

I'm going to have to distance myself, for her sake and mine.

Edris placed a cup of tea on the desk and pulled up a chair.

'I'm really sorry about Gwen, it must've been difficult for you to bring her in. I don't understand how it could've been missed in the original investigation.'

You've no idea how difficult.

'Gwen had lost her memory and there was a dead girl with an unidentified DNA sample under her fingernails and signs of sexual activity. Matt did attack Bethan even if he didn't kill her, the crime scene was compromised. It makes sense to assume that someone was in the shack with the girls and attacked them. Gwen was devastated by the news of her friend's death, there was no reason to believe that she had anything to do with the attack, especially given her horrendous injuries.'

'But you worked it out.'

'Only because we had more information this time around. Gwen gave us most of the information and it was just a case of fitting all the pieces together. Even then, we nearly put an innocent man away.'

'I don't think Matt is completely innocent. He could've come forward at the time and if Gwen hadn't walked in on him that day, who knows what would have happened? I feel sorry for the children, both parents in custody. Do you think that Gwen will get bail until the hearing?'

'I don't see why not, but then Matt could also get bail.' Meadows sighed. 'What a mess. He knows that we've charged someone with Bethan's murder and it's only a matter of time before he finds out that it's Gwen. I dread to think how he will react. I expect under the circumstances there will have to be a restraining order to keep him away from Gwen. Maybe Gwen won't apply for bail and stay in custody until sentenced.'

'I think that would be best.'

'It's ironic, all these years Matt thought he was protecting himself by staying close to Gwen.' Pain gnawed at his stomach. He picked up his cup and took a sip. He didn't want to talk about the case anymore. 'So I guess you're going to go back to work with Blackwell.'

Edris pulled a face. 'I would rather stay working with you if you'll have me. If not, I'm putting in for a transfer.'

Meadows laughed. 'I'll see what I can do. Go home and get some rest.'

'How about I buy you a pint?'

Meadows looked at Edris. Despite his initial reservation he had enjoyed working with him. He just didn't feel like going out and putting on a show. All he wanted to do was to go home, smoke a joint, and think about what might have been.

'I know you don't feel like celebrating but I'm a good listener and not a gossip,' Edris said.

If he's going to stick around then I guess I have to get to know him.

'That sounds like a great idea.'

He closed Gwen's file, stood up and picked up his jacket. 'Come on, let's get out of here.'

List of characters

Bryn Mawr police station:

Detective Inspector Winter Meadows
DC Tristan Edris
Sergeant Dyfan Folland – custody/desk sergeant
DS Rowena Paskin
DS Stefan Blackwell
Chief Inspector Nathaniel Lester

Others:

Gwen Thomas née Collier – survivor
Matthew Thomas – Gwen's husband
Ariana Thomas – Gwen's daughter
Alexander Thomas – Gwen's son
David Collier – Gwen's uncle
Sue Collier – Gwen's mother
Blue – Gwen's husky dog
Bethan Hopkins – victim
Samuel Morris – Bethan's boyfriend
Doreen Hopkins – Bethan's mother
Giles Epworth – headmaster

Catrin Evans – school friend
Fern Meadows – Winter's mother
Wayne Allen – schoolboy
Gary Lane – schoolboy
Steven Powell – schoolboy
Carl Perkins – schoolboy

If you enjoyed this book, please let others know by leaving a quick review on Amazon. Also, if you spot anything untoward in the paperback, get in touch. We strive for the best quality and appreciate reader feedback.

editor@thebookfolks.com

www.thebookfolks.com

Also available:

When the boss of a care home for mentally challenged adults is murdered, the residents are not the most reliable of witnesses. DI Winter Meadows draws on his soft nature to gain the trust of an individual he believes saw the crime. But without unravelling the mystery and finding the evidence, the case will freeze over.

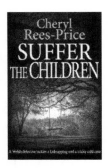

When a toddler goes missing from the family home, the police and community come out in force to find her. However, with few traces found after an extensive search, DI Winter Meadows fears the child has been abducted. But someone knows something, and when a man is found dead, the race is on to solve the puzzle.

When local teenage troublemaker and ne'er-do-well Stacey Evans is found dead, locals in a small Welsh village couldn't give a monkey's. That gives nice guy cop DI Winter Meadows a headache. Can he win over their trust and catch a killer in their midst?

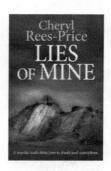

A body is found in an old mine in a secluded spot in the Welsh hills. There are no signs of struggle so DI Winter Meadows suspects that the victim, youth worker David Harris, knew his killer. But when the detective discovers it is not the first murder in the area, he must dig deep to join up the dots.

When a family friend is murdered, a journalist begins to probe into his past. What she finds there makes her question everything about her life. Should she bury his secrets with him, or become the next victim of Blue Hollow?

All available FREE with Kindle Unlimited and in paperback.

Made in the USA
Columbia, SC
18 December 2021

52015734R00155